The Magic Mirror

The Magic Mirror

Concerning a Lonely Princess,
a Foundling Girl, a Scheming King,
and a Pickpocket Squirrel

SUSAN HILL LONG

ALFRED A. KNOPF
New York

Library of Congress Cataloging-in-Publication Data.
Names: Hill, Susan.
Title: The magic mirror : concerning a lonely princess, a foundling girl, a scheming king and a pickpocket squirrel / Susan Hill Long.
Description: First edition. | New York : Alfred A. Knopf, [2016] |
Summary: From the time she was a crippled baby, left in a church, Maggie's life has never been easy. But when she glimpses her destiny in a magic mirror, she goes off on a quest to find her father and, along the way, finds happiness, as well.
Identifiers: LCCN 2015022145 | ISBN 978-0-553-51134-5 (trade) | ISBN 978-0-553-51135-2 (lib. bdg.) | ISBN 978-0-553-51136-9 (ebook)
Subjects: | CYAC: Fairy tales. | People with disabilities—Fiction. | Magic—Fiction. | Foundlings—Fiction. | Adventure and adventurers—Fiction. | BISAC: JUVENILE FICTION / Fantasy & Magic. | JUVENILE FICTION / Family / Orphans & Foster Homes. | JUVENILE FICTION / Action & Adventure / General.

For Molly and Eliza

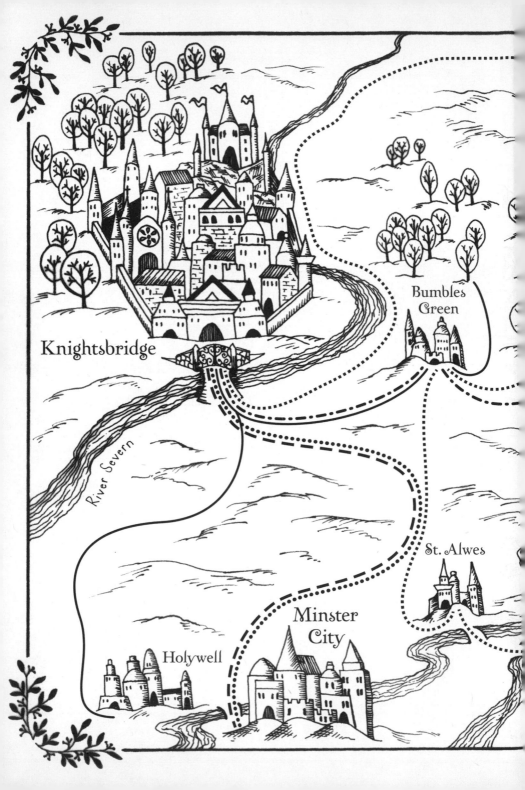

Knightsbridge

Bumbles
Green

River Severn

St. Alwes

Holywell

Minster
City

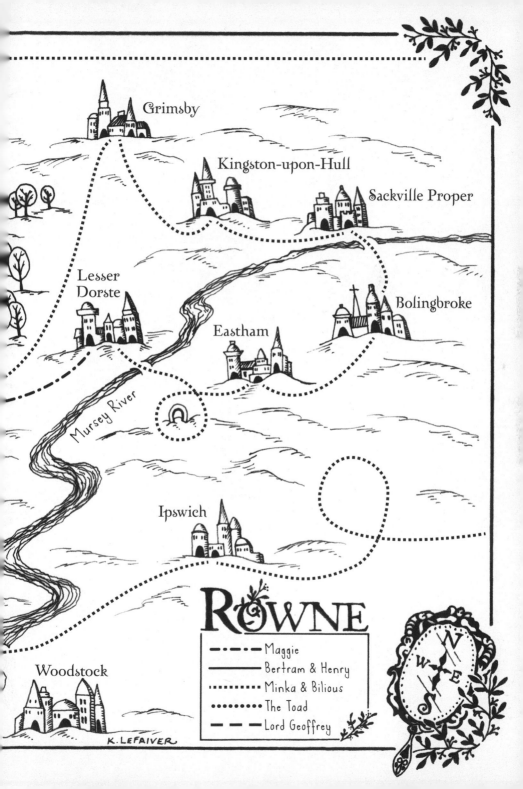

"Tell me, Nature," said I, "the best craft to take up."
"Learn loving," said Nature. "Leave everything else."

XX 206–207
PIERS PLOWMAN
William Langland

The Glass-Painter's Gift

*I*N KNIGHTSBRIDGE, IN DAYS GONE BY, there lived a glass-painter called William the glazier. Will had learned to make glass at the knee of his father, learned which metallic salts—cobalt and copper, gold and iron and manganese—to add to the molten sand and beechwood ash to create the most glorious colors.

But Will was born also of an alchemist, and at his mother's side he learned the secrets of combining common things of nature to create a new thing, something not of nature, not quite, something close to magical. In those days, unless it hinted of heresy, magic was tolerated at its most innocuous levels: the soothsayer did brisk business at the fair, for example. Will's

1

mother reasoned that if she could learn the secret of turning something worthless into gold, the same method might be used to make more worthy the human soul. Alas, she expired—the result of an unfortunate experiment—before she could prove her theory, and Will let alchemy alone. Mostly.

But one day Will thought to combine his two interests—alchemy and glass—to make a gift for his wife. Something special, something rare. And it worked. Like magic.

✤

"A mirror," Catherine breathed.

It was near sunset, and the cathedral was empty, except for the glass-painter and his wife and a pair of jenny wrens who'd got in through the half-completed wall of stained glass. Will had been hired by the old king, Ranulph, to create the great rose window—years in the making—that would finish the cathedral's west end.

"Not just any mirror," said Will, coming round the long worktable with the object—a circle of pale glass, bound and backed with lead, and with a handle of carved bone. "I've made a pair, as we two are a pair." Will glanced around, as if among the solder and snips and shadows there might be another ear to listen, then gave the mirror to Catherine. "Look! Look into it!"

Catherine ran a hand absently over her belly—the baby would be born before the month was out, by the midwife's measure—and lifted the mirror. First her face clouded with confusion. Then her eyes lit up and her lips twitched.

"What do you see?" Will held his breath.

"I see you!" Catherine smiled and cupped Will's cheek, then looked again into the mirror. "Your eyes, green as spring," she said, gazing into the glass. "What is it about? How . . . ?"

Will grinned wildly and raked his hands through his hair so that tufts stood alert in all directions. "Several attempts, many secret hours at the kiln. Cherrywood ash instead of beech. And to the ash I added this and that: chamomile for love, coltsfoot for visions, dandelion root for divination, fern leaf for clarity, and"—he rubbed his hands together—"*prim*rose. I'm quite proud of the primrose. That's where the *truth* comes from. Yes, that's what I meant to say! The mirror reflects the beholder—inside and out!" He grabbed the glass from Catherine and ran his fingers over the words etched on the back. "I call the magic mirror *Lux Vera*."

Catherine shook her head, uncomprehending.

"'True Light.' You see?" Again Will touched the words. "Because it shows the heart's true light, just as my great rose window shows the true light of God. When I look into the mirror, I see you, my love. And this proves I've done the magic right, for you see me!"

Catherine's delighted laughter was cut short by the scrape of the west porch door on the stone flooring.

"William Glazier!" came a shout. Lord Geoffrey, king consort, had been checking Will's progress on the rose window with irritating frequency.

Will shoved the mirror on the shelf beneath the worktable. He didn't trust Lord Geoffrey. Just last week he'd seen him toss a mouser from a parapet.

The king consort advanced along the aisle, the hem of his mantle swirling with the force of his stride. When he reached them, the cloak swelled and settled like a vulture's wings.

"My lord!"

His Lordship acknowledged Will's greeting with a curt nod and turned his attention to the worktable, on which a panel of stained glass was taking shape. There, three figures met between lines of lead.

One was Queen Isobel, daughter and heir of Ranulph, hair flowing in saffron swirls and waves, while down her cheek trailed a widow's tears.

The second, fair Armand, her late husband, dead in the wars not one year past.

The third, Armand's closest comrade: Lord Geoffrey himself, husband now to Isobel and, as such, the new king consort. Will had painted his likeness—thin nose, hollow cheek, and pointed tuft of beard—with confident brushstrokes, as he had all the masterful detail in the great rose window under construction. Then he had fused paint to glass in the kiln at Knightsbridge Wood.

Geoffrey stroked his beard, then tugged at the tips of

his leather gloves, removing them finger by finger. "We fought for God and kingdom, Armand and I," he said, and tucked the gloves in his belt. "Thank the saints I could be of comfort to his widow."

Catherine smiled fondly. "And how is Queen Isobel? Expecting any moment, the midwife tells us?" Catherine, a distant cousin of Armand, could afford this slight familiarity with the royal family.

"Our little heir," Geoffrey crowed. "A son this night, I pray."

"But . . ." Will glanced at the queen and Armand in the glass. "What of . . ."

"Poor Armand, never laid eyes upon his infant daughter." Geoffrey sniffed. "I'm honor-bound to raise the girl as my own, of course. For I loved Armand like a brother."

"Of course." Will swallowed. There had been rumors. . . . The midwife had said Geoffrey was clearly displeased that Armand's child, and not his, would one day rule. As Will said a quick prayer for the continued health of Queen Isobel, Geoffrey all at once bent and swept up the mirror from the shelf.

"No! It's—it's a gift for Catherine," Will stammered. He put his hand over the mirror.

But Lord Geoffrey pushed the glass-painter aside. Lips parted, he drew the mirror closer in the fading light, and suddenly his grip on the bone handle whitened his knuckles. He pressed the mirror to his chest, then looked again with open hunger at the glass. "God's wounds," he sputtered at last, "what magic is this?"

"Magic?" Will twisted the hem of his tunic in his hands.

Now Lord Geoffrey spoke slowly, distinctly. "The power to make such a mirror might be judged born of the Devil," he said. "There are tests, Will Glazier."

Catherine gasped, and Geoffrey glanced sharply in her direction.

"The hot iron, the sinking in the River Severn . . . ," Geoffrey went on. "A trial by ordeal can never end well. But," he said, stroking his pointed beard, "I wonder if we might work . . . together." Geoffrey smiled coldly at Will. "I'm a generous man. I will keep secret your talent. You have my word." And he thrust out his hand.

Will hesitated only a moment before taking Lord Geoffrey's right hand in his. At the same time, he reached to the mirror with his left, glanced at the glass, then stared, transfixed. "That's . . ." Will's eyes cut to Geoffrey's face, and back to the glass.

For long moments the two men were locked in strange, silent battle; then the mirror dropped to the flagstone with a delicate, final, crack.

"Idiot!" Geoffrey's cheeks reddened with angry spots.

"An accident, my lord. Apologies. So clumsy." Will knelt to pick up the shards of glass with hands that shook.

"You saw something," Geoffrey hissed, breathing with effort. "What was it?"

6

Rising, Will forced himself to look steadily into Lord Geoffrey's eyes. "I—only you, of course. I can make another mirror. One fit for a . . . king."

Geoffrey yanked the gloves from his belt and tugged them on, jaw clenched, his gaze never leaving Will's face. "I will have another." His voice dropped to a whisper, but it seemed to fill the cathedral. "Just like that one."

Will and Catherine stood still as stone while the sound of Geoffrey's boot steps faded to nothing. The west porch door scraped the floor once, twice. The brilliance of the rose window guttered with the setting sun and went dark.

Will's knees buckled. What in God's name had happened?

"The second mirror," he said to Catherine. "It's at the kiln in the wood. Go gather what you need for the baby and meet me there." He put both hands on her belly and took in a juddering breath.

"Will, you're shaking; you're frightening me. Tell me what's happened!"

Will gripped Catherine's shoulders. "When I took Geoffrey's hand and looked into the mirror, I saw a vision most . . ."

The vision—horrid vision!—played again in Will's mind. "Geoffrey and Armand, sharing a laugh. Armand turns, smiling. All in one swift motion, Geoffrey unsheathes a knife and drives it deep in Armand's back."

Catherine gasped.

At the sound of fluttering wings, Will looked up. Two wrens perched in the unfinished rose window, balanced there only a moment, until one and then the other flew out into the dusk.

Will pulled Catherine to him. "Hurry," he said, releasing her. "We must fly. I'll meet you in the wood."

Will heard the door swing shut behind Catherine as he collected his tools in a sack. Grozing iron, stippling wand, squirrel-hair brushes, paint.

"*Lux Vera,*" he whispered. He did not doubt the mirror's true light.

He must warn the queen. And he must away.

Will dropped the shards of broken mirror into his sack and turned to go, then stopped cold. The west door scraped open once again. In the vast darkness of the cathedral, Will could not see how many men approached. But he could hear their heavy boots upon the stone.

Accidents of Birth

Margaret set down her market basket, which was large for a child of five or six to bear, leaned upon her crutch, and looked at the beggar, who stuck out her hand and said, "Please." Margaret shook her head; she'd nothing of her own to give. But she didn't turn away as she'd been taught. The beggar looked to be about Margaret's own age; who had put her out on the street? If the widow Minka thought to turn *Margaret* out, she'd be a beggar too, and bad luck, that. Minka had said so oft enough.

The beggar sat in the dirt scratching at her filthy tunic—Margaret could see the fleas from where she stood—and then she took up a thing from her sack, a brown, furry, dead-looking thing, and cradled it as if it were a baby, soft and sweet. "Dolly," she murmured.

The stench was appalling. Still, the kind and tender way the beggar rocked the thing in the crook of her elbow made Margaret's nose stuff up and her eyes sting, and not from the horrible smell.

"Oi, Maggot! The cripple and the beggar are friends—of course!" came a boy's shout, followed shortly by a hurtling rock. The beggar covered her head with one arm and with the other clutched the doll to her chest. Margaret took a sharp breath and glared at their tormentor. It was Thomas the miller's son. Her heart beat like a rabbit's, but she squinted her eyes and bared her teeth the way she thought a lion or a dragon would. Thomas came running at them, and she drew up her crutch like a lance and held it steady. Crutch met bone, the boy fell back, and much wailing ensued.

"Ah, quit yer crying, Thomas, and leave a poor cripple alone," said the boy's mother, coming after him and giving him a whack. "Vex me much more and I'll turn you out, boy. Then *you'll* be on the street, same as that one," she added, with a glance at the beggar. "Accident of birth," she muttered as she hurried Thomas away, "the both of them."

Margaret thought of the butcher's sow, which bore a runt and ate it. She supposed *that* was an accident of birth, but she didn't know what it had to do with her.

The beggar sniffed loudly and rose from the ground, giving off a pong and upsetting legions of fleas as she did. But for a moment Margaret caught sight of their reflection in the surface of the brook. Two girls, side by side, poor as piglets and marked by God's displeasure. She heard the girl's stomach growl. The beggar, she knew, was worse off than even her miserable self.

Margaret stared at her face in the water and decided something. She took the market silver from the belt at her waist and pressed a coin into the girl's palm.

The beggar's jaw dropped. "A penny entire? Why, I'll dine with the duchess!" she said, and stuck out her heel for a curtsy. Then her mouth made an O as she had a thought. "You can have my dolly in trade," she said, gently stroking the brown thing with the tip of her finger as if it had a downy cheek, and then thrusting it at Margaret.

Hair is what it was. A thick plait of matted hair that never was, nor ever would be, a dolly. "No." Margaret shook her head. The beggar looked relieved and quickly tucked the thing into her belt and patted it.

"Sommat else, then, for stabbin' that boy and givin' me a whole penny."

And while the beggar knelt and rootled around in her filthy sack for something else to offer, Margaret saw etched on the back of the girl's bent neck a pale scar or mark of birth: two separate, slender stems curved outward and joined in a crotch at the top, resembling nothing so much in size and shape as . . . *a wishbone!*

Margaret rootled through a knot of wishes in her mind—*I want not to be et by a sow; I want Thomas drowned in the river; I want two straight strong legs*—but in the end she whispered the wish that beat a steady rhythm on her heart: *I want not to be so alone.*

The Miserable Coin of Life

Ten Years Later

"Don't linger," the widow Minka squawked from the window of a steep-roofed mud-and-timber house. "Don't dawdle, don't dally, don't speak to strangers." Minka paused to take a breath, and all went still in the unexpected silence: her linen headdress, her doughy cheeks and quivering jowls.

Margaret stood beneath the window and stared at her reflection in a puddle. Spring had come slowly to Lesser Dorste, and the late-April morning carried a chill. "I'll be on my way, then," she said. She picked up a large woven basket with her left hand; then, with a practiced movement, she hooked her crutch beneath her right arm.

"Don't forget you've got that crooked leg," Minka screeched, remembering at last the final thing Margaret shouldn't forget.

Margaret grunted. As if she could forget the crooked leg that had dragged behind her all her life—fourteen or fifteen years, by Minka's reckoning. She pointed her too-tight shoes toward the town center and began the walk—*clump-slide, clump-slide*—to Market Cross.

Pestiferous, Minka had often called her, and worse. Margaret took a step. *Clump-slide.*

Putrid, beetle-headed scullion was a favored taunt of Thomas's. *Clump-slide.*

Eye-offending offal, Otho the sniggler called her, as though an eel-catcher should judge. *Clump-slide.*

A pox on them all, thought Margaret. *Clump*—

"Wait!" came Minka's cry. Margaret stopped.

"You'd forget your own left foot if it didn't drag behind you," Minka yelled, and shook a small purse of jingling coins. Scowling, Margaret limped back below the window. From the purse Minka pinched a silver penny. Margaret held out her hands to catch it, but Minka paused, turning the coin one way and the other.

"There are but two sides to the miserable coin of life," Minka said from under the protection of the overhanging roof, while the rain dripped down on Margaret. "The good luck and the bad. The two of us, Mags," she said, "we fall on the bad luck side every time, sure as Beady Bone."

Margaret shuddered at the name of the poor beggar girl who had been browbeaten and bullied and finally run out of town. Margaret knew she'd have shared the same fate were it not for Minka's benevolence, such as it was. Minka reminded her of this fact often enough to keep the girl in her thoughts. But mostly Beady haunted her in dreams of a dark and frightening sort.

Minka tossed the coin and withdrew from the window. "Oats and fresh fish, don't forget," she said, and banged the shutter.

Margaret bent and collected the coin. Then she hitched her crutch and stepped warily through the mud and muck.

Only last night she'd woken from a dreadful dream of Beady Bone, and then the rain had kept her awake as it dripped through chinks in the wood-tiled roof. She'd listened to the gale, worrying the scrap of soft green velvet she kept tucked beneath her bed of straw. She might have wondered where the wind was going and where it had been, but to wonder caused Margaret a sadness that was beyond her understanding, and anyway it didn't do to dwell.

A yellow cat appeared in the lane beside her. "Hello, Cat," Margaret said, and the cat, smoothly matching Margaret's halting pace, meowed intelligently. "Would you believe me, Cat," Margaret said, "if I told you that the rain"—she glanced at the cat—"well, that it spoke to me last night?" The cat flowed like water around and between her ankles, and then sprinted off. "Hmph," Margaret said to the departing yellow tail.

But it was true. She had strained to understand the sound of the rain dripping steadily into the crock in the corner: *pitter-patter, bitter-butter.* But then the sounds had slowed to a rhythm that spoke more clearly. *Better tell her, better tell her, better tell her, shhhhhh.*

Better tell her what? Margaret wondered. Tell me what?

Nothing about the poor and lonely circumstances of Margaret's life had ever given her reason to hope, but if there *was* magic in the world, it seemed possible she'd hear it on the rain. Mayhap it would heal her crooked leg.

Pick-a-pickle, pick-a-pickle, plinked the rain in the puddles now. She walked on into a narrow alleyway darkened by upper stories that jutted out and closed in over the street.

"Oi! Cripple-noggin!" came a shout. "Maggot the Crutch!"

Margaret glanced back. Thomas the miller's son! Her awkward gait sped to match the beat of her heart: *Clump-slide! Clump-slide! Clump-slide!* She hurried toward the glimpse of sky at the far end of the alley. But then the way ahead filled with the figure of Otho the sniggler, so big he blocked the sky. Behind her came Thomas. She was trapped.

Margaret gripped her crutch and raised it up like a knight's lance, wobbling in her effort to gain balance.

16

She had much practice in self-defense, but gone was the time when she could poke Thomas in the eye and send him running to his mother. As the town boys grew bigger and rougher, her efforts served her less. Now Otho, as slippery as the eels it was his job to catch, slithered near and grabbed at her. Margaret swung the crutch wide, but Thomas kicked high and sent it skittering. Margaret dropped to the ground and scrabbled toward it on hands and knees.

"Go away, wantwit," she growled. "Leave me be!"

Margaret and Thomas grabbed the crutch at the same time, him on one end, her on the other; like vicious dogs tussling over a bone, they tugged and pulled and fought. She would have that crutch! They rose, each gripping an end of the stick. Thomas tugged with all his might, leaning, leaning. . . . Margaret let go, and Thomas fell on his rump, knocking over a reeking bucket of waste. Margaret snatched up the prize.

"Ah, Thomas," cried Otho, "you look like my ma's old rutty sow! Ha!"

Margaret shoved the wooden stick beneath her arm and limped with all haste to the top of the narrow alley, where it spilled out onto Milk Street. She could hear Thomas fumbling to his feet and Otho already giving chase. Just then a cheese cart came rolling down Milk Street; quickly Margaret crossed. She let the wagon come between her and the alley, and kept pace with it as it moved away.

When she came to the churchyard, Margaret ducked

inside the gate, hurried to the graves, and dropped behind a marker. She waited in the shadow of the church. Years ago, when half the town had died of the black death, one aisle of the church had been chopped away to make the building smaller. Now the church was crooked, like herself.

Margaret was thrown off balance by her feelings, muddled as the Mursey on wash day. She'd seen the miller kick his son hard enough to crack a rib. Thomas was a beast, but he was born of one, and for that he could not be blamed. He was as much an accident of birth as herself.

She peeked around the gravestone and watched for Thomas and Otho to pass. The stone marked the grave of Minka's husband, dead these twelve years.

Margaret knew well the story of Minka's bad luck, a tale woven into Margaret's own history.

Minka was a nurse, those years ago. One day a man was brought in, near drowned. He'd fallen into the Mursey River burdened with a suit of mail, and so he sank quickly to the bottom. His chain tunic, winking in the sunlight, had caught the eye of John the sniggler, Otho's father, who had managed to pull the stranger's head above the water.

The soldier slept for seven days. Minka, captivated

by his handsome though eel-bitten face and his silent disposition, spoke shrilly in his ear, called him Sweetheart, and stayed by his side night and day, so hers was the face he opened his eyes upon when he woke from death.

"Holy God!" he exclaimed.

It was a miracle he lived. Another miracle that he fell in love with Minka. And then, bad luck. One evening, Minka walked with Sweetheart along the riverbank; he'd been going to ask her to marry him. He knelt— would this be the question?—and at that moment a knight, a red-bearded stranger, approached on a galloping steed. They both turned in astonishment. And the "yes" that Minka had at the ready turned to "No!" For the stranger's piebald horse spooked and reared and trampled poor Sweetheart to death. The ring in his fingers rolled away, into the dust and gone. Minka collapsed. The priest called the marriage near enough in God's eyes and made Minka a respectable widow.

When Father Bernard knocked at Minka's door on the following day, the feast day of St. Margaret, it was to offer condolence and to ask a favor. He'd found a crippled child abandoned in the church and hoped Minka would take her in. The priest expected that someone would come for the child, a girl of three years or thereabout, for she was no street urchin—she was clean and cared for and dressed in a fine gown of green velvet. But no one ever came.

In time, the priest assured Minka, the girl would give comfort and service, despite her tiny crooked leg. And, in time, she might offer love, much like what Minka might have known from her own offspring with Sweetheart, God rest his trampled soul.

And so Minka resigned herself to her bad luck. She took up spinning and brewing. She put the sign of the bushel and the pike outside the door whenever she had ale to sell. But with the exception of an annual trip to church to give God a piece of *her* mind, she never left the house again.

🎵

When Margaret heard Otho and Thomas pass by the church and head away up Milk Street, pitching stones at the poor yellow cat, she deemed the way safe enough and continued on it herself. Nearing the marketplace, she smelled cooking meat and burning wood and heard the thud of the butcher's cleaver. She saw carts of grain bound for the mill, pickled meat and salted bacon, fresh fish, tanned hides and sacks of wool.

"Hot peasecods!" came the cry of a street vendor.

"Rushes fine and green," sang another.

"White wine, red wine!"

"Ribs of beef and savory pie!"

Margaret's stomach rumbled loudly, for Minka ate the queen's share of everything Margaret brought home. Her purse hung lightly from the belt at her waist. She could imagine many and varied ways to part with money, if she had it. Sweet figs and dates, oranges bursting with juice. A hot pie, full of steaming meat and sweet plump currants. A visit to the tailor, maybe, to purchase a new kirtle: emerald-colored, with purple laces up and down the sleeves. But Margaret didn't spend much thought on nonsense, and she brought to mind instead her duty: fresh fish and a sack of oats.

She carried on with her errands, sniffing the fish before selecting it and digging down in the oat sack to be sure the grain wasn't rotten beneath the handfuls of good oats on top.

"You doubt my honesty, miss?" came the tart accusation from the merchant.

"This way I don't have to," she replied.

"Meowww!" The yellow cat streaked by. Close on its tail came first a skittering stone, then Thomas and Otho, joined now by some other rough boys.

"Maggot!" shouted Thomas, forgetting about the cat now that better sport was at hand.

Margaret clutched her basket in front of her and looked left and right but saw no escape. Thomas caught her arm and drew her so close that she could count the lice in his hair. Breathing foully into her face, Thomas pinched her cheek hard enough to sting.

Margaret drew up her shoulders, shut her eyes against Thomas's leering teeth, and turned her face from the dark smell of his breath, gathering strength and wits for another scuffle.

"Ripe for the kissing, that one is," Otho taunted. Thomas laughed and kissed her cheek rudely, and then he wiped his mouth with his dirty sleeve. Her face burned with anger and shame.

"You, boys, watch yourselves!" came a shout. A dull old chestnut mare was stepping and dancing, the butcher's well-fed terrier at her hooves, causing everything in the cart she was pulling—brass pots and bronze bowls, scissors and bridles and beads—to jiggle and twinkle like sparks from a fire. Seated in the cart, a man round and friendly as a pumpkin spoke softly to the horse, shushing and cooing and gentling the mare and then smiling. He struck Margaret as being the very opposite of sneering Thomas, who now, saints be praised, retreated a pace.

"Step lively, dearie!" cried the peddler. Margaret drew up her skirts and stepped—*clump-slide*—to one side.

"Maggie the Crutch ain't much for stepping lively," Thomas jeered. "Cripple and lame she is!"

The peddler scratched his chin and leaned back on his perch in the wagon. He watched the girl hop-step to the edge of the street, trying to avoid the people, the little yapping dog, Old Penelope's hooves, and a pile of steaming droppings. He watched her struggle to walk in the mud, watched the boys taunting in a laughing pack, while other folk pulled back so as not to touch the cripple.

"It's like that, then," he muttered. He laced the reins to the hitching post and hopped down from the wagon to light beside her.

Neat as a tumbler at the fair he was, and him with one leg cut off above the knee and a peg leg below it. He bent the one knee and peered into Margaret's face. The peddler's eyes, searching hers, crinkled merrily. Here was a one, she thought, who would not harm her any more than he would harm his old mare or the little dog at the mare's feet or the tormented yellow cat.

The peddler raised a menacing fist at the boys. "Be off with you, rascals!" he shouted. He lunged in their direction as if to deal a blow, succeeding in running them off but failing to keep his balance on the one leg. Margaret, thinking to help, grabbed at the peddler's cloak, but with such force of will that she, too, went wobbly, landing them both in the mud.

"God preserve me!" cried the peddler. "Will you try and kill a poor fellow?" But he laughed, and Margaret, after a moment's hesitation, laughed with him. Her crutch stuck fast in the muck like a pollard tree, and the peddler reached for it to help him up.

"Between us we've got two good legs, my girl, and that'll do," he said. "Maggie, is it?" His smile was broad and kind as he helped Margaret to her feet.

"My thanks for running them off," she said.

"My pleasure," the peddler replied. "They'll be back, of course."

"Don't I know it," said Margaret, rubbing her cheek where it hurt.

"I've bought a hot meat pie," the peddler said, jerking his head to the wagon. "I'll gladly split it, and I've a dozen tales I'll gladly share as well." Margaret tried not to appear too eager. "What would you think if I told you that in my travels I have seen a unicorn?" Margaret drew back and squinted, doubting, but he nodded fervently. "What's more, I've put my palm upon a whale, the briny monster!"

At that, Margaret snorted. When the peddler grinned widely, apparently satisfied with her response, she saw he had but four teeth in his head. Unicorns and whales? Stuff and nonsense. But . . . enticing all the same.

The peddler introduced himself as Bilious Brighton. The two of them sat by the side of the road in front of the town well, and it was quiet between them while they shared the promised meat pie, no longer hot but very good.

"Your leg," Bilious began. "Does it pain you?"

Margaret shrugged. "Not so terrible much," she said. "Does yours? Where it used to be?"

Bilious wiped his chin with his sleeve. "It itches. I want to give a good scratch, but there's no flesh where the itch is, confound it." He knocked on the peg and shook his head. "The leg haunts me is what it does."

Margaret was quiet, and her thoughts went unbidden to her mother, the one who must have left her in the churchyard. Her mother was there and then gone, and, as with Bilious's leg, the thought of her was very like an itch that she couldn't scratch.

"Have you really seen a unicorn?" she asked after a moment, licking the last bit of piecrust from her fingers.

"Of course!" Bilious exclaimed, looking wounded. "You don't believe an old man? You've cut me to the quick, by God."

"It smacks of magic, is all," she said.

At that very moment, as the word *magic* crossed Margaret's lips, the church bell rang noon. But whether to confirm or to scold, she did not know.

A Bit of Magic

"What do you know of magic?" said Bilious.

Margaret blinked. She'd come close to magic only last summer, in the soothsayer's tent at Grimsby Fair.

"I've seen a two-headed goat," she said to Bilious. "And"—she heard the soothsayer's words in her mind, saw the faraway look in his eyes—"I've had my fortune told."

"Oh? Did the seer tell of the handsomest peddler in all of Rowne?" he joked, grinning with all four teeth.

Margaret shook her head slowly, pulling on her lip before speaking the words she'd put to memory:

"'In a glass glimmering, a green-eyed man awaits.

Seek him, but soft! For he is touched by death and danger.'" The seer had peered at Margaret even more closely then—so near his breath had made her blink. "'Just because you limp doesn't mean you can't heal.'"

Margaret looked at Bilious sidelong, judging his reaction.

"A strange portent," murmured Bilious. "Gibberish to me. Sometimes these seers are only in for the penny, one can't be sure, and if I could grow a new leg I'd have done so by now," he said. "Now, then," he went on, "I have one—only one—bit of magic that I've picked up on my travels. Here, let me show you."

He rummaged in his sack and pulled out a circular object the size of a bread loaf, ringed round with lead and with a slender handle fashioned of bone. Bilious turned it over, and it flashed. A hand mirror!

Margaret smiled. "Rare," she said, "but magic?"

"My own dear wife gave it to me when we married. She was given it by a knight errant she'd nursed to health before we met, name of Harold, or Hobart, or Hy. Something haitch-ish." He looked to the gray sky as if the knight's name might be delivered from above, then shook his head and shrugged. "She followed its charms for a time, till she took up with me and put aside the mirror, after which she counted what blessings she had and longed for nothing more."

"What does it do?" Margaret's skin tingled. She sat up very straight.

Bilious scratched his bearded chin. "That's the question, all right. The future? The past? The heart's longing? True love? Over time I've thought it shone them all." He glanced at Margaret and brushed his fingers over two words etched on the back. "Mayhap these would tell us what it's meant to do, but I canna read, and I'll warrant nor can you."

Margaret shook her head no. "Does it really work?"

"The magic works, one way or another. I know, because I saw my own dear wife in it, God rest her soul," Bilious said, and wiped a tear. "A more able woman I never met in all my travels. She could fell an oak and have a fire laid afore you could say 'jackrabbit.' She'd have downed a bit of game and popped a stew in the pot, all in the time it took me to climb from the wagon and set the nag aright." He shot a look sideways at Margaret. "What with my absent leg, you understand." He smiled fondly. "Had a laugh like a wheezing bagpipe, she did."

"What happened to her?" Margaret's gaze slid to the mirror, but she forced her eyes back to Bilious's face.

"She died a bleak and ignominious death at the hands of the thief John Book." His face reddened. "I've sworn to avenge her death," he said in a low voice. "I'll cut off his hands if he crosses my path. I'll make him eat his own shoes." He pointed at Margaret as if she herself were the thief John Book.

He looked once more to the mirror and smiled. "Truth

is, now the most I see in it's a cup of ale." He shrugged. "I'm a simple man. Or perhaps I've learned not to want too much."

Margaret sat quietly. What might she see in the magic mirror? She had no real memories of her mother or father, and though she'd been abandoned in a churchyard, somehow she felt she'd been loved. Or maybe it was wishing that made her feel so. She had a picture in her mind of a mother: ginger hair like Margaret's own, dressed in a glorious gown of green velvet just like the scrap of rich cloth she kept under her pallet—and she'd have tiny, pretty ears for whispering secrets in. Margaret's sadness was brought about not by missing a parent, as Bilious missed his dear wife, but by never having known one at all. Would her pain be greater had she known a mother and lost her? She wasn't sure, but she thought probably. Poor Bilious. She reached out a hand and gently patted the peddler's arm.

Bilious closed his eyes and nodded. "Now I'd sooner gaze into a pond or a river, sommat teeming with life, than stare into this magic mirror and waste away with longing. Oh, it gave comfort for a time, but no more." He beamed at Margaret with a smile more gap than teeth. "I don't want it. And you're a good lass, I can tell." He held out the mirror to her. "It's yours," he said.

Margaret stared a long moment at the mirror, but she did not move to take it. Was she a good lass? She wanted to have it. But she had nothing to give in return, and she would not be beholden.

"No, not for me," she said at last. She licked her dry lips. "Thank you anyway."

Though she refused the gift, she squeezed her hands together like a beggar hides a penny, and her gaze never left the shiny surface of the glass in Bilious's hand. She could no more conceal her desire than she could her disfigurement.

"Wait, then." Bilious rubbed his chin, looking over Margaret's belongings. "The basket is doubtless too dear to her mistress," he muttered, "and as well the goods within. . . ." He cleared his throat and, like wise Solomon, raised a finger. "If you won't take the gift outright, the mirror is yours, let us say, for a price. It's yours," he said, pausing, "for the price of one stout crutch."

Margaret swallowed. The crutch? But she needed the crutch. She'd found the right stick herself down along the Mursey, washed bare and clean from its journey downstream. She'd polished it smooth.

Rain began to fall again, and she blinked against it.

But the mirror! How it shone and sparkled and promised! She hesitated a moment more and then thrust the crutch at the peddler.

Margaret took the mirror greedily and gazed into it. Her heart drummed in her chest. What would she see? A mother? A father? What in the world would she see?

She squinted. The silvery surface was mottled and

gloomy, no better than a bucket. She angled the mirror into better light, and some rain dropped on it, obscuring any hope of reflection. Now the glass seemed to ripple like wind-pushed water. *Better tell her, better tell her, better tell her,* pattered the rain.

She shook her head and lowered the mirror. She was afraid she'd see nothing. Nothing but her own plain face.

"Look again," Bilious said, kindly.

Fearful, hopeful, she wiped the surface with the sleeve of her cloak, bent over the mirror to shield it from the rain, closed her eyes, and dared to pray. *If it please God, let me see my heart's true longing.* Then she opened her eyes.

She stared. The mirror was gray, nothing but rippling gray like the sky and the rain. It didn't work.

In frustration and despair, Margaret shook the mirror. And then came a jolt as sharp and dizzying as a knock to the kneecap, like waking in the night from a dream she'd swear was real, and then waking yet again to understand that the time awake, too, had only been a dream. And with all that came a rushing in her ears so that she barely heard Bilious's voice asking what was the matter, and after several moments—who could say how many?—she could hear the rain again. She felt it too, clear, cold, pricking her skin, and in the mirror now the ripples cleared and an image began to settle: the face of a man.

Bilious was saying something, but she waved him away.

The man in the mirror had wild fair hair, and his eyes, too, were wild. Green eyes they were, as green as new grass, as green as her precious velvet scrap—*as green as the soothsayer's prophecy*, she thought with a start—and he was muttering soundlessly and fiddling with objects on a wood table, tools of a sort she'd never seen. He scratched his ear, picked up a small tool, set it down, rubbed his bearded chin. Who was this man? Now he was looking with alarm at something Margaret could not see, something outside the frame of the mirror. Behind him she could see an arched window, crossed with bars, and beyond the bars a bird flew, and beyond the bird . . . but now the image was fading. Margaret shook the mirror and the glass rippled and went dark.

Margaret slumped, as if she'd been held up by a puppet master's strings and was now released. What on God's earth had just happened?

"Are you unwell, Maggie?" came the peddler's voice. "What did you see?" Margaret raised her head, looked into Bilious's seeking eyes, and saw concern and caring there.

"I don't know," she managed. "But I'm all right. I think."

Bilious nodded, satisfied. "Well, I've trades to make, though I'll not match the one I've just accomplished," he said, thumping the crutch upon the ground and using it to pull himself to standing.

Margaret, still reeling, rose stumblingly to her feet and grabbed hold of the side of the peddler's cart. Pain stabbed her twisted foot and she gasped. How would she manage to walk without the crutch? Never mind how, she thought, wincing. She *would* manage.

"Magic, mystery . . . have a care with the mirror's power," Bilious said as he began to poke through the items in his cart. "My departed wife, bless her"—he paused to wipe his eye—"she was wise as she was loud, and I will say to you what she said to me. 'Bilious,' she said, 'do not ask what is my true love's face, or show me the riches I long to claim. Ask instead, "Who am I and what am I about?" Time and tide you'll need, to seek a true reflection—and never magic at all.'

"Go well, then, Maggie dear." Bilious began to put out his pots and pans, his hides and bronze bowls and wooden spoons.

"Goodbye," Margaret said. "And thank you."

She slipped the mirror into the pocket of her cloak. Who was the green-eyed, wild-eyed man? How was he in any way what she longed in her heart to see? She frowned in confusion. She had so many questions. Even so, she thought, in some manner the magic worked. For Margaret the Crutch, the magic worked. And that was enough. She patted the mirror in her cloak, gritted her teeth against the pain, and turned for Milk

Street and home, bearing oats and fish in her basket and hope in her heart. Everything the same but everything different. Now, though she went with no crutch, her stumble and lurch seemed almost like a spring in her step.

A Hideous Proposal

The going was slow without the crutch, and Margaret limped along, lost in thought, one arm holding the basket and the other stuffed in the pocket of her cloak, where she could keep hold of the mirror.

"Margaret, good day" came a familiar voice in greeting. It was Hugo the hunchback, whose words grated like a nutmeg on a rasp.

Margaret blinked and mumbled a reply. She had heard his whine too often of late; he'd visited with Minka at Martinmas, and again on the eve of the Feast of St. Fergus. He and Minka had whispered and tittered across their cups of ale, huddling as if to share a secret. As if—she shuddered to think—they were in love.

"On your way home, are you?" Hugo asked, and stepped closer.

Margaret nodded. She lurched a step back, to keep her distance.

What if the secret they kept was their desire to wed? She pitied Hugo, but she didn't want him to live with them in their small house. The way his head dipped, it was impossible to look directly into his eyes. One eye lolled in such a way that she could never be certain whether he was looking at her or at someone three paces to the left. Margaret knew well that Hugo's deformity was God's will and not Hugo's own, but she did like to look a person in the eye. Did his gaze skitter and start like Tim the baker's, who sold bread gone green? Or did he smile and crinkle, like—well, like Bilious the peddler? With Hugo the hunchback, she simply couldn't tell.

"I've only just come from there," Hugo was saying. He took another step toward her.

Margaret brought her attention around. The hunchback's tunic dragged in a wide puddle, a dark spread of filth creeping up the cloth to his knees. When he smiled, he showed a set of yellowed front teeth as blunt as a mule's, worn down to the nub as if by gnawing and grinding.

"From where?" she asked, stepping backward once again.

Nearby, the butcher's cleaver hit its mark with a sick-ening thump; Margaret swallowed hard and returned a thin, uneasy smile. What would become of her if Minka wed? What if they put her out on the street just like Beady Bone? She'd not seen the beggar in many years, and reckoned her dead of cold or hunger or worse. Margaret shivered and pulled her cloak tight around her throat.

"From your house," said Hugo. And then he winked, whether by intention or to clear the eye of its putrid-looking ooze she could not be sure. He took yet another step closer.

Pulling her basket across her like a shield, Margaret stepped backward so hastily that her foot caught on the hem of her cloak, and she tripped and lost her balance and would have fallen except that Hugo's hand darted out and he caught her arm and pulled her roughly to him. She could see into the steady eye now, inches from her face, and she did not like what she saw.

"Let me go!" she ordered.

"You might thank me for saving you," Hugo whined, but after a moment he released her, tipped the brim of his ragged hat, and walked on down the street in the direction Margaret had come.

Margaret straightened her shoulders and settled her basket once more upon her arm. The mirror rested pleasantly against her hip, and after a glance over her shoulder to be sure Hugo wasn't watching, she reached her hand into the pocket of her cloak, pulled out the mirror, and peered into it.

As before, the mirror rippled, then cleared. But instead of the face of the wild-eyed man, she saw Hugo the hunchback.

Margaret's stomach clenched, and she felt the ghost of Hugo's grip on her arm. Repulsed, she pressed the mirror to her stomach and looked away down the road. Hugo was well distant, and could not possibly be reflected in the glass. What on earth? She blinked her eyes rapidly and slowly raised the mirror. Thanks be, the vision had faded and Hugo was gone.

Margaret shivered, shoved the mirror in the basket, and made her slow way home.

When Margaret arrived home at last, she was soaked with rain and muddled with confusion. Her bones ached from the effort of walking without the crutch. Minka complained of the fish ("foul!") and the oats ("damp!") and struck her with a spoon for being late. ("You are well aware how I suffer, unable to set foot outside the house for fear of strangers and tramplings, and yet you keep me waiting all the day!") And then she found the mirror.

Margaret made a grab for it, too late. "It's mine," she mumbled, too fast.

"Yours," Minka drawled. "And how did you come by such a pretty as this?" Minka drew her finger along the smooth handle and glared at Margaret from beneath her wimple.

"Please," Margaret said. Even had it not been magic, the mirror was a singular thing, a treasure. Excepting the bit of green velvet and a small horn comb, she'd never had anything fine, and hadn't Minka taken that little horn comb—so pretty with its delicate carving—and kept it for herself? And the mirror wasn't just a pretty. It was magic! "I traded for it," she said, and then realized her mistake.

"Traded for it?" Minka bellowed. "And what would you have to give in trade?" Minka looked about the room; her gaze caught on the empty peg by the door. "The crutch!" She whipped around. "Knotty-pated prat. Well. Never mind. More's the fool who took it in trade for this," Minka said, a look of triumph crossing her face as she flourished the mirror like a rondel dagger. "Better for me to keep it. Hugo expects no dowry, and will never be the wiser."

Margaret's heart sank. A dowry. A wedding settlement. So she had been right about Minka and the hunchback sharing a secret. What would become of Margaret? Would Minka throw her out?

Margaret braced herself for the blow. "You are to be wed, then," she said.

Minka blinked. Two bright spots pinked her plump cheeks. "I?" she said, hand at her throat. "I, wed the hunchback?"

A chill crept along the back of Margaret's neck. Minka didn't mean—she couldn't mean—

"It's all arranged," Minka was saying. "It is you who shall wed the hunch—who shall wed Hugo the wool-monger. Don't look that way, Mags, as if you've a curdled stomach. He's a freeman with an income of five pounds a year," she said, shrill voice rising with each word, "and he owns a proper house built all of stone!"

"But I don't want to marry!" cried Margaret. "And he is so old, and he slaps women on the bottom, and his—his hump!" she said. "And his eyes!"

Minka switched her with a wooden spoon and called her a clay-brained baggage but then, for once, fell silent. She motioned Margaret beside her on the bench, and Margaret stumbled to her and sat.

Minka remained silent several moments while she removed her starched white wimple and scratched her head. Coarse growth pale as straw sprouted a good inch back from a customary hairline. Minus the head cover, Minka looked bare and raw, like a chicken gone to molt.

Minka looked at Margaret with a tenderness that, by its rarity, frightened Margaret. "You have no family, Mags, no prospects. Marriage to Hugo will protect you as I cannot," she said. "Marriage will make you proper, give you a place. That he is old, so much the better!" she exclaimed, and dropped her hands to her lap. "He will all the sooner die, leaving you a respectable widow with property, and better still, he'll leave you with your heart in one piece to beat another day." She wrung her wimple in her hands and sucked in a ragged breath. "Would that I'd been so lucky."

Margaret still felt the sting of Minka's spoon, but when she looked into Minka's eyes, she saw there something she had never noticed before. Was it sorrow? Was it . . . love?

"It's for your own good, Mags," Minka said, shaking out her wimple and settling it back on her head. "And if he is a bad husband, why then, you'll simply pray to St. Wilgefortis." She stroked her chin. "I'll wager a bearded-lady saint knows much of suffering."

Margaret sat on the hard bench, feeling nothing, for if she let herself feel anything, she would split apart like a milkweed, and everything inside her would burst forth and blow away. Surely this was the lowest she had ever been in all her life.

Minka had apparently forgotten all about the hideous news she had just delivered, for she was fiddling with the mirror, primping and fussing. She lifted the mirror to her face.

Minka's primping hand went still. Her pinched lips parted; her jaw went loose. She held the mirror at arm's length, then drew it closer, stuck her neck, gooselike, toward it, squinted, squawked, then all at once thrust the mirror deep in her apron front and used both hands to cover her mouth, which gaped like a fish.

"Bad luck!" Minka wailed. "The thing is cursed! What black magic is this, sent to bedevil me!"

"What did you see?" Margaret said, alarmed. "What is it?"

Minka pulled the mirror from her apron and dropped it on the table as if it burned her hands. "Look!" she said, pointing to it. "It's the Devil's work!"

Margaret picked up the mirror. There again was the wild-eyed man. Did Minka see him too? Did she recognize him? She faced the glass to Minka.

"Do you know who he is?" Margaret asked.

"Of course I know who he is! Sweetheart! Handsome as ever he appeared in life! Oh, but he cut a fine figure in his knight's tunic. And such good, strong teeth!" she wailed, and twisted her hands in her apron.

Margaret's brow knotted with confusion, and she brought the mirror close. There again was the wild-eyed man. And now a scene was unfolding in the glass. Margaret could see more of the man's chamber. She could see a pallet on the bare floor, and pieces of glass and metal, and on the wooden table were more strange tools and shallow bowls and small vials. The man was fiddling with a large disk of gray glass, picking it up and setting it down, bending to look at it from different angles. She could see, as well, out and beyond the barred window, which framed a sky purple and gold as if lit by a dozen setting suns. There were tree branches, rooftops, and sky and clouds, and a pair of great tall spires, and beneath and between them a huge round window.

Minka grabbed at the mirror, but Margaret wouldn't let go. Surely she knew of that great rose window. Where was it? What city? Shoulder to shoulder, Margaret and Minka each tugged at the mirror, their fingers entwined on the bone handle.

"There!" Minka looked from the mirror to Margaret and back again, tugging, tugging. "It is Sweetheart, God rest his soul. My soldier, my own true love, killed on our wedding day!"

Now it was Margaret—tugging—who looked from the mirror to Minka and back again. The wild-eyed man in the glass faded, rippled, and then a man dressed in a knight's tunic came into view. He was not handsome, but he did have strong teeth, large and square as fence posts. And there, too, was a younger Minka, smiling coquettishly. Margaret blinked in surprise and let go the handle.

Minka elbowed Margaret out of the way, clearing ample room to beat her breast in anguish with one hand and grip the mirror tightly in the other. "Bad luck, this!" Minka wailed. "This wretched fate is what I save you from, by marrying you off to the hunchback! While I, I am cursed to revisit the greatest torment of my miserable life, all over again!" She stared hungrily into the mirror. "And again!"

Things were not making sense. The magic didn't work

the way it ought. While Minka ranted and moaned, Margaret stared into the hearth and went over in her mind everything she'd seen in the mirror. First she'd seen nothing but gray. Then she'd seen the wild-eyed man. Then she'd seen Hugo. And just now she'd seen the wild-eyed man again, and as well the view outside his window. And then she'd seen Sweetheart in the glass. What was the meaning of it all?

Margaret's musings were interrupted by a heavy hand upon her shoulder; Minka was leaning on Margaret as though she were the traded crutch.

"Oh, I cannot bear it!" Minka moaned, and with another squeeze of Margaret's shoulder she retired to her room behind the chimney, taking the mirror with her. Margaret could hear her crying.

It was the touch, Margaret understood with the suddenness of a cool breeze before a rainstorm. Hugo had grabbed her, pulled her to him, and after that she had seen him in the mirror. And it was when Minka's hand had touched hers, tussling over the mirror, that she'd seen what Minka saw: Sweetheart.

Deep in thought, she rubbed the back of her neck. The magic worked differently for her than for Minka. Minka had not been able to see the wild-eyed man at all. Not even when their hands touched. Minka saw her own vision in the glass, but not Margaret's.

The wild-eyed man. She wrapped her arms around her middle. Why would he appear to her? She would focus on the man, crazed though he seemed. The bars on the window. The scene beyond the chamber. The spires. Something shifted in her mind. The spires. The great round window, a web of masonry and glass. Could it be the rose window of Knightsbridge? The cathedral in the royal city was famous for its wall of glass. Even Minka had considered leaving the house and facing the whims of the world to kneel before the rose window, if only she could be sure she'd not be trampled to death by the speckled horse of a red-bearded stranger.

"Is the man in the glass . . . my father?" Margaret whispered. She wanted to make the notion real by saying it aloud. "Is he alive? In Knightsbridge?" She dared to think it so. To be certain, she needed the magic mirror, which anyway belonged to her and not to Minka.

Margaret stood. *You have no family, no prospects,* Minka had told her, and so she had engaged her to Hugo. Margaret had always thought of Minka as family, and though it wasn't much, they had each other, didn't they? Yet how readily Minka would pitch her away, like so much slops in the bucket. What if she *did* have family, *and* prospects? Then came another thought, as new as dawn: mayhap she had a place in the world. Not as wife of Hugo the woolmonger, nor as the town Maggot. Someplace good.

She would go to Knightsbridge and find there what she would.

At an hour just past the lowest of her life, she vowed—to God and to herself—to run away.

A Stowaway

Later, Margaret set about preparing a measly supper, noisily putting on the table no fish (Minka had tossed it out the window) but bread and ale and turnip soup. Reflected in the murky broth, Margaret's face looked back at her in a very un-magic way.

"I know what you're thinking, Mags," Minka said with a sidelong glance, "but the mirror is mine, and I've hidden it away. For what if the magic has a limit?" she wondered aloud. "I must be sparing. I must mete it out like salt." She spent the rest of the evening planning how best to conserve the magic.

Maggie said nothing and bided her time.

When the hearth fires were banked and the lights extinguished, Margaret dressed in both her kirtles, the russet and the gray, and quietly put into her satchel her few belongings: an extra pair of hose with a hole she'd yet to mend, the scrap of soft green velvet from the dress she'd been found in as a babe, a pretty blue feather, and a cup. Up in her sleeping loft, Margaret lay on her straw pallet, clutching the satchel, and waited for Minka's snoring to begin.

There. Like the snort of the peddler's nag.

A quick search turned up the mirror under Minka's mattress ticking. Another moment and she had it in her hands. She peered into its surface but could see nothing in the dark. She shoved it in her satchel. Minka groaned and rolled over. Margaret froze, but Minka slept on. She thought to shove her hand again beneath the mattress, and a slow smile spread across her lips as her fingers found what they sought: the little horn comb. Into the satchel with it.

Grab the food, don the cloak. Done. Margaret reached for the latch, pulled open the door, turned. Her gaze moved slowly about the room, blue-lit by the moon: the table and the hard bench, the heavy cauldron on the hearth for brewing day, every common thing silvered and softened in the indistinct light. She fancied this must be like looking out from inside the mirror.

She swallowed hard. The silence of the house seemed

a reproach. By what faith did she believe herself fit for such a journey?

An arrow of guilt shot through her at leaving the one who, though bitter and mean, was nevertheless her caretaker and companion. She would have liked to explain. To say, after all, farewell and Godspeed. If she could write, she would have left a message. But Margaret could not write, nor could Minka read.

Minka gave a fart and snorted in her sleep. Margaret would not be sentimental. Pinning her cloak close about her throat, she lurched crookedly out the door into the dark night. Even without her crutch she felt unexpectedly strong: if she ran afoul of Thomas the miller's son this night, she did believe she'd box his ears.

Margaret kept to the shadows and hastened to Market Cross, for it was late and the taverns would be closing. Her plans went only as far as finding the peddler Bilious and hoping he could be persuaded to travel west, the way toward Knightsbridge.

Bilious was not to be found. A blow, to be sure, and again Margaret thought to turn back. She saw a couple of travelers and asked them where they were going; when they referred to cities and townships she thought to be east, she hurried away without answering their questions.

But a new scheme presented itself soon enough. Margaret listened to the men outside the tavern, most of them drunk on ale and chatty as geese. The tinker who spoke of Bumbles Green, he would be traveling west.

It was a simple matter to find the man's cart, with its collections of shears and snips and nippers for patching pots and things. Simple enough to climb into the back and conceal herself there beneath a heavy canvas. Simple enough to pray she'd not be discovered, for what else could she do?

She must have slept, for the movement of the cart woke her some hours later. Dawn neared, and she was on her way.

Margaret's thoughts bounced along with the cartwheels, rolling over and over her circumstances. She was a fool to venture out alone and without protection on the road. What if she never found her way to where she was bound? What if she was wrong about the man being in Knightsbridge? Minka would never take her back. Margaret was terrified to end like Beady Bone, wandering and begging, beaten and bloodied. She could leap from the tinker's cart even now and soon be back at home on her bed of straw in the attic, and no one the wiser, including herself. She sat up straight in the cart and held her satchel to her chest, watching the road run away.

She might still jump from the tinker's wagon! Should she?

As if deciding for her, the horse gathered sudden speed; the resulting jolt pitched her onto her back in the wagon. The clomp of the horse's hooves, the *ka-lump* of the rolling cartwheels, and the very beating of her heart carried her farther and farther from everything she knew.

Minka Leaves the House

In the morning, Minka stretched her arms up and gave her head a good scratching. With a sharp pang of joy she remembered: Sweetheart! She smiled, cheeks tightening with the unaccustomed movement. But when she groped beneath the mattress, her smile slipped. She tumbled out of bed. On her knees, she stuck her hand under the mattress all the way up to her armpit and swept the ticking. She stood and brought the bedding with her, tossing it to the floor. No mirror.

"The knotty-pated baggage," she hissed, "she took it, I'll wager, or my name isn't Minka Pottentott!" Minka stormed out of the room and bellowed, "You clay brain! You muddy-mettled oaf!" Snorting like an ox, she waited for Margaret to climb down and cower, but was met instead with stone silence. "Get down here, you beetle-headed scullion, before I climb the ladder and pitch you down myself!"

Minka prayed that Mags would come down, for she certainly could neither climb the ladder nor pitch a well-nigh full-grown girl over the side, even so slight a one as Mags.

Nothing, not a sound.

Minka stared at the ladder. She stared at the dead embers on the hearth. She stared into her room at the back, where the missing mirror was. Or would be, that is, were it not missing.

The limping, timid mouse, she'd never gone any-where save the town market, and once the fair at Grimsby. Always at hand she was, since the day Father Bernard dumped her like a runty lamb in Minka's care. Always underfoot, always at the table, always coming or going to market, always sleeping in the house they shared. Minka caught a breath. Always here, with her.

No, Mags would not simply go out. She'd not sim-ply go for a stroll beyond the hedgerows, or to picnic with a friend. She hadn't any friend. No one but Minka, and Minka was no friend; she wasn't meant to be. She tugged her wimple over her wild straw hair. No, Minka thought. Maggie was gone. And with her, the mirror.

"Bad luck, that!" she gasped. "Oh, dear. Oh, me. God's wounds!"

And after only a moment of hesitation, despite having

not set foot outside the house in months, Minka decided. She took up her good kirtle and pulled it on over her linens. "Surely it's shrunk since last I wore it," she said, stuffing her arms in the sleeves and attempting to tug the center closed across her bosom. "I wouldn't bother for that frothy, dismal-dreaming baggage," she huffed, "but I must have the mirror!"

Minka found an old felt hat with a deep brim, and put it on her head on top of her wimple, leaving a ruff showing below the hat all around. The assemblage looked like a cowpat atop a puff pastry. "Oh, that miserable, muddy-mettled crookshank!"

She pulled the too-tight kirtle tighter still across her broad chest, and attempted to fasten the open front with laces too short to span the gap. "Bad luck," muttered Minka. She tied the dress as far up the front as the laces would go. Then she took a wooden spoon and stuck it through the holes in the kirtle's front facing, to secure the remaining gap, and prayed the spoon would hold.

As she grabbed her cloak, her gaze caught on the peg where the crutch used to hang, before Margaret traded it away for the magic mirror. Minka shook her head. How would the poor little ninny manage without it?

"Oh, Mags, my girl," she said softly. "What have you done?" She closed her eyes and put hand to lips to stifle a single cry. "What have you gone and done?"

Then, shaking herself with a burst of trumped-up

gusto, Minka opened the door on all the bad luck out-side it and stepped into the street.

"Saints preserve us," Minka muttered as she hurried away from the house.

By the time Minka stomped her way to the village cen-ter, it was midmorning. No one had seen Margaret—not the cooper's wife, nor the butcher, nor the miller's son—and all were surprised to see Minka out and about. "You might not stare so," she said, "as if I've grown a second head."

All the while, Minka looked round and over her shoulder, knowing bad luck typically approached from a slant. She preferred to face bad luck head-on, lest she be trampled to death by it like poor Sweetheart, God rest him. She put her hand to her cheek, thinking of his image in the magic mirror. She must find it!

She looked in the church and at Market Cross and down along the river and behind the mill and every-where. Margaret was not to be found. She was gone.

Gasping from the brisk walk and unaccustomed emotion, Minka stood in the street outside the tavern and took several deep breaths.

"Forgive me, madam, but I couldn't help noticing your distress" came a voice.

Minka turned and gave the rough stranger a squint,

on guard for bad luck: an itinerant, by his traveled appearance, humped over from driving a cart, no doubt, minus most of his teeth, missing one leg from disease or accident or the wars, and supporting his bulk upon . . . She gasped. Yes, by St. Matilda! Upon a too-short crutch! Minka's gaze snapped to the man's face, and she began to shout.

"You eye-offending, gorbellied thug! What have you done with her?" She shook her fist at the man. "What have you done with her, I say! Where is she?"

"Who?" demanded Bilious, for he was only moments awake, and still, if truth be told, a bit drunk. "What?"

"The crutch! How came you by that crutch?" Minka lunged for him.

Bilious reared back to escape her. "I traded for it, fair and square," he said, "if it's any business of yours."

Minka put her hands on her hips in a threatening manner. "It is my business," Minka said, her voice rising steeply, "since the object belongs to me, and its bearer also belongs to me. Furthermore," she went on, her voice now reaching the pitch of a falcon shrieking before plunging to seize its prey, "the whereabouts of such bearer is certainly business of mine, and what do you know about it?"

With that, Minka yanked the crutch from under Bilious's arm and began to beat him over the head with it.

"Stop, Dame Beat-About! Stop, I say!" he cried.

Suddenly exhausted, Minka let go the crutch, and it

fell to the ground at their feet. Bilious, on guard for further menace, slowly bent and picked up the crutch, and then held it firmly under his arm.

"I am innocent, good dame," Bilious said, "excepting an honest trade for a bit of . . . glass." Eyes narrowed, he peered sideways at her. "A mirror it were."

Minka shifted uncomfortably. "Er, yes. I believe my girl may have said something about a mirror." She glanced left and right. "She showed it to me, in fact."

Bilious leaned forward. "Did you, errr, see . . . anything in it?"

Minka put her hands to her cheeks. The hat brim rolled like the belly of a dying fish. "Yes, by God, I did."

"And now you want it back?"

"Yes, by God, I do!" Minka cried, her hands in fists. "And I want *her* back, as well!"

"The one the village boys call Maggot?"

"Maggot! Why, you cursed cur!" With that, Minka set upon the sluggard again. He covered his head with his hands until Minka's fury was spent. Then he sat down on the bench outside the tavern and waited while Minka muttered and paced.

"But where on God's earth would she go?" Minka stopped pacing and looked at the peddler, noticing as she did the four teeth in his head, which seemed to point in the four directions of the wind. "North?" she said. "South? East? West?" Minka turned all around. Dizzy, she tipped dangerously to one side.

Bilious hopped up and tried to catch her. Buckling under her weight and thrown off balance, he still managed to ease the woman down gently in the street and keep her from landing on a steaming pile of ever-present dung.

"You might have caught me!" Minka panted.

"I might have, if I had two good legs, and you didn't weigh twelve stone and ten!"

"Well! Hands off! Off, I say! Poor defenseless woman."

"Poor defenseless woman, my absent leg," Bilious muttered, rubbing his head.

"Well, help me up, then!" Minka cried. "A gentleman would help a lady!"

"A lady would cover up her plump knees and great bosom so that her linens didn't show!"

"Oh! Humph! Whatever's to become of me! I must go after her! I must find her and save her from—from—from bad luck! Since you've taken the poor girl's crutch, she'll not have got far on foot," Minka huffed. "She'll have found passage with a"—she gasped—"a stranger. She's off in who knows what direction with a stranger traveling who knows where!" All this while, she was reaching one hand back to draw round her cloak, and clutching with the other the front of her kirtle to attempt to meet the two sides in the middle, but her efforts failed, as did her makeshift button, which popped like a cork. She looked around the cobbles in dismay.

Bilious picked up the fastener.

"Your spoon, my lady," he said gallantly. "Bilious Brighton," he added, introducing himself with a broad smile that exposed all four teeth to best advantage.

Minka could not have known how very imposing an impression she made upon Bilious, who reckoned any woman who would wear such a hat and make such a fuss was a fearsome and magnificent creature.

"If I might suggest it," Bilious said, bowing deeply and taking note of the woman's stout shoulders and ample hips, "for a fair fee, you might ride with me to Eastham." She could probably be counted on for some heavy lifting, and that misshapen old hat could be used to gather tinder for the fire.

"Certainly not!" Minka said. But even as she uttered the words, she knew that by this hour all the other merchants had traveled on, and that his was the only ride she'd get. She looked Bilious up and down. He was fat, and he smelled, and those teeth! She didn't know if they made her want to laugh or stuff his head in a grain sack. Nonetheless, though lacking leg, teeth, and looks, this Bilious brute was in possession of wagon and nag.

"I'll pay you two pence and not a penny more."

"I'll take a halfpenny and nothing less," countered Bilious, generously.

Within moments they had struck a bargain in her favor, and then off they went in the wrong direction.

Oats and Beans and Barley, Oh!

Margaret hunkered lower in the tinker's cart. Every so often she peered out to determine where she might have come to on the road. She did not know the distance between Lesser Dorste and Knightsbridge, nor where she should depart the wagon. But the east-west road would surely lead there.

She knew next to nothing of the royal city. She'd heard of the princess who would one day rule, when she was of age. The princess was a motherless girl, like Margaret herself, and for a time, when she was much younger, Margaret had liked to imagine that she and the princess were sisters who didn't even mind having no mother, because they loved each other that much.

She heard the occasional horseman galloping by, followed by a period of long quiet pierced with birdsong. Every so often she heard the rushing water of a stream or river, and she longed for the driver to stop so that she might steal out and drink. But he did not stop. The wheels kept up their grumble and creak, the horses their faithful clop, the birds their song.

Then she heard another song. Curious, she drew back her covering. At first she saw only the country: the fields with the beginnings of wheat, oats, and barley, some goats and sheep. Then the cart overtook a group of people on foot. Pilgrims. She'd seen pilgrims before in Lesser Dorste, stopping over for lodging in homes and in the churchyard.

A boy was singing with obvious delight at a volume all could hear. He was taller than most of his twenty-odd companions, and his dark hair curled merrily into glossy swirls and peaks. As the wagon rolled slowly by the traveling party, Margaret forgot herself and watched the boy. Head high, he smiled as he sang, and by his easy stride and swinging arms seemed to have not a care in the world.

> *"Oats and beans and barley, oh!*
> *Do you or I or anyone know,*
> *How oats and beans and barley grow?"*

Suddenly the boy tipped his head to her as if he'd known all along she was watching. Their gaze caught, held. She put a finger to her lips. He winked. She yanked the tarp over her head.

From under her cover, Margaret heard the boy's song carry on.

> *"Oats and beans and barley, oh!*
> *Dance your partner to and fro.*
> *Someone spies where someone hides,*
> *Oats and beans and barley, oh!*
>
> *So now you're married you must obey,*
> *You must be true to all you say.*
> *Someone knows where someone goes,*
> *Oats and beans and barley, oh!"*

Margaret lifted the cloth and peeked again. The boy waved, and now he threatened with a bagpipe he produced from over his shoulder. He screwed a pipe deftly into the body of the instrument and blew into it, inflating the bag.

Someone spies where someone hides! Would this bad-mannered boy expose her? Well! She pulled the cover over her head once more and prayed he'd keep her secret.

The boy's bagpipe, bleating sourly, offered no promise whatever.

The wagon rolled on. Margaret thought of the boy—that wink!—and then opened her satchel to pull out the small curved comb, and fixed back a lock of hair. She smiled to feel the pretty trinket in her hair; it was a triumph of a sort that she'd managed to steal it back from Minka along with the mirror. She had always imagined the dainty ornament had belonged to her mother.

Margaret slipped the mirror from its green velvet wrapping and peered into it. The surface of the mirror shone dull gray. Then, as she watched, an image formed. There again was the wild-eyed man. Again he was working with a large disk of glass, taking its measure with a rule. He set down the rule and picked up the glass, peering at it intently.

All at once, a hawk flew over and its cry pierced the air; Margaret jumped. At the same time, in the magic mirror a great flock of blackbirds erupted from the spires in the distance behind the wild-eyed man. The man looked up in terror at something or someone outside the frame; the glass disk slipped from his hands and shattered at his feet.

The mirror went dark.

In a glass glimmering, a green-eyed man awaits, the soothsayer had told her. *Seek him, but soft!* Was the man in the mirror "touched by death," as the seer had said? Was he in danger?

Later, Margaret stirred to the sound of water rushing, and shortly the wagon stopped and the driver got out, murmuring to the horse. Her heart beat faster; would he come around and discover her? She peeked from under the canvas. She slid out and crouched. No sign of the tinker.

Margaret stumbled and ducked behind a briar patch. She spied the driver off in the other direction, his back to her, apparently answering the call of nature. She pulled up her skirts and crouched to do the same. The sun felt good on her face, and she shut her eyes and listened to the birdsong and wondered at her bravery thus far. She had left Lesser Dorste! For better or worse, she sought the wild-eyed man. She was on a journey sure as any pilgrimage. No more Margaret the Crutch, she thought. No more little Maggot. Why, she'd give herself a new name. Margaret the Brave. Margaret the Strong. Something befitting such a take-charge, clever sort as she.

A noise roused her from her reverie. The cart! The wagon was pulling away without her! She lurched out of the briar patch after the cart. The wagon drew farther away. With no prayer of catching even the slowest of plodding horses, Margaret threw all care to the wind and yelled.

"Wait! Wait, good sir! Wait for me!" she shrieked, stumbling, dragging her crooked leg, but the cart driver did not hear her over the creak and rumble of the wagon and the rushing of the river. Her foot caught on a stone; she staggered and fell to the dirt, crying, "Stay! Stay!" He did not hear. He did not turn. He did not stop.

Margaret pulled herself to standing. The wagon grew smaller and smaller to her eye; soon it was very small. Then, as she watched, the cart rode up and over a hump in the road and disappeared, and with it, she realized only then, went her satchel. The magic mirror was gone.

❧

Margaret the Dull. Margaret the Moronic. What would she do now? She was alone and unprotected, and night would fall, and it would be cold, and all hope of discovering who she might be and where she belonged seemed gone away with the magic mirror.

She touched the horn comb in her hair—the only belonging she had left.

Margaret's thoughts did not fly straight, but darted and twitched like sparrows. She stood in the middle of the road with her shadow short beside her and looked back the way she had come: back to the churchyard where she'd been left a foundling child, back to her pallet in the attic with the rain her good companion, back to the streets she knew by every clump of crutch and slide of foot, back to the hunchback, the town boys, and Minka. All in that direction was known to her, and there was comfort in knowing, even if what she knew was bad.

She faced the hummock beyond which the cart had disappeared. In that direction were only questions:

Why did the wild-eyed man appear in the mirror? What or whom did he fear? Was he somehow what her heart longed for? And why? Was she addlepated, to run away on nothing but the magic of a gap-toothed peddler? Yes, that was it. Margaret the Addlepated.

A quail with quaking plume started out from behind a tump of grass, leading the way for seven trusting babies, which sped across the road after her. If only she, too, had someone to follow. She hadn't sure feet to carry her; she hadn't any guide. She watched the birds until all she could see was the mother's plume amidst the reeds, and then that, too, disappeared.

After a few moments she stepped to the side of the road and rooted around the ditch till she found a stick. She tested it; it was not of hard wood, but neither would it yield like a willow wand. Not a crutch, but a walking staff to help her move along.

Margaret raised the staff and with it struck the road. She would simply have to pretend to be the mother quail, leading her own self. She turned away from Lesser Dorste and walked on, *clump-slide, clump-slide*, traveling west toward Knightsbridge, the way of the setting sun.

Margaret walked and walked, stumbling and lurching till she thought her legs would snap and her feet would turn to pudding. Hunger gnawed at her stomach. She might have asked for food and drink—she met a few people coming and going—but she knew she was in danger, traveling alone, and feared to speak to anyone. She walked with purpose, and kept her head low.

By late afternoon, the weather had changed. Storm clouds approached from the north, bringing with them a chilling overcast. Shadows disappeared with the sun, and Margaret was all alone on the road. When the rain began to fall in earnest, she shuffled to a sheltering grove of ash trees, pulled her hood up over her head, and settled herself to wait out the storm. Thoughts of Minka and of the magic mirror were pushed aside by baser senses: Hunger. Thirst. Cold.

When a magpie soared overhead, Margaret searched the surroundings for the bird's companions, the old counting rhyme running through her mind like a town boy's taunt: *One for sorrow, two for mirth. Three for a wedding, four for birth. Five for silver, six for gold, seven for a secret not to be told.* She looked around, rubbing from her upper arms a crawling dread. There. Another bird flew up from the branch of a linden. Eight. *Eight for hell,* and—there, another—a ninth magpie flew up and followed the others. Margaret felt the damp and chill creep about her throat, and clutched her cloak more tightly.

And nine for the Devil's own self.

Minka Has a Heart

Having departed from Lesser Dorste late in the day, Minka and Bilious bickered and bungled, traveling east toward the middle of nowhere until dark threatened, and it was then that Old Penelope threw a shoe.

"Bad luck, that," said Minka, looking gloomily at the slumped and sagging horse. She glowered at their bleak surroundings. "We are neither here nor there, and wherever we are, it's some distance from a farrier. At this rate of travel we shall never catch up to Mags. Though a cripple and a half-wit, she's a sharper one than you, I'll wager," she said, pointing with her chin at Bilious.

Bilious scratched his stubble and eyeballed the toolbox, the horse, and Minka's stout figure in the gathering darkness.

"What are you looking at?" Minka screeched.

Bilious gave a loud sigh. "I was only thinking of my dear wife, God rest her soul. She could fell an oak, chop it up, and lay a fire, quick as lightning." He wiped a tear from his eye.

Minka humphed. "I whittle a fair toothpick."

"Ah, but the wife!" Bilious groaned. "She were handy with the hammer and horseshoe."

"Do you not think I can wield a brute tool?" Minka huffed. With that she pushed up her sleeves, thrust her arms elbow-deep into the toolbox, and tugged out rasp and hammer, nail cutters and clinchers. Soon enough she'd got the shoe nailed back on, and Old Penelope was happily munching from a feed bag.

Bilious set up a simple camp. "We'd best stay here tonight and make our way onward on the morrow. We've lost the light."

Minka nodded. She was, in fact, quite tired from wrestling with Penelope's shoe.

"My wife," Bilious said, eyes misty once again.

"What is it now?" Minka snapped.

"She could cook a meal fit for a king, is all, out of two stones and a burdock root!" Bilious shook his head sadly. "Fine woman."

"God's wounds!" Minka exclaimed. "Such a woman never walked the earth," she muttered, but soon had cooked a meal of fried rabbit and tender shoots of spring nettle.

"Have you no children to aid and assist you?" she asked, after they'd supped and passed a jug of ale between them. Bilious was reclined against one end of a fallen log, and Minka sat primly at the other end of it.

Bilious frowned. "Never had any offspring. Not for lack of trying!" he said, leering comically. "But God did not see fit to bless us with a child."

"Pity," Minka said. "Bad luck, that."

"And you? Have you no issue?"

"Naught but the one we seek," Minka said. "I cared for her all her life." She sniffed. "Pretty as a pink piglet." How Minka had loved to cradle the little thing on her lap, and rub ointment of radish and bishop's-wort on her poor little leg. How Mags had clapped her wee hands with happiness when Minka sang a ditty as she worked the wool or brewed the ale on brewing day.

Bilious cleared his throat, and Minka brought herself back from the past. "But as she grew, I did not want to grow overfond. She were bound to leave, and then what?" She saw in her mind's eye Margaret's face—the shock!—when she announced the betrothal to Hugo the hunch—the woolmonger. And though Minka's stomach soured to see Margaret's horror again in her mind, she adopted a bluffness. "I arranged a marriage for her, to both our advantage. And now she has run off, as I knew she would all along."

"Everyone leaves," Bilious said. "Leaves or dies. That's the way of it."

"I know that well enough, don't I? I need only that magic mirror now," she said, and sniffed loudly. "I'll not be soft of heart again and suffer for it."

"Then you'll not live a proper life," said Bilious.

"So be it."

"So be it."

Minka seemed to be done with the subject, and Bilious made to rise from the fire ring.

"I'd sooner hit her than hold her in my arms," Minka said. Her voice climbed up the sentence like a ladder, and quavered at the top.

Bilious sat back down.

Minka went on, now arguing with herself. She spat impressively into the fire, and Bilious raised his eyebrows. "Bah. I made it easy for her," she said, reaching for the jug of ale. "I toughened her hide. She's bound for bad luck, what with the crippled leg, and dumped as she was in the churchyard like a sack of onions."

Minka swigged from the bottle, wiped her mouth on her sleeve, and straightened her back. "She'll do well to be hard of heart, as I am," she said. "By my own example I've taught her well."

Bilious sat quiet, seeing in his mind the girl's balled-up fists in a show of bravado at the boys' taunts, and remembering, too, the tender way she had patted his arm when he'd told of his dear wife. How she'd spoken a volume of sympathy with her simple touch. Bilious grinned. Hard of heart—ha!

"Minka, my good woman," he said, "you have failed." Then he laughed out loud. "You've failed miserably!"

When it came time to bed down, Bilious climbed in the back of the wagon with Minka; a moment later, he tumbled out. He made a bed on the ground beneath the wagon, grumbling but smiling.

In John Book's Camp

The storm passed; night fell. Miserable and afraid, Margaret made her way deeper into the woods, well away from the dangers of the road at night, she hoped, and tucked herself in between a pair of boulders before which a tangled lilac grew. People lived in the woods, she knew, mostly honest folk who meant no harm, but who had no homes and no means and so were unwelcome to stay the night without sponsor in cities or towns. But roving in the woods too were wicked outlaws and bandits, and they were what Margaret feared. At first alert to every sound, gradually her body relaxed; at last she slept.

She dreamed of Beady Bone. Always, when the dream began, Margaret saw a bent figure in the Potter's Field. Mist covered the field, slithering and coiling like eels. She hobbled nearer to the figure: a girl, no taller than herself, dressed in grain sacks, her feet wrapped up in rags instead of shoes. The girl was doubled over, urgently searching for something.

Dream–Margaret spoke, her words muffled and indistinct. *What do you seek, Beady Bone, Beady Bone?*

The girl unfolded, turned. Her face was hideously scabbed with sores and filth. She did not answer, but moved as if by flight to stand before Dream–Margaret, grabbing her hand in her own. And then, as it always did, the face of Beady Bone began to change, and it was Margaret's own face then, upon the bent figure.

It is the truth I seek, whispered the poor beggar.

Then there was a burning smell, and the sound of crackling and hissing, like the fires of hell.

Margaret woke to the sound of a guttural oath. Alert to danger, she leaned forward, her head close to the ground. Only luck and a dark-colored cloak had kept her hidden. Through the branches of the lilac she could see a crackling fire and a group of men—she counted eight—setting up camp. Their movements, animated by dancing firelight, were jerky and exaggerated, like those of puppets at the fair.

One of the men tripped and fell into another; that one whipped a knife from his belt, and in a moment he had the man in a hold from behind, knifepoint at his neck. But the next moment, the man with the knife laughed roughly. "Back to work, Robert, you lousy sluggard," he said, pushing away the one called Robert. Robert staggered and nearly fell into the fire. These were no rough boys who would taunt and jab, but men with sharp knives and dull wits.

A woman came into the clearing, bearing a brace of skinned rabbits. She was the only woman in sight. She worked the game onto a spit and set it over the fire, then huddled apart from the men, alternately stepping close to turn the spit and stepping away again, worrying at the long, dark braid that fell thick as rope to her waist.

Margaret was seized by several instincts at once. She wanted to flee, to get far away from these rough men. She needed to eat, and there was food. She needed to drink; there were leather bottles and ale. She needed shelter; there were hides and covers. She would wait and watch.

As the night wore on and the men drank, Margaret quaked to hear boasts of cruel capture, thieving, and plunder: all in a day's work for this crew. The one the men called John laughed and cheered at their bounty of the day, a haul taken from a merchant on the east-west road. Another, the man who'd earlier held his mate at knifepoint, replied, "He'll tell no tales, that one, John Book."

Margaret's heart beat like wings of magpies in her

chest. It was the thief John Book and his band. John Book, who had killed Bilious's dear wife.

"A fair take today, lads," Book gloated, tossing sacks of goods. His voice was low and rough, rocks ground under a heavy foot. "Sort it, stack it; let's see what we've got." Three of the men rose from the fire ring and began to pull out items from among a heap of sacks and barrels. A silver tureen; a sack of grain and another of oats; a necklace of gold links, crusted with colored stones; a brooch big as a fist; a satchel.

Margaret sucked in a breath. *Her* satchel!

She crouched down deeper behind the bush to watch, to keep guard of herself, to wait.

It was a long wait. The men ate, messy and crude, the fat of the cooked rabbits dripping down chins and wrists. The voices were so gruff and coarse as to be a foreign language. After a while the talk turned to song, and then, at last, to snoring. She waited longer; the prospect of stepping any closer to the men sent ice water through her veins. But once sleep had come to the men, they fell fast and hard, as she'd seen Minka do on brewing days, after drinking too much ale.

Clouds fled, and the moon was high. She waited till the fire was but coals. Then she stepped out from behind the copse, *clump-slide*—Deus!—*clump-slide*. Closer to the men, very quiet, very close now. She took up the satchel, felt by its weight and shape that the contents were within—the mirror!—and stepped away from the clearing. *Clump-slide, clump-slide, clump-slide;* her eyes focused on the sleeping shapes of the men, and she prayed fervently that she would not be heard. *Clump*— God's wounds! Her step landed on a twig, and it broke with a tiny snap.

It was enough to wake John Book.

A hand darted like a snake, gripped her by the ankle, and felled her with one yank. Then he rose from where he'd slept on the ground, put his hands on his hips, and laughed, a girlish giggle that froze Margaret's heart in her chest.

"Ah, we've snared ourselves a big rabbit, aye, boys?"

Several but not all of the men were waking, groggily standing or sitting, clearly ready to do John Book's bidding. The man called Robert stood and, grunting, stoked the fire, which roared up and cast shadows across the bandits' greasy faces. The firelight seemed to glint off scores of lances and knives, sharp and cruel as John Book's nose.

Without warning, John Book booted Margaret in the ribs; she wheezed and wrapped her arms around her middle, doubling over in agony.

"Don't think this one'd fetch a ransom, eh? Nor would anyone pay us to keep her!" John Book leered at her. A couple of the men nodded and laughed, a sound like beasts barking and braying. The woman with the long braid stepped into the light of the fire ring and looked hard at Margaret. Margaret looked at her hopefully, but the woman only lowered her gaze, turned, and stepped away again.

Margaret tried to keep from eyeing her satchel.

But John Book saw. "Yours, is it?" He swooped the satchel up and dumped out its few contents. Out tumbled and flung wide the cup, the feather, the extra hose, and the mirror partly wrapped in a velvet scrap. The dancing firelight caught silver, and the mirror shone like fire itself. John Book took two strides and plucked the mirror from the dirt. The men roared with laughter as he giggled, primped, and posed.

Margaret prayed to God the mirror would fail to work for thieves and murderers.

Then John Book stopped fussing. His eyes lit with greed. He stared into the mirror as if lost, until a string of drool dripped from the corner of his mouth and roused him from his stupor.

"Gold!" He giggled like a madman. "Jewels, heaps of coins tossed about by pink-powdered ladies and fat-fingered men!" He grabbed Margaret's wrist and wrenched it. "What is this mirror? What is its power? Where is the treasure it shows me?"

Margaret cried out. "It's mine! Give it here! Give it!"

John Book yanked her to him. Pressed to his barrel-like chest, she could smell the ale on his breath and see the stubble on his greasy chin. Suddenly there was a knifepoint at her throat; she felt it prick her skin.

"I can read the mirror!" Margaret shouted. "I—I alone! I can read it."

"Then do!" John Book tossed the mirror to her; she fumbled and caught it as tenderly as she could. "You will tell me what you knows, or I'll be done with you and good riddance." There was no ghastly giggle now.

She held her breath and gazed into the mirror. All the gold and jewels for which John Book's heart lusted sparkled and shone, heaps upon heaps of them, and John Book himself sat in the middle of it, a lady's large necklace on his sweat-soaked chest. Bristles of hair leaped from the neck of his tunic.

The image faded, and there again was the wild-eyed man. It was dark now, in his chamber, and he sat by candlelight at his table, scribbling and scratching on a parchment, dipping his quill into an ink pot, scribbling again with furious purpose.

"Quit mooning and tell me what it means!" boomed John Book. "Tell where the riches can be found!"

Margaret breathed deeply, willing her heart to slow, and cleared her throat. She looked into the mirror.

"I . . ." Her voice froze. "I see a coach," she lied, "a great painted coach, stopped beside a campfire and leaning to one side. A—a spoked wheel is off its post and lying, broken, upon the ground." She swallowed hard. John Book shook her arm, wrenching bone and socket—she winced and went on. "There is the crest of a noble family on the door of the coach. One of six horses in the line is missing. A rider must have gone for help. A guard paces, keeping watch."

"The crest? What does it look like?"

"Corners colored dark, and a . . . a bird."

"What bird?"

"Er, a falcon."

John Book rattled her wrist. "Where is the coach broken down?"

Margaret shook her head. "I see only—only woods such as these."

John Book twisted her wrist once more to yank the mirror from her hand, and let go her arm. Margaret clutched her shoulder where it hurt. She began to shiver and could not stop. She thought her lie was convincing. But now what?

John Book stared at her a moment more, then stuffed the mirror in her satchel and spat upon the ground.

"Wilfred of Woodstock." John Book picked up a jug from the ground and swigged from it, tipping his head back and staggering. He didn't bother to wipe his wet mouth. "That's how the crest reads. And within the broken coach will be his lady, or his daughter, or his aged mum, else travel would be by wagon. I smell a chance," he said, "to aid and comfort a noble in distress!" The one called Robert snorted.

Margaret's breath came shallow and fast. She glanced at John Book and found that he was staring hard at her, as if figuring the value of a cut of beef. When they didn't find a broken coach, would he kill her? Or would she have to lie again? Could she?

"The south road, then," John Book said. "We move to

Woodstock with the dawn." Margaret silently prayed her thanks to God, and thought too of Minka's two-sided coin of luck: John Book had believed her. 'Twas good luck!

Then Book turned to Robert. "Bind her!"

Bad luck.

Robert laced Margaret's wrists behind her expertly and painfully, and shoved her to the ground. John Book drank again, a long pull, and then he lay down beside the fire ring.

Within minutes the thief was snoring, followed one by one by his mates. The watchman's head drooped, nodded, until his chin settled on his chest and then he slept. Margaret tried to untie herself, but she could not. She looked hopefully for the braided woman, but did not see her. Her wrists ached and burned, and her stomach crawled with hunger and fear. She lay in the dirt hour upon hour, until at last she began to drift into uneasy sleep.

All at once, a hand covered Margaret's mouth. She struggled to breathe, tossing her head, twisting, turning to see: curling dark hair, bright eyes—a wink!

It was the pilgrim boy!

A Rescue

Without a word the boy sliced away her bindings, then replaced the knife in his belt. Margaret smiled her astonished thanks, then turned and reached to gain her belongings, strewn dangerously close to the snoring John Book. She managed to grab the scrap of green velvet, but in the next instant the boy threw her over his shoulder like a sack of grain, and off he trotted. Being swept off her feet was not at all as she'd expected, she thought dryly.

After a while the boy stopped, and Margaret slid from his back. She could glimpse only his white teeth in the moonlight, whether set in smile or grimace she could not tell. He remained silent, no song or bagpipe now. They stood a moment, breathing like horses, listening like rabbits. They'd got away from the slumbering John Book, and for that Margaret was grateful. But the young pilgrim had rushed her away, shushing her protests, without giving her the chance to steal back the satchel and the mirror. She used the scrap of green velvet to stab the tears of frustration that had collected at the corners of her eyes. Though her heart felt the loss cruelly, reason told her it would have been folly to test the limit of John Book's slumber. He slept with a knife in his fist.

They walked on in silence. After a few steps the boy held out his arm, and she took it, and this enabled her to keep up with his long strides, though she could tell he shortened his natural gait for her benefit.

In a while the boy stopped and held up a hand. He disappeared into the trees. When he returned, he pulled her gently into the cover of a small grove of aspen quaking in the breeze. To the east, the dark blanket of sky leached to gray wool, and Margaret could see the boy's face in the dawning light. It was grubby, smudged with dirt and stained with what looked like black-currant jelly, but improved by a certain pleasantness of features balanced almost perfectly between dark, thick eyebrows and a strong chin, and between a set of ears that poked out like the handles on Minka's cook pot. His eyes were dark and large and smart, and his wide mouth was bracketed by dimples, deepened now by smiling. It seemed he thought the danger past, but Margaret was not so certain. She winced at the sound of his voice, loud after so much silence and fear.

"Now we can rest our bones," he was saying, "at least long enough to catch a breath and properly introduce ourselves." He put a hand to his chest and dipped his head. "Forgive my rudeness, lady. I am called Bertram Stanground, and I am at your service."

"I am Margaret—Margaret of the Church." What other name could a foundling claim than the place where she was found? Margaret spoke it in a whisper, as if thieves might be lurking behind every tree. "Thank you," she said. "And for before: when my wagon passed your band, you kept my secret."

"*Your* wagon?" He sat back. "And did the driver know you owned the cart?"

"You almost gave me away with your song!" She flushed, remembering suddenly the lines about dancing, and marriage. "How happened you upon me?" she said.

"I was gathering herbs and medicinals found only in the light of the moon. Good luck I lost my bearings. Rough company you keep. Where are you going? And how came you to be separated from your cartwheels?"

It was such a long story. The rush of capture and escape past, Margaret felt suddenly faint and weak with hunger. She did not speak, but put her head in her hands.

"Never mind; there will be time enough to tell your tale," Bertram said. "My companions will have food and drink, and you'll be safe with us, no matter what your crime."

"Crime!" She jerked her head. "I—"

But she could see in the growing light that Bertram was smiling, and she knew he was only teasing.

"Do you think you can travel a bit further?" he asked kindly. Margaret nodded at him. The smile lines disappeared. Instead his face was writ all over with concern.

"Wait," he said. He was gone just a few minutes, but during his absence Margaret began already to worry, her mind wandering back through the woods to John Book's camp, to the danger she'd escaped, and to the magic mirror she'd been so viciously parted from. Again.

Bertram returned carrying a sturdy stick with a wide fork at one end. He quickly took her measure, broke off the stick's excess using a foot as a lever, and then presented the crutch to Margaret with a courtly bow. She thanked him, and they began again to walk, and to talk. She told Bertram how she'd come to be captured by John Book. The way was easier, now, and the crutch helped, and the cheering sun was up over the hedgerow. Soon they came out of the trees and onto a field, and from there they could see the road winding in two directions.

"Ah, the open road at last," Bertram said, and began first to hum, and then to sing, as they made their way along the road.

> *"Maiden, mother without peer, with mercy sweet*
> * and kind,*
> *Pray to him that chose thee here, with whom*
> * through grace did find,*
> *That he forgive us sin and mistake*
> *And clean of every guilt us make."*

Then Bertram grinned, and his song took a turn.

> *"Ale makes many a man to stick upon a briar,*
> *Ale makes many a man to slumber by the fire,*
> *Ale makes many a man to wallow in the mire,*
> *So doll, doll, doll thy ale, doll, doll thy ale."*

"My mistress brews ale," Margaret said.
"A worthy skill. What is your mistress called?"
"Minka," she replied.
Bertram threw back his head and began again to sing.

> *"Minka makes a man to stumble on a stone;*
> *Minka makes a man to stagger drunken home.*
> *Minka makes a man to break his bone—*

Join me now!"

She shook her head shyly, but he grabbed up her hand and swung it in time to the song, the beat of which matched her *clump-slide* surprisingly neatly.

"So doll, doll, doll thy ale, doll, doll thy ale."

Margaret smiled in spite of her hunger and weariness. She was out of danger for the moment, and although she had lost her mirror once again, she was alive to walk another day. And, thanks be to God, her rescuer had not brought his horrid bleating bagpipe.

"Doll, doll thy ale, doll thy ale!"

An Addition to Our Party

The sun cast early-morning shadows as Bilious's cart bounced into Eastham. In no time he'd paid tradesman duties and fees for pontage and pavage, set out his wares, and begun to hawk them.

"Ten-penny nails! Shining pots of brass and copper plate! Pennywhistles and port! Darning needles, thistledown, fine soap!"

Minka humphed. "If you've fine soap, why then do you smell so ripe?"

"Soap I use on my person is soap I cannot sell."

"Soap you'll *not* sell if ripe you smell," countered Minka. "Consider sampling such wares as soap and scent, and see what *then* you sell!" She smiled and crossed her arms across her bosom.

Bilious grinned. "As you wish it, I shall sample the scent." He bowed low, then rose and rooted around in a wooden box. At last he pulled out a tiny vial, which he opened and passed beneath his nose. "Good stuff," he proclaimed, eyes watering, and dabbed a bit behind each ear.

"Good God," said Minka, waving a hand in front of her face. "I couldn't say what's worse—your natural aroma or whatever vile sack of skunk is in that bottle."

Bilious had a customer. "Observe," he said to Minka, and turned to the approaching fellow. The customer, tall and skinny and gaunt of cheek, fairly jingled with coin. "Good sir!" said Bilious. "May I interest you in a—"

The man held up a hand. "Have you any needles?"

"Needles? Needles? Of course, my good sir. I've needles of any size you may require. I've needles fine enough to stitch a lady's dainties, wink-wink, or tough enough for saddle leather."

"I'll take one fine and one sturdy," said the customer, "and never mind what use I make of them."

"Of course, of course, dear sir." He eyed the man's garb and the quality of his shoe, and arrived at a figure he thought he might afford. "That'll be a halfpenny for the pair."

"A halfpenny! For a pair of needles! Certainly not. I'll give you in trade a hunk of beef jerky."

"Hardly!"

"Fine jerky," the man said, "fine as this needle."

"Fine jerky for the fine needle, then," said Bilious, "but I'll not include the saddle-weight."

"Fine."

The deal was struck and the fellow strode away.

Bilious turned to Minka. "Now you see how it's done," he said, and stuck a bit of jerky in his gums.

Minka turned up her nose, then turned to go in search of Margaret. "The value of the trade would depend on the eye of the beholder."

"What's true of trade is true of love and beauty," said Bilious, chewing vigorously and economically with his few teeth. "It's all in the angle of the squint."

❦

Minka returned a time later. She'd asked after Margaret with no luck, but Bilious seemed happy.

"I see by the foolish set of your head upon your shoulders that you are well pleased."

"I've come away with an uncommon good trade," he admitted. "I began with a basket and traded for a bucket. Next a broom of clustered twigs for a tallow candle." He ticked the items off on his fingers. "One item for the next, if you follow: a funnel, two tin plates, a large brass pot, a remnant of cloth, a rug of blue linsey-woolsey, and a cup made out of a coconut!" he finished.

Minka nodded eagerly. "A cup made out of a coconut?"

"With small silver feet."

Minka marveled at Bilious's skill. "Silver feet! I admit you've come out far ahead. Well done! Where is this rare cup made out of a coconut and finished with silver feet?"

Bilious beamed more brightly, if it were possible, and leaned toward Minka. "The cup made out of a coconut were not my final trade." He stood back triumphantly, stomach out, as with hands on hips he grinned and waggled his eyebrows, waiting for Minka to ask what it was he'd acquired.

Minka, frowning, shrugged. "It matters not to me," she said. She sighed and removed her squashed hat, scratched at her scalp beneath her wimple, then placed the hat once more upon her head. She puffed out her cheeks and let the air go in a great whoosh. She whistled a snippet of a dirge. At last she said, "If you're not going to come out with it, you vexing man, then I'm sure I care not what the item is. *At all.*"

Bilious guffawed, and clapped his hands. "As you're so eager to know, I will show you," he said. "Allow me to place something small in the pocket of your cloak."

"I'll allow it," she said, smiling a little, in anticipation of the outcome of the trade. "Is it small as, say, a pearl, a pretty, a jewel?"

"Wait, wait," Bilious said, and indeed slipped something into her pocket.

"Wait, wait," he said again when Minka reached for the pocket, and so she put her hands on her hat, resigned to whatever game Bilious would play. He stood back, and with a sly look unfastened the small brown satchel that hung newly from his shoulder.

As Minka watched, out from the satchel came first a pair of tiny tufted ears, followed by a russet-furred little round head and bright black eyes.

Minka drew back. "Noo," she began.

In an instant the creature leaped from Bilious's satchel to the ground and ran daintily up Minka's cloak, scarcely disturbing its drape, and dipped into her pocket and out again, as all the while a guttural sound was building from a low, deep place in the very core of Minka's being, up, up, up and out her throat.

"Noooooooooo!" Minka hopped about, arms wild in the air. "No, no, no, and no again, no!" she cried. "Get the beast off me! Get it off, I say!"

"Pip is hardly a beast," said Bilious, calmly welcoming the little red squirrel, for that was what it was, back into his small sack, first taking from it the prize picked from Minka's pocket: a halfpenny.

"Pip? Pip? The beast has a name?"

"Of course he has a name, Minka, as you have a name and I have a name, and he likes shiny things, same as you."

"You would compare a wretched rodent to a human being made in the image of God?"

90

"Certainly, for he is a pet with wit and charm in great abundance. Pip will make a right jolly addition to our party."

The squirrel poked his head out of the sack, and Bilious scratched the fur between his ears. Minka leaned against the cart and fanned herself with her hat.

"What a profitable morning it's been," Bilious went on. "I'd just accomplished the trade for the cup of coconut, if you can imagine—"

"I can *well* imagine the rare thing!" Minka wailed.

"—when a young lad happened by in need of a gift for his bride. The lass is all a-sneeze around Pip, says the lad, but myself? I wonder if she sneezes more at petty thieving than at the humble squirrel, who is clean as a whistle, after all, with no dander to speak of. Anyway," Bilious went on, "the lad was pained to part with his pet, what he'd trained to, yes, pick a pocket, but also to do little flips and capers for show."

"A regular squirrel *cirque*," Minka muttered.

"Precisely my thought! Pip will draw a crowd to my wagon, and increase my trade." He rubbed his hands together gleefully. "Beautiful."

Minka rolled her eyes. "As you say," she growled, "it's all in the angle of the squint." She slapped her hat against her leg to knock the dust out, and then plopped it back on her head. "I'd have rather had the coconut cup."

To Be Healed!

Margaret and Bertram walked until their shadows stretched not so far ahead of them as when they'd started out upon the road. Soon they came upon a group of gray-robed travelers breaking their fast beneath a stand of silver birch. A pair of old men sat on the ground upon a cloak, playing a game of dice. A plump woman sliced rounds of sausage as quickly as her little girl could gobble them up. The smile that split Bertram's face and showed his crooked teeth told Margaret what she wanted to know: this was Bertram's traveling party, and she was safe.

"Come, Margaret Hopalong," he said, grabbing a

piece of coarse bread and some sausage and passing it to her, "come and meet my cousin Henry. I am bound to him in service, and have been these seven years."

Bertram led her to a man of an age better than Father Bernard but less than the bishop, sitting upon a field-stone. A dark felt hat's broad brim did not obscure the nose, which squatted left of center and was flattened at the bridge. He wore a heavy woolen cloak fastened with a pewter pilgrim's badge. At their approach, he leaped from his perch and reached a hand to Bertram. His cloak opened to reveal a plain brown cross stitched to the front of his cassock.

"Bertram, back from the wars, you've found us once again. I was sure you'd been et by wild pigs." Henry smiled at Margaret, curiosity lighting his eyes, and removed his broad-brimmed hat. She saw his head was shaved above the temples, leaving a ring of red hair all around, tonsured in the manner of a friar or monk.

"I see, Bertram," the man went on, "that you've collected a friend! I am called Brother Henry, friar of the Brethren of the Holy Cross, and I note we've something in common. My brotherhood in Dale's End is known commonly as the *Crutched* Friars!" He chuckled and pointed at her crutch and at the same time patted the crutch, or cross, on his torso.

Margaret frowned, tucking the crutch Bertram had given her behind her back. The friar seemed kindly, but she didn't like her infirmity to be spoken of so openly.

Brother Henry's face gentled as he sensed he'd troubled her. "Come and sit, child," he said. "I must know how you came to be in Bertram's company, which I trust has been gentlemanly."

Bertram bowed regally, sweeping his arm low along the ground, and then introduced Margaret, relating the story of her capture and rescue, while she sat beside the friar and ate the bread and sausage, too hungry and weak to add a word to Bertram's dramatic retelling.

"You've no need to worry," said Henry when Bertram was done. "With us you'll find safety and companionship, and never a threat shall harm you."

Though his gaze was serene and sure, the friar seemed ill equipped to carry out such a promise. Doubt must have shone in Margaret's gaze, for in the next moment the holy man sprang from the rock and, dark robes whipping all about, turned a set of perfect cartwheels! One, two, three!

Margaret, who couldn't have been more surprised if fire had spewed forth from his ears, dropped the rest of her bread and clapped.

"Well done, Cousin," said Bertram, laughing. Margaret noticed how laughter was never far from Bertram's lips, and what a nice laugh it was.

Brother Henry settled himself beside Margaret once again on the rock and caught his breath. "Though you may not imagine by the cut of my clothing and the cut of my hair, I was once capable of great feats of strength.

Oh, yes. I could leap upon my destrier fully armed, without putting foot to stirrup. I could scale the underside of a siege ladder, using only my two strong arms. Indeed, it was not uncommon for me to turn cartwheels in full armor!" He raised a hand skyward in triumph, then let it fall to his lap. "And in a coat of mail," he said softly, "to dance."

"But . . ." Cartwheels in full armor? Warhorse? Dancing? He was a holy man!

"I was not always Brother Henry, under vow of poverty and chastity. In another life, another time, I was a knight, you see," Henry explained, as if hearing Margaret's unspoken doubts. "I served Ranulph, the old king, among others," he added. "I was a fine knight, if I say it myself." He stroked his chin. "Oh, and such a fine red beard I had," he said. His voice trailed off wistfully. "But," he declared, slapping his thigh, "if beards funded salvation, then all goats would be saved."

Bertram laughed heartily. "Perhaps they are, Cousin!" he said.

"Blasphemy!" roared the friar, and he switched Bertram on the rump with a willow wand. Bertram howled, dancing about, knees high, as if his bottom were on fire. Margaret couldn't help but snort.

"Maaaaa!" Bertram was bleating and tugging on his chin as if he were a billy goat. Then his eyes lit, and he leaped to a sack upon the ground and pulled from it his bagpipes.

Margaret cringed when he inflated the bag and blew a few tentative notes.

"Getting better all the time, Bertie!" said Brother Henry, shouting to be heard above the din. "Keep up the good work, but"—he pointed vaguely in the direction of the woods—"mayhap over there. . . ."

Bertram's face reddened with effort, and he waggled his eyebrows and moved off a bit.

"Here, Margaret, I've gone and told you something of myself, and you've told me nothing," said Brother Henry. Margaret had meant to keep her own counsel. But the friar was so kind that everything spilled out— Minka's plan to marry her off, the soothsayer's prophecy. The magic mirror.

Henry stroked his chin where his legendary beard once was and said nothing for a time.

What must the friar think of her? Margaret wondered. Might he imagine her burning in hell for heeding a soothsayer's prophecy? For courting images in a magic mirror?

But when he spoke, it was a cipher. "Things are not always as they appear," he said. "You are now on a journey, magic mirror or no, and none may travel that journey for you."

"But all is lost! The mirror is gone, and I know not how I shall find the wild-eyed man without the mirror's aid."

Henry fingered the ring on his littlest finger, head down, deep in thought.

Who was he to advise this young girl? Henry's thoughts traveled back in time across the fields of his own life. *All is lost.* On his own darkest day, had he not uttered those very words?

How well he remembered that day, and his failure.

After the king consort Armand died, Henry had been kept on at court, but grudgingly. He'd been riding the countryside on a fool's errand—sent by that ape Lord Geoffrey, Queen Isobel's new husband. He was always inventing ridiculous quests to occupy the knights in the new time of peace. Then word came that Isobel's child, heir to the throne, had gone missing and was feared dead. "The queen lies ill and dying of grief," the messenger said. "All are to return to court and join in the search for the missing child."

Henry was making ready to leave when a crone approached, her face in the shadow of a shawl.

"The queen yet lives, and so there is hope," said the crone.

"All is lost, I fear," said Henry.

"Not all, not yet." The old woman withdrew from her apron a small package wrapped in linen, tied around with twine and sealed with wax. Henry looked upon the object with curiosity. "Take this to the queen without delay," she said, "for it may yet be of use. But mark me: take it only to the queen, the queen alone, and do not open it. Do I have your word?"

The crone peered up from her stooped posture and fixed him with a dark, bright eye. He promised his word was true, and true it was. He would not break a lady's trust.

Henry squinted at the sealed, linen-wrapped package. His heart beat with a strange curiosity. "But what is the gift, good woman?"

She glanced at him, her gaze troubled with—what? Mistrust? Had she doubted him, then? It turned out she was right to doubt.

"Let us say it is a tool of truth," the old woman said, and pressed it into his hands. "Take it. I beg you, take it from me!" She closed her eyes and turned away. "Now ride."

And so Henry mounted his horse, a massive pied destrier called Gilly, and rode away at top speed. And as he rode, his mind went back, again and again, to the gift he bore, this tool of truth. What truth might he learn, were he to open the package intended for the queen? And while he picked and plucked at the package in his mind, foolishly craving whatever it might yield, he scarcely noticed the travelers on the road. Trees and fields and hedgerows were all a dizzy blur, and then—

His horse reared up and roused him from his stupor. In a flash he saw a river, a man, a woman. But before he could act, Gilly's hooves, with unlucky precision, struck the man down. He tried to rein the horse back around and saw the man's head, bludgeoned beyond reach of life, before Gilly, wild and out of control, carried him off.

He had taken life before, in service to God and the old king in time of war. But as he clung to his panicked steed, he vowed that if he survived this ride, he would not take life again. The guilt of his carelessness settled heavily on his shoulders. Let God take a life, not him. Not him.

Later, when Gilly had calmed, he rode back to the scene, but the people were gone and the doors of the town were shut. Sick and trembling with remorse, he feared his mind was playing tricks: He thought he saw the crone, held captive by the royal messenger, crying, "She needs me!" *The queen?* He squeezed his eyes shut against the vision—cruel taunts of a guilty conscience!— and went to the river. Something blinked in the moonlight, and he knelt and found a silver ring in the dirt along the riverbank. He wore it to remind him of his vow. Over the years, the ring had dug a gully in his flesh.

🍂

"Brother Henry?" Margaret said. The friar seemed lost in thought, fingering the little ring he wore. A token of his faith, no doubt.

The friar cleared his throat. "Tell me what you saw in the mirror," he said.

"The man, and . . . blackbirds flying from the spires

of what must be Knightsbridge Cathedral. I think," Margaret added. "At least, it had a great stained-glass window."

"Round? A rose window?"

Margaret nodded.

"Ah," said Henry. "This is why you travel west."

She nodded. "To find the green-eyed man of the seer's prophecy."

Bertram had wandered near, and now his bagpipes deflated gustily. "But the seer foresaw death and danger with the man in the glass. Would it not be wiser to travel in the direction opposite? It's foolish!"

"It's brave!"

"Peace," said the monk, laughing gently. "You knew to travel west. You wisely left the mirror behind, as you value your life, and the life of him who came to help you," he added, nodding to Bertram. "You've charted a course, alone and friendless."

Margaret smiled at Brother Henry. "*You* are too kind, sir," she said, with a sharp glance at Bertram.

The friar slapped his thighs. "As we are heading west ourselves, you must continue your journey with us. In the royal city we may bide awhile. My old friend Father Sebastian is at the great cathedral and will ensure we have a place to sleep. Let us walk together."

"I fear I am quite slow, and will tire," Margaret said.

"How came you by your infirmity?" asked Henry.

"I believe I was born thus," Margaret said. "I know not my true history."

Henry nodded again. "One need not know his history to know his nature. In fact, for some it is best to walk away from that history with deliberate strides, and pray to discover one's true nature on the path." Pensive, he twirled the ring on his finger, then stood and offered Margaret his arm. She rose. "We will be fine companions, for I am strong but weary of spirit, and require frequent rest along my way."

The friar's rugged, broken-nosed face clouded, and Margaret imagined secret regrets and lost loves, pictured him dancing, dressed in his coat of mail.

Now the sun was high, and the warmth felt good on Margaret's bones, which were stiff and sore from bumping for miles in the tinker's wagon and spending half the night tied up in John Book's camp. Bertram walked slowly beside her and never seemed to mind the pace.

"It's a good fit?" Bertram said, pointing to the crutch he'd cut for her.

"It does me fine," Margaret said. "I did have a good crutch," she added, "but I traded it." Her face flushed. "For the mirror."

"A right fair trade!" Bertram assured her. "The adventure!" he cried. "The hope! The very nerve of the trade!" he exclaimed. "Margaret of the Quest, I'll call you." His expression went thoughtful, and his fingers moved as if playing the pipes. "Deserving of a song, I'd say."

Margaret suppressed a smile. "I'll not introduce myself so grandly," she said. "When I meet the man in the mirror, if ever I do, I will say, 'I am Margaret Church. Who are you?'"

"A fine introduction, none finer," Bertram said. "And will you curtsy?"

Margaret flourished her free hand and bent low her good knee.

Bertram bowed in return. "May I have this dance?" he said, and grabbed her around the waist. Margaret spun about in his arms, laughing, her new crutch flailing wide, her cheeks grown warm.

Bertram released her, and they began to walk again. "Sometimes I dance or skip to relieve the steady step-step-step," Bertram said. His face turned serious. "Henry walks with a burden. I know not what it is, but he has confided that he has done harm to another. Grave harm, for which he must atone." But as quickly as his face had darkened, it cleared. "Many's the tale of what relics of the saints we've seen along the way," he said, glancing at Margaret with a sly grin. "St. Francis's hair shirt, for one," he said, "and the Virgin Mary's milk. At Wimborne, some hairs from Christ's beard and a shoe of St. William, and a tooth from the grin of St. Philip! It's astonishing what remains of the saints, and how gloriously the bits and parts are enshrined!"

Margaret shuddered gleefully. "What else?"

"Toenails!" Bertram drew his bagpipe more comfortably across his shoulder as he warmed to her curiosity. "And I near heaved when I saw the finger St. Thomas used to touch the rib of the risen Christ, I can tell you!" he said. "In one holy shrine, some desperate soul bit off a piece of the holy cross and stole it away in his cheek!"

"Desperate, or hungry," Margaret said.

"Ha! He'd have done better with the piece of manna we saw in Santa Croce, a relic of the miraculous food God fed to the starving Israelites!"

"I fear I would not have saved the manna for the ages," Margaret said, "but et it on the spot."

Bertram burst out laughing. "I never thought it," he said, "but now I do wonder what starving Israelite chose to store instead of eat this God-sent food!"

Bertram suddenly stopped grinning. "But of course! Come with us to St. Winifred's Well, where we are bound! I know you've a quest, but won't your way be easier if you are healed by the waters? St. Winifred is the patron saint of the crippled, as you must know! I mean no offense," he added hastily.

"None taken," she said.

"Think on it." Bertram began to walk on.

Margaret stood still in the middle of the road. To be healed! To set out, and to come back different. *Just because you limp doesn't mean you can't heal. . . .* Is that not what the Grimsby seer had told her?

She busied herself with the effort of catching up to Bertie, *clump-slide, clump-slide, clump-slide.*

Farther Along the Wrong Way

Having bickered the better part of an hour while the sun moved across the sky, Minka and Bilious determined to travel farther east to Bolingbroke. Pip had picked a farthing from the purse of a nun—"An accident!" Bilious insisted in the face of Minka's glare—and they'd decided as one mind to depart Eastham with all haste.

The cart rolled into Bolingbroke late in the day, and Minka called out to the townsfolk, "Has anybody seen a girl with a crooked leg? A skinny thing, capering and stumbling and looking for all the world like a muddle-headed prat?"

Bilious frowned at Minka. "Now, then," he called,

"has anybody seen a ginger-headed girl, slender of waist and intelligent of eye, walking nobly but with an unfortunate limp?"

Minka humphed.

Bilious looked sidelong at her. "Is the girl not ginger-headed?"

Minka nodded. "She's not as fair as I."

"And is she not slim as a whip?"

"She never et much."

"And is she not bright and smart as—"

"I suppose she did bring back the proper coin, most times, when she went to market."

Bilious smiled. "There now," he said. "I'm convinced we're looking out for the same girl, then."

They stopped the wagon at the center of town and set out on foot to search the streets, and to inquire of everyone they saw.

"A girl with a crooked gait asked me what direction I might be traveling," said a merchant, "and when I said east to Eastham and on to Bolingbroke, she thanked me and moved away in a hurry." The merchant let out a great fart that rumbled long and deep as hell's own thunder.

"I should say she did!" said Minka.

"When did you see her? Where?" Bilious asked the merchant.

"Day afore last, I think," he said, mulling it over for a moment, "back in Lesser Dorste."

"Bad luck, that!" Minka moaned.

"And yet we know now that she did not travel east," Bilious suggested. "That's something we didn't know before."

"Oh, but what if it were another girl with a crooked leg what spoke to the odorous merchant?" said Minka. "How are we to know?"

Bilious pondered. "Let us assume, for lack of better instruction, that it were indeed she. We will travel north from here, for north is not east, and discover what we will."

"Oh, bad luck we've come the wrong way!" Minka moaned again, and wrung her hands.

"It were she," the merchant piped up. "And she might have stole a meat pie from me as well, now I come to remember it," he said, eyeing Minka's supper.

"She never done it!" cried Minka.

"She were hungry!" said Bilious.

"A thief, now, is she, as well as a cripple-noggin!" said Minka.

Bilious pulled Minka aside. "Rest easy, we're on her trail now. We know sommat more than before, and I'll wager she never stole any meat pie. Let's do some custom here, and then early tomorrow we can be on our way north to Sackville Proper."

Minka sniffed and nodded. "All right." She wiped her nose on her sleeve.

Bilious smiled. "You can't hide your tender heart, Minka, not from me."

"Tender heart, my bunioned foot," she said, then smoothed her skirts and sniffed once more. "It's the mirror I seek, as well you know."

"I do know what you seek," said Bilious. "Mayhap better than you know yourself. Now, then," he said, unfastening his satchel and sizing up the crowd, "let the squirrel *cirque* begin!"

"Gah!" Minka hurried off, to spare herself the company of the rodent Pip.

The Very Rain That Falls

Two days passed upon the road. Whenever a pilgrim stubbed a toe or patched a blister, Bertram would play a tune on the bagpipe to take away the pain, and each time, the ailing pilgrim would hasten to assure him that the bagpipe had done the trick, and that he need not play any longer on their account. For all her travel, Margaret felt no closer to the man in the mirror, be he real or—the thought had crossed her mind—invention. But there was no question now of turning back, no matter how often Margaret wondered whether she'd have been better off had she never set out. Margaret Quest indeed.

Once, the road ran close to a dark wood, and Henry

and Bertram walked one on either side of Margaret. She looked deep into the forest for a sign of John Book, but they passed by in safety. Once, they passed through a village and drank some ale that was not as good as Minka's, nor as strong, and once, a storm howled in the night as they slept in a shed, and the rain on the roof roared *Minka-Minka-Minka!* to her ear.

Sometimes Margaret would stop to rest and the others would go on, but Bertram always stayed back with her, talking and joking until she caught her breath and grew strong enough to continue. He never seemed troubled by her slow pace, nor did he seem to prefer another's company. And by the light of the evening fire, he whittled designs to pretty her crutch.

She wasn't used to so much chatter. Bertram had ready an endless supply of questions, and songs to share, and curious interests; gradually her shrugs and scowls gave way to real conversation. Even so, time passed as often in pleasant quiet as in talk and merry singing.

One rainy morning, Bertram's step was not lively. His bagpipe drooped beneath his arm. He shuffled, grim-faced, his eyes sunk in dark hollows.

"You look like you've et fish gone bad," Margaret said, though she knew from the slope of his eyebrows and the hang of his head that the trouble was not his gut.

"I cannot shake the dream I had last night," Bertram replied, "for it's as well known to me as my own feet. I dreamed of my sister. My dear companion, when she lived."

"I—I'm sorry, Bertie," Margaret managed. She wished there was something she could do for her friend. She recalled the good peddler back in Lesser Dorste, who'd kindly asked about her leg instead of ignoring it or cursing it.

"It pains you," she said, "to think of her?"

"When I was ten years old or thereabout, my parents died of the black death. It happened quickly, and sadness was overtaken by worry. I had myself to care for, and my sister, younger by two years. We lived in St. Alwes, and I thought to travel to Minster City, to find work and food. On our way, we stopped to wash in the river. She went under and never breathed again. I dove in and found her struggling in the reeds, vicious as eels and strong they were. I grabbed her under her arms, but . . . in the end . . . I let go.

"I dragged myself from the river and up the bank. It was then I remembered the knife in my belt. Why had I not thought of it before? I returned to the water and cut her free, but she was dead. I buried her on the riverbank, marked the place with a cross of stones, and prayed God her soul to keep.

"She and I will meet again in heaven, if I mind my step," Bertram said, "and Mother and Father, too. Dear little Taggot."

"Taggot!"

"Yes, that was her name. Taggot."

Margaret took Bertram's arm, and he stopped and looked at her. "What is it?" he said.

She reached up and tugged at his hood so that it fell to his shoulders, and the rain fell freely on his curling black hair and on the tops of his ears.

"Listen," she said. "Do you not hear it?" She gripped his arm like a vise.

"I hear the other pilgrims," Bertram said. "I hear your voice. I hear the rain."

"Yes, the rain!" Margaret said. "It speaks her name all around us! 'Taggot Taggot Taggot'! Do you not hear?" To her ear it had often sounded "Maggot," but, she thought now, it could as well be "Taggot." Not insult but benediction.

Bertram shook his head and yanked his arm from hers. "It's only the rain."

Margaret dropped her crutch and took both his arms, stumbled, and caught herself.

"I hear it," she said to him. "I hear your sister's name. In some way she is everywhere. All around us."

Bertram stared at Margaret a long moment. Then he stooped to pick up the crutch from the ground and gave it to her. "Margaret Church, Maggie Hopalong, Maggie Quest, she who hears kindness in the very rain that falls," he said. "You have a sweet and tender soul."

Margaret held her breath. Bertram thought that lovely thing of her.

Knightsbridge, We Greet You!

Margaret was the first to see it—the cathedral! Two more days had passed along the pilgrimage route. The rain had stopped and the sun had come out, warming their backs and drying their cloaks and hoods and then, as the day wore on, moving ahead of them, a shining path for them to follow. The trees began to grow thin along the road, and suddenly there it was, immense and splendid in the evening sun. The great roof of the twin-spired cathedral was built all of pointed lead. Sets of flying buttresses bristled around it, and the spires pointed higher than every other structure in sight, even above the great stone wall surrounding the city.

"Knightsbridge, we greet you!" cried Bertram, raising Margaret's hand in triumph. While Henry bowed his head, overcome by private emotion and humility, Margaret quaked in the shadow of the great cathedral. This was no common church like the one—humble, half-crumbled, and skewed—where she had been found in Lesser Dorste. The great spires seemed to reach straight to God in his heaven, while their shadows ran over the wall and across the ground and directly to her feet. She shuffled away from the creeping dark so that she might escape God's notice.

The party walked on toward the gatehouse—two magnificent towers flanking a pointed arch, and with a painted statue of the queen in a niche above the entrance—and soon their feet trod a bridge across the River Severn, which flowed around and shaped the eastern boundary of the city. With the steep cliffside there, it formed a natural defense of the royal castle. The river carried with it detritus of all type; the foul stink of it was horrid. Margaret put her velvet scrap to her nose and mouth and stepped gingerly across the bridge to the other side.

The church bells began to chime the hour, and Margaret looked up. A great cloud of blackbirds exploded from the cathedral's two towers, just as she'd seen them do in the magic mirror. She stopped and held fast to her crutch. She felt in her bones that the wild-eyed man was flesh and blood, as real as this cathedral built of stone and glass.

"I am Margaret of the Church," she whispered. "Who are you?"

Margaret felt Bertram at her side, and firmly took his arm.

"He is here, Bertie," she said. Her heart beat like wings against the cage of her ribs. "Now I've only to find him."

"I'll never find him!" Margaret shouted, midst the music and singing, the color and movement and people. So many people!

Once they were through Isobel's Gate, as it was known, and inside the city proper, Brother Henry went straight to the cathedral to pray and then to arrange lodging in the lady chapel there, as was the pilgrim custom. The rest of the party broke away in small groups: the plump missus and her daughter to seek the marketplace (perhaps to buy more sausages), a few of the men and women to sample their choice of nearby alehouses. Margaret and Bertram staggered about the city, marveling at the crowds and the costumes of merchants dressed in rich red, bright yellow, deep blue. Margaret's ear caught words in foreign tongues, and she wondered whence the people had come. She'd walked seven days. How far from home were these great throngs? The streets were wide, some twenty feet side to side, and yet so peopled there was barely room to spare.

"Are you sure you *want* to find him, Maggie?" Bertram said. "Do you not recall what the soothsayer said? About the danger? The death? I expect this fellow's a madman, mayhap a murderer, and I'd be glad if you never set eyes upon him."

"He is why I'm here, Bertie, and why else would I have seen him if I wasn't meant to find him?"

"Perhaps you were meant to find another," Bertram suggested solemnly. "Such as *me*."

A few people stopped and stared at them; Margaret supposed she and Bertram looked more travel-weary than she could guess. She tugged her cloak around her as best she could, but there wasn't much she could do to hide the grubby state of her clothing, nor the curse of her crutch.

Margaret's stomach trembled with eagerness, and she felt weak from walking, from nerves, but above all because she sensed she'd arrived at the end of a journey, and that now she would begin another sort of journey altogether.

But to have set out, and to have found the very place where the wild-eyed man must be, danger or no? What luck! What excellent good luck! Could it be that Minka was wrong about the coin of life? The thought of Minka made the back of her throat sting. But Minka wouldn't be missing *her*, she told herself.

Her belly groaned. Smells of meat and baking bread and fresh-brewed ale teased, but she was too excited to eat. They wandered through the marketplace, where stalls displayed all manner of wonders: a supposed unicorn horn (she thought of the peddler Bilious), a selection of inks on a wooden tray, stylish hats and boots. A soothsayer winked knowingly at Margaret and crooked a beckoning finger. If she'd had a penny she'd have dared, but she did not.

All the while, they were making their way toward the castle on the far side of the city, opposite the cathedral. They could see turrets and towers and the top of the mighty keep.

"Petronilla pies!" shouted a baker, setting out a tray of heart-shaped tarts that glistened with deep red filling. "Princess Petronilla pies, try Her Majesty's favorite," he called. He turned to his companion. "Tasty, wouldn't you say, Wife?"

"Bitter they are, just like Her Royalship," the baker's wife muttered.

"Indeed, and dark as blood," the baker added, snickering. When he caught sight of Margaret, the snicker stopped short in his nose; he snorted, then sneezed, while his wife pounded him on the back to assist his recovery.

"God's wounds!" cried the baker, pressing palm to chest. "You gave me a start, you did!" He elbowed his wife in the ribs and pointed at Margaret. "Would you look at that one?"

"Oh my, yes," the wife agreed. "Upon my soul."

The baker motioned Margaret closer. She hesitated, glancing at Bertram, then approached the baker's stall.

"Has anybody told you, you are the very image of the Princess of Hearts, er, of Her Royal Highness?"

Margaret looked at Bertram. Bertram shrugged. "Who?"

The baker nodded vigorously, chins quivering in accordance. "The Princess Petronilla, by my honor!" He looked her up and down. "Excepting the dirt, and the burr-infested hair, and the filthy layers of clothing what no doubt crawls with fleas, and the tattered shoes, and above all the damnation of a cripple!" He nodded rapidly. "But elsewise the very image."

He leaned conspiratorially over the trays of tarts. "I know a jester, up at court," he said, "happens my wife's sister's husband's brother Quimby, and he pre-forms quite the amusing theater. Why, he rides in on the back of a dog, and it's all laughter and bawdy songs and juggling apples and plates! The princess might find it funny, might she not, Wife," he said, turning to the woman and nodding, "to have a cripple act out her part—a sort of comedy, like."

"*I* know, *I* know!" shrieked the baker's wife, nudging him out of the way. "These two could act out the *wedding*! This one could be the bride, and that one"—she pointed to Bertram—"nah, too tall and thin; the groom's a right fat fellow, in't he though, and a droolin' idiot, I hear!" She chuckled, then, eyes wide, made an O with her fleshy mouth and clapped. "The dwarf! The royal dwarf could play the role! I see it now, right up here in my mind." She tapped her temple, leaving a splotch of flour on the side of her head. "Can't you picture it, Husband?" She punched the baker's shoulder.

"Yes, yes, if this one were to play the part, it might be good fun, eh?" The baker scratched his chin. "Then again, Her Majesty might not like it one bit, and then what? She'd have your head!" The baker and his wife guffawed at length, finally turning their attention to another customer.

Margaret shriveled inside. She turned, wide-eyed, to Bertram. "Bertie," she began.

"Right, then," said Bertram. With a quick movement he pulled up Margaret's hood and tugged it forward, so that her face was shadowed. "It would seem sensible to hide your face till we know more. But fear not. What do those two know? The baker's wares were attractive enough to the flies, *that* much we know and no more."

They hurried back the way they'd come, and farther on to the cathedral, where they found Brother Henry in the lady chapel, in conversation with a priest clothed in black.

"Lux Vera," the priest was saying, and both men were gazing rapturously at the great rose window.

"The True Light," Henry said, and put a hand to his chest and bowed his head. "The window was not yet finished when I left the royal city years ago."

Henry turned, smiling, at the approach of his young friends, and introduced them to Father Sebastian. "Sebastian will let us stay here in the lady chapel for as long as we wish."

"Fleas!" said Father Sebastian.

"Fleas, Father?" said Bertram, after a pause.

"Our lavender incense discourages them," Sebastian said. "Not so at the abbey," he added, "as you would soon have found, had you lodged with our brethren on the other side of town."

"A boon indeed, Father," said Henry, "and finer accommodations than we've enjoyed in many weeks."

Sebastian's gaze lingered long on Margaret's face. "I'm sorry for staring," he said to her, smiling, "but you bear a remarkable resemblance—"

"To the princess!" Bertram was forgiven his interruption, and they told Henry and Sebastian of the strange looks Margaret had received, and the odd exchange they'd had at the baker's stall.

"They hinted at something unsavory about the princess," Bertram offered, "and swore Maggie could be her twin."

Henry stroked his chin. "Hmmm. A look-alike, eh? Stranger things have happened," he said.

"The similarity is quite remarkable," Sebastian said again, "and I am aware of rumors, but regarding her sanity, I'm in no position to judge."

Father Sebastian smiled sadly at Margaret. "Let me tell you what I know of the Princess Petronilla's tragic young life." Sebastian told them a tale that any person in Knightsbridge could have done, for though it was frowned upon to speak of it, still it was a story well known in the manner of gossip.

When old King Ranulph died, the young Queen Isobel and Armand wed happily, and for love. But their love could not last; Armand died in the wars the very day his child was born, a daughter who was called Beatrice. For protection and alliances, Isobel hastily wed again, to Geoffrey, by all accounts Armand's closest friend; he'd been with Armand when he died. Together Isobel and Geoffrey had a child, Petronilla, and the two daughters, half-sisters, were scarcely a year apart in age. One night the elder daughter fell from a great height atop the castle wall and down, down into the River Severn and was presumed dead, though her body was never recovered. The queen fell ill and died of grief, leaving Petronilla heir to all of Rowne. Her father, now the regent, Lord Geoffrey, would hold the throne until his daughter came of age.

"I know Geoffrey, and even served him for a time," Henry said. A storm of emotion had crossed the monk's face as Sebastian spoke, and now his face darkened. "As young knights we jousted. He was cruel to his mount. I liberated the horse." He winked at Margaret before glancing heavenward, hands folded piously at his chest. "Another sin for which I must atone."

Father Sebastian bowed and took his leave, after offering his assistance with anything they might need.

Bertram cleared his throat. "If, as we are led to believe, they look alike, the princess and Maggie," he said, "and the two are near enough in age as well . . ." Bertram's voice trailed off. "Maggie doesn't know her true history. Could it be that—"

"The child fell into the river, Bertram, presumed dead—"

"But never found, Henry, never *found*—"

"It's too unlikely, Bertie, too unlikely by half."

"You've said yourself the Lord moves in mysterious ways—"

"His wonders to reveal, yes, but—"

Margaret sat very still and let their words flow over her. Her blood pulsed in her temples, and she felt a two-pronged stab of fear and anticipation. Was it possible? she wondered. Could she be . . . someone?

The Castle

They supped early on thin soup and thick slices of rye provided by the priests, and Brother Henry put down his traveling cloak on a pallet in the lady chapel, where they would sleep in the company of other pilgrims. Beside him was a stub of candle, and he sat on his cloak and bent over a Bible.

"Brother Henry," said Bertram, "Maggie and I are going to take a stroll about the city."

Henry barely looked up, but raised a hand and mumbled, "Mind you're back before curfew."

They walked out of the chapel and heard another exhortation from Henry. "And don't go to the castle! It's trouble, Bertram, to entertain your fancy—trouble!"

They passed through the huge open nave of the cathedral, and Margaret saw at the end of it, filling the west end of the edifice, the great round window. She realized she was seeing, from inside, the same window visible from the wild-eyed man's chamber. Where must he live?

"Bertram," she said as soon as they'd left the church, "there's a little light left in the evening; let's explore in the other direction. I want to see what's on the other side of the cathedral."

"Tomorrow," he said hastily. "Won't that be soon enough?"

"But—"

"Come on, let's go to the castle," he insisted.

"Brother Henry said—"

"Yes, but these royals, sometimes they make an appearance at the close of day, greet the populace, toss out some bread, that sort of thing," he was saying, all the while fairly pulling Margaret along. "No harm in looking, no trouble there."

"All right," she said, laughing, "all right! To the castle!"

They made their way through streets narrow and wide till they came to Castle Street, and followed it from there straight to the gate in the wall that ringed the castle grounds. They looked up at the top of the wall, and beyond that the tops of the castle towers, and, rising above that, the castle keep.

They stood. They waited.

"I've half a mind to storm the gate," Bertram muttered after they'd stood a long while.

Margaret turned and pulled up her sleeves and thrust her arms to her elbows in the fountain outside the castle wall. She hadn't skill to braid and coil her hair like a lady, but she quickly raked her fingers through her hair from scalp to ends, and fixed a lock behind one ear with her little horn comb.

"Might we"—Margaret shrugged, shaking out her sleeves—"knock?"

"Yes, let's." Bertram pantomimed knocking at a door. He cleared his throat to address an imaginary someone.

"Sir, we have come"—he gestured to Margaret—"my good companion and I, at this late hour"—he faced the invisible gate again—"to gain audience with Her Majesty. What business, you ask? Er, why it's a matter both personal and private, at once peculiar and propitious. Do you not see that my companion could be a royal twin? Blasphemy, you say? Off with their heads, you say? Nonsense. Now let us in. Stand aside." Hands on hips, Bertie turned slowly and looked at Margaret.

Margaret turned now to explain their presence at the imaginary gate. "Yes, it is true we are filthy, and my companion did fart just now as loud as Minka Pottentott, and though I am lame, what of it? He sings like an angel, and I . . . I . . ." She searched for what she might say she was—"I . . ."—and failed.

"By the Mary, she is a mystery worth solving!" Bertram said with feeling to the guard who was not there. He turned to her, a smile twitching the corners of his mouth. "I sing like an angel, do I?" he teased.

Margaret flushed, and was saved from further embarrassment by the night that seemed to come down around them as sudden as a shutter darkens a room, and by the sound of an approaching ruckus.

A group of rowdies came tumbling toward the entrance to the castle grounds. At the same time, the bells rang announcing curfew, and a pair of guards laughingly prodded the stumbling drunkards.

"You rascals been at the ale again, I see," said one of the guards, his falchion at rest but ready in a scabbard across his back. "Look sharp, now, Edgar. Jem, there's a good lad. Best get you in before we close the gate on you and lock you in the dungeon!"

The other guard laughed coarsely. "Your wife won't take kindly to that, now, will she, Edgar?"

"Or better yet, we might do his missus a favor and shut him out, eh?" The guards laughed again.

Bertram squeezed Margaret's arm. "Follow me, Maggie," he whispered. "We'll go in with this lot."

"But . . . curfew!"

Bertram shook his head and put a finger to his lips. Then, just as he'd done the first time she'd laid eyes on him, and again when he'd rescued her from John Book's camp, he winked.

Oh well, then, Margaret thought, flushing with a mix of annoyance and amusement. She huddled beside Bertram and moved as gracefully and unobtrusively as was possible. Bertram pulled his hat low across his brow and began to sing a drinking song.

"Doll, doll thy ale, doll thy ale!"

The others sang along heartily, and Bertram and Margaret joined the band of rowdy men and passed through without detection. The heavy gates closed shut behind them. They were inside the castle.

The castle walls protected not just one, but an assembly of buildings. The enclosure was about a hundred yards across, and at the left was a cluster of low buildings. There was a well in the middle of the courtyard. Opposite the gate, rising above the ramparts on the far side, was the great column of the keep. And at the right, taking up most of the enclosure, was an enormous stone palace. A liveried servant was beginning to light lanterns here and there, and Margaret watched his movements warily.

They entered the palace house by way of the kitchen

shed, a merry, singing band. Margaret peeked at Bertram from under her hood and raised her eyebrows: *What now?*

Just then, a harried-looking woman stopped the carousers by thrusting a laden tray in their direction.

"Oh, Maynard, not again, you drunken sod! And me fit to be tied, with Her Majesty in a stink as usual! 'I don't care for the soup,' she says, and 'I don't care for the roast lamb,' she says! 'Bring me supper in my room,' she says!" With each explosion of words the woman tipped the large tray, threating to dump its contents—steaming crocks and stewed meats and crystal stems—across the stone floor. "And now you show up here reeking like a brewery!"

In answer the man called Maynard leaned toward her, turned his head to the side, and vomited.

"Gack!" the woman cried. She turned and shoved the tray into Bertram's arms. "Are you drunk?" she demanded of him.

Bertram shook his head. "No, missus!" he said, while Margaret made herself small in the shadows behind him.

"Then take this to her chambers. Hurry, now! Knock hard at the door and wait."

Then she spun round to Maynard and stuck a bucket over his head.

"Shoo, then!" she shot back at Bertram over her shoulder.

"I'm not—" Bertram began.

"Up the passage, up the second stairway, through the arch, second doorway—now shoo! Shoo!" she snapped, and returned her attentions to Maynard.

Margaret slipped ahead of Bertram so that she would be hidden by his form, and they hurried away with the tray. No one gave Margaret so much as a glance, though her heart pounded so, she was sure the noise of it would draw attention. Gratefully, she noticed that the action of her crutch was near silent, wood upon stone. They followed the kitchen maid's directions and found what they hoped was the door to Petronilla's chambers.

Margaret's knock on the heavy wooden door sounded with more bravery than she felt. "I am Margaret Church," she whispered. "I am Margaret Church." Blast it, how had she got this far, and why had she gone along with Bertram's wild hare? There was bravery, and then there was stupidity. But then there came a voice.

"Come!"

Bertram pushed open the door.

There, across the chamber, stood Princess Petronilla. She was a bit taller than Margaret. Her hair was fair, parted in the center and wound round in a ramshorn coil above each ear. She wore a gown of glorious blue brocade with scarlet laces up the sleeves, a close-fitting tunic of yellow linen over the top. Her fingers dazzled with rings, and she held in her arms a large white rabbit. And her shoes! Peeking from under her gown were two slippers fashioned of spotless silk and beaded all over with pearls.

But what captivated Margaret most was her face. It was true. They were alike as . . . sisters. Margaret stood unmoving at the threshold of the chamber, legs gone to lead and mind to mush. She wanted to hide within her hood and never mind any of this madness, and at the same time she prayed the lady would look and see for herself the remarkable likeness between them. But in the manner of royalty, Petronilla was not even glancing at her supposed servants.

The princess waved a white hand to a table. "Put it there," she said. Now Bertram looked feelingly at Margaret, and she roused herself to enter the chamber and close the door behind her. Her stomach turned to butterflies, fluttering thickly and rising in her throat.

Petronilla glided to an ornate hutch, fresh herbs among the rushes on the floor giving off a good scent with each step of her slippered feet. She opened the door, kissed the rabbit's nose, and settled the pet inside. Then she crossed to a little table, lowered herself gracefully into a dainty chair beside it, and began to write. The goose feather bobbed with the speed and passion of her words, and Margaret wondered what words those might be. Without looking up from the vellum, Petronilla said, "Why are you still here? You may go." The voice was final.

But Margaret couldn't go, not when she'd come upon such a strange coincidence. Margaret Quest would not turn and go. Wrapping her cloak more tightly about her, by which she concealed leg and crutch, she glanced at Bertram for courage.

"I am Marg—" Margaret's name froze in her throat.

Petronilla's quill stopped dead at the sound of Margaret's voice, and she snapped her gaze to Margaret, cold as stone.

"You would dare speak?"

Margaret's mouth went dry. Why had she let Bertie talk her into coming to the castle? Why hadn't she simply gone and looked for the wild-eyed man? Was she *afraid* to find him? She'd be wiser to fear the princess— the baker said she'd have their heads!

Margaret took a deep breath and tried again. "Highness, I am Marg—"

Petronilla stood abruptly and pointed a regal finger, first at Margaret, then at Bertram. "What are you doing in my chambers? Did Miriam send you?"

Bertram shot a look at Margaret, still shadowed by her heavy hood.

"I am Maggot!" Margaret blurted.

Petronilla turned to her, mouth slack with surprise. For a moment there was no sound but a soft rustling from the rabbit hutch. Then Petronilla tipped her head back and laughed.

"Oh, ha-ha! Maggot, yes! Maggot, I like that!"

Margaret's cheeks burned furiously and she glared at the princess.

"Show her," Bertram whispered. "Show her your face."

"Fine." Margaret yanked her hood from her head. "Feast your eyes, Princess."

Petronilla's brow creased in confusion, rude laughter dying on her lips.

Now that she had Her Royalship's full attention, Margaret was glad her long cloak concealed her crutch and twisted leg.

Petronilla stood very still. Her eyes widened, and then she seemed all at once to shrink, for one hand went across her middle, the other to her lips, and she gave a gasp that was barely audible.

Bertram took a step. "So you see it too, Your Majesty, how you"—he inclined his head—"and Margaret here"—he gestured to her—"well, you're alike as two peas!" he said brightly. "Is it not a wonder?"

Petronilla once more went rigid and regal. "You must be mad. To suggest that she—that she and I—that there is some resemblance—" Petronilla scoffed, turning to Margaret and looking her up and down. "You smell of dung! You're a disgusting ruffian, and a sneak, and yes, quite possibly insane!" She bit her lip. "Yes! More insane than I!"

"But—surely, Princess, you can see—" Margaret said, pointing to her own face. In for a penny, in for a pound, she thought. What was the worst that could happen if she pressed her point?

Suddenly Petronilla ran across the chamber and threw open the door. "Guards!" she shrieked. "Father! Intruders!"

Ah. That could happen.

The Comb

Heavy feet thundered down the hall. Triumphant, Petronilla turned in the open doorway. "You see? They come at my call. They'll lock you up and swallow the key!"

Bertram held out his hand to Margaret; she reached for him, stumbled, and her cloak fell open. Petronilla took in the crooked leg and the crutch; the cold smile slipped. She looked at Margaret's face, her gaze lingered there, and then she fell against one side of the doorframe, collapsing as if punched in the stomach. Her gaze searched Margaret's face, her leg, her face again.

Footsteps pounded closer. "Your Highness!" came a deep cry.

Petronilla glanced behind her out into the hallway. Then all at once she swung round, slammed the great door shut, and threw the bolt. She ran to Margaret and grabbed her arm roughly.

"You'll hurt her!" said Bertram.

Quick fingers darted, pulling Margaret's hair. Petronilla's purpose became clear—she tugged Margaret's horn comb from her head and held it inches from her nose. "Where did you get this?" she hissed.

"My comb? I—I've always had it," Margaret said. Alarm coursed through her veins, and she grabbed for the comb. Petronilla snatched it out of reach and held it high in one hand. "I didn't steal it, if that's what you mean!"

"He told me you were dead!" Petronilla whispered, explaining nothing. "He told me that I—" She shuddered.

"That you what?" demanded Bertram. "What are you talking about?"

Petronilla pitched Margaret's comb to the floor and held up her hands. "I don't understand," she said, backing away. "I don't understand any of this, I tell you!"

Fists banged on the door.

"Hide!" Petronilla said, her voice urgent and low.

Margaret looked about in a fever. Through the rounded archway was an alcove, but no cover, and no door but the one they'd come in, and upon which now came urgent knocking.

Petronilla pushed them roughly toward the bed. They fell upon red silk and pillows. Heavy bed-curtains that draped to the floor enclosed them. They heard the rustle of Petronilla's garments as she went toward the door.

"Quick, Maggie!" Bertram whispered. They slipped down over the edge of the bed and huddled side by side underneath its carved wooden frame. At the last moment Bertram tugged her crutch, and it too disappeared beneath the bed.

"Danger, Bertie!" Margaret whispered hotly against Bertram's ear. "And probably death!" He shook his head to shush her.

❧

Petronilla unbolted the door and let the men inside.

"It was no one, Father," Petronilla said, pretending petulance. She settled her skirt and patted her hair, addressing a tall man, lean and balding, dressed in a quilted doublet and rich brocade. His beak of a nose and the hunch of his shoulders gave him a birdlike aspect. "Father, I fear I'm on the verge of one of my fits."

Her father looked round the chamber and pulled on his tuft of beard. "Your cry was most convincing."

"No one here, Lord Geoffrey," said a guard.

"I thought I saw . . ." Petronilla's brow wrinkled with confusion; she shook her head as if to clear it. "She looked like . . ."

"What, Petra? Looked like what?"

"A ghost," she said. "A ghost, a dream . . . just one of my spells. I'm sorry, Father." Now she regretted calling for the guards and, most of all, for her father. By the saints, none could know of this look-alike girl, Father least of all, leastways not till Petra could discover more. She cast the concealing drapes a furtive look.

Lord Geoffrey, noting her glance, strode to the bed and drew aside the drapes.

Petra stifled a gasp but let out a shriek. "Why? Why am I plagued so!"

"Calm yourself, Petra, my sweet," Geoffrey said, turning from the bed and letting the curtain fall.

❦

Lord Geoffrey, crown regent, kept his daughter under careful, constant control. "Guards, search the castle and the grounds, to be sure my daughter is under no threat."

One of the guards shrugged, then went to kneel and peer beneath the bed, and narrowly avoided the kitchen tray Petronilla hurled onto the floor, scattering crockery and smashing glass. She was even more agitated than usual. Too much oil of henbane in her daily dose? Geoffrey wondered. She seized her ink pot and flung it against the wall. She began to scream and cry and tear her hair. Yes, Geoffrey thought, a bit too much henbane for his liking.

"Petra, stop," Geoffrey said, his voice rising to be heard above her tantrum. He jerked his head, and one of the royal guards approached and stood at attention, head solicitously bowed.

Geoffrey drew the guard to the alcove and spoke into his ear so low that none but the guard could hear.

"A calming elixir for my daughter again this evening," he said. "Make it so her sleep is deep."

The guard nodded curtly. "Of course, my lord." He reached into his tunic and withdrew a small clear vial of amber liquid.

Geoffrey squinted at the bottle. "Good. I'm afraid I expect another . . . incident." He looked meaningfully at the rabbit hutch.

"I understand, my lord."

From across the room Petra wailed, "I'll never live to be queen, Father. I don't want to!"

Geoffrey met Petra with the little bottle. "Drink this, my sweet." Petra turned her head away.

"My elixirs help control your humors, Petra; you know that," Geoffrey said soothingly. "The red one in the day, the amber one at night."

"But, Father, they make me so muddle-headed I can't think. Please, Father."

"Petra," he scolded, "without them . . . ?" He used

his old trick, the thing that scared her most, kept her in line. "Do you want to end up like the madwoman in the dungeon?" he asked.

Petra wilted. Father still occasionally dragged her down, down, down to that horrible place, and forced her—horrified, terrified . . . curious—to look at the old woman. Darting eyes sunk deep in a wizened face. Clawlike fingers clutching the bars of the cell. Wild gray hair a storm about her head. *Do you want to end up like that?* Petra always yielded to him, always trusted him in the end. She had to, for he alone knew what she really was. *Madwoman.* What she might do. She took the vial, tipped it back, and swallowed.

Geoffrey led Petra to her bed. "Tomorrow I travel to Minster City, to settle the wedding. You will wed Frederick de Vere, and I assure you, Petra," he said, patting her hand, "you'll be a fine queen. And I will always be here to guide you." He eased her back against the heap of pillows.

"Yes, Father," Petra murmured. "Thank you, Father." Petra's eyelids began to droop, and her mouth went slack. In moments she was asleep.

🌿

Bertram and Margaret could not remain hidden in the princess's chamber all night. After what seemed an age, they crept out from under the bed, first peering from under the drapes, then cautiously rising. Margaret spied her horn comb among the rushes on the floor and picked it up. Then she stole one more look at Petronilla.

Petra's eyes fluttered; she woke. Under influence of the elixir, she appeared not enraged, as before, but fearful. Her gaze fell first on Bertram.

"Are you . . . are you my death?" she asked.

Bertram almost laughed. "No, Princess, not I."

When Margaret stepped closer, Petronilla's eyes lit with recognition, and she reached out a hand and grasped Margaret's arm. "And you? Are you a ghost?"

"No. Not a ghost," Margaret said, "but a girl, bone and blood, like you. Very like you, as it happens." She smiled, but Petronilla's eyes had already closed; her hand fell away, and she was once again asleep.

Margaret and Bertram exchanged a look that held all of their questions. *Was* the princess insane? What of the elixirs this Lord Geoffrey administered? And how would they make their exit?

Bertram pulled his hat down low to darken his face, and indicated to Margaret that she pull up her hood. "There's no way out but through," he whispered. "Follow me, and stick to the shadows."

The Princess Petronilla

Petronilla dreamed. Her mother lay dying. Her father wept fat tears, and then, voice thick, he said to Petra, *You are my beloved daughter.* . . . In parte insana—*you are sick in mind and heart. For why else . . . Your half-sister is dead: you pushed her from the castle wall.*

In the dream, her father gave a tender smile. *Only we two will know what you've done; we two, and God.*

The face of the madwoman appeared, bony fingers beckoning.

Petra tried to wake; she tossed and turned. Her half-sister was alive; she had come home! Petra dropped back into sleep.

In the dream the girl appeared. The girl with her own

140

face. The crippled girl, leg ruined, mayhap by a fall from great height.

I am Maggot.

Petronilla fell deeply asleep and dreamed no more.

❧

In the morning, Petra was slow to wake. The splash of the chamber pot being emptied by her maidservant on the other side of the bed-curtain roused her, and she lay with her eyes closed, loath to break the spell of her dreams.

"I saw my sister last night, Emma!" she said. And just like that, Petra knew that what she'd dreamed was true. That face! The girl Margaret could be no other but her own half-sister, long thought dead. With every bone in her body, Petra believed it.

"Did you dream of her again? Another nightmare?" Emma said, her voice muffled by the curtain.

"Not at all—that's not it at all!" Petra opened her eyes and stared up at the dark drapery of the canopy high overhead. Father was wrong; all this time, he'd been wrong! She had not killed her sister! And if she hadn't killed her sister, then she wasn't wicked and depraved, *in parte insana.* Mayhap Father was wrong about that, too.

And then Emma drew open the bed-curtain—and screamed.

Petra bolted up and saw her white rabbit, his neck at

an unnatural angle, a trickle of blood running from his nose.

"Holy Father, it's happened again," whispered the maidservant, fear and revulsion in her eyes.

Petra pulled back in horror, and her hands flew to her mouth; she whimpered animal sounds. She touched the rabbit; the body was cold. She cried out and covered her head with her arms, and Emma took the dead rabbit away.

Petra curled into a tight ball. She was bad, still, after all. She must be insane, just as Father said! Sick, sick in the head, sick in the heart. She tossed her head side to side.

She had not killed her sister. But hadn't she tried? Father had seen her do it, seen her push her sister from the wall. Not dead, thanks to God—but injured dreadfully.

She jumped from her bed and rushed to her dressing table, scrabbling through ribbons and pins and ornaments . . . there! The horn comb, the match of the crippled girl's—the proof. It was her mother's comb, the mate long lost until last night. She cupped it tightly in her hand till she could feel the teeth in her palm.

Somehow, her sister had *known* her. Some way, she had come to her, a gift. Petra would not turn away from such a gift. She would not deny Margaret, and she would not deny herself.

But she must take care. The moment this Margaret heard the rumors—and surely there were rumors—

about Petra's true nature . . . a girl who would strangle the life out of her dear pets, who would push her own sister from the castle wall, a girl the doctors called *in parte insana*. If Margaret knew, she would hate her. If Petra presented her sister to the court, she'd surely find out, and their sisterhood would end—again—before it could begin.

No. If Petra wanted to know a sister's love at last, then she had to keep Margaret's very life a secret.

Emma returned to the chamber and placed a glass of amber liquid on the dressing table. "You can't help it, lamb," Emma said, smoothing back Petra's hair. "You can't help how you are." She patted her hand. "Now drink this, and go back to bed," she said. "Sleep is what you need."

"I will."

But Petra did not drink it. She would keep a clear head, no matter the cost. She would go out and find her sister, but with care, in secret. Petra would keep her nature a secret too. She would have to pretend she wasn't insane.

Another Addition to Our Party

The peddler's cart bumped and rolled into Sackville Proper. Minka grumbled to Bilious, "I pray we find her here. My arse cannot stomach much more of this barrow you call home." They'd traveled north from Bolingbroke for many days, inquiring in villages along the north-south road, and suffering many delays from bad roads and bad ale and bad temper.

They looked round and asked for a girl with a crooked leg.

"Oh, yes, yes, sure and I seen such a maid, or one near enough," said the blacksmith by the forge. "She were ugly and worthless, she were."

"I should say not!" Minka objected. She stalked away from the blacksmith stall and purchased a meat pie at a nearby vendor.

"Yet you yourself have pronounced her thusly," Bilious observed.

"It is my place to say it, and not the right of that blighter," she said, indicating the blacksmith with a toss of her head and biting into the pie.

The blacksmith heard her and pulled on his beard.

"For a share o' that meat pie," he called, eyeing the steaming pastry, "I will tell you what I know, which is a sight more than you know."

Minka narrowed her eyes but strode back to him, split the pie in two, and gave him one piece.

"I prefer the greater half," he said petulantly. His voice was loud and bold, but his eyes betrayed a fear of the big woman.

Minka frowned. Yielding, she swapped her larger piece for his smaller one, and they began to eat.

The blacksmith jabbed a thumb in a vague direction. "She went off that way not long ago. Gimping along with her, uh, with her crutch, she was," he said, and took another bite.

Minka seethed. "My charge has no crutch, sir. As *you* well know," she said, purposefully turning to glare at Bilious. She put out her hand to the smith. "And for that useless bit of information, I'll thank you to return what's left of my pie."

The blacksmith opened his mouth, chock-full of chewed meat, and belched.

"Never mind, you blasted oaf," Minka said, and strode away from the offender, moaning, "Bad luck is ever my lot!"

On they went, to the butcher and chandler and innkeeper. But no one had seen a not-so-hideous lame girl. Minka did see someone, though, huddled beneath a blanket behind the baker's shop: a girl, covered in filth, with hollow cheeks and hungry eyes.

"What those eyes have seen I'd not care to," Bilious remarked.

The girl swung a stout stick—not a crutch, but a weapon—in their direction. They jumped.

"Gack, what a stench!" Minka covered her mouth and nose. Bilious staggered two paces back as if slapped.

"You talk as if I ain't got ears," the girl said, causing them both to jump again, "but I do hear you!"

The girl shivered, appearing more human for her obvious suffering, and wiped the back of her hand across her dripping nose, smearing dirt and gunk across her cheek.

"Oh, more bad luck I run into!" moaned Minka.

"It's the girl here who seems to've had a run of bad luck," Bilious said. "What is your name?" he asked the girl, shooting Minka a warning look.

"I am called Urchin," said the girl, rising from the ground in a cloud of vile odor.

"Mother of God," Minka gasped, and pinched her nostrils shut. "Urchid?" she squeaked, with her nose plugged.

"Right," said the girl, "named after my mum: Her *Royal*ship the *Lady* Urchin, of Hemminy Haw-Haw." Urchin tugged her stinking blanket daintily out to either side, tucked one foot behind her, and curtsied.

Bilious smiled at the girl; she tilted her head fetchingly and grinned, revealing a twinkle in her eye and horrid gray teeth. "I like your little fellow," she said, pointing at the satchel slung at Bilious's side, out of which Pip's tiny russet-tufted face was peering.

"Ahem," said Minka, elbowing Bilious in the ribs. "We'll be on our way, then, as you are not who we seek, and we shall not pass another moment in your pungent company."

"But, Minka," Bilious began.

"Not another moment!" Minka said, glaring at Bilious, and she pulled at his sleeve with the force of an ox until he yielded. Pip ducked back inside his sack.

Urchin, interested in the pet squirrel, and having smelled meat pie on their breath, rolled up her flea-infested blanket, tossed her sack across her shoulder, and followed.

At first Minka and Bilious did not notice Urchin trailing them. She was downwind, and they were bickering loudly about what direction to travel next.

"We began by traveling east," said Bilious, "and met

a man who by his word indicated she had not traveled east, herself. I proposed north, and here we are, and here Margaret is not."

"I suppose she traveled west or south instead of east or north," Minka countered, "and so our time has been in vain, on top of which I have endured your company for the whole of it. But let's away now south or west, for the sooner we find my Mags, and my mirror, the sooner the two of us shall be parted."

"That day cannot come soon enough for me, madam," said Bilious, "and the mirror does not belong to you, I might add."

The pair of them bickered several more moments. Urchin made herself comfortable on a stump and sat and watched the proceedings. "Jollier than Punch and Judy puppets," she murmured happily, and she scratched her skull to satisfy a profound itch.

"I say we carry on to the south," said Minka, hands on hips, a bead of sweat dripping down her forehead.

"And go back the way we came, through Eastham?"

"Not to Eastham, then, but rather to Ipswich," said Minka.

"I do poor business in Ipswich," Bilious countered. "I have a ruthless competitor that has run me out in the past."

"Our travels are not about you and your business, but about me and my business," said Minka. "Did I not pay my passage?"

"A halfpenny, God have mercy, does not assure my service for all time, Minka," Bilious said.

Several moments passed in such bickering before the wind shifted and they noticed Urchin upon her stump, beaming as if she had every right in the world to enjoy their sport.

Both Minka and Bilious stopped speaking and stared at her.

Urchin took advantage of the pause. "Spec-ta-cular sunset, eh?"

Both turned, beheld, nodded.

"How I longs to gaze into them beautiful colors, and have a full belly, and a clean blanket, and hop in a cart and go on and on, and on," she said as she blissfully closed her crusted eyelids. "Why, then I could lie down, happy as pigs in clover, and die." She cracked open one eye to judge their response, and quickly closed it.

Minka and Bilious glanced at each other. A smile tugged at the corner of Bilious's mouth, and somewhat gently he elbowed Minka in the ribs. Minka for a moment imagined her own Maggie's face upon the disgusting beggar before her, and softened. She harrumphed with grudging admiration.

"She's a bold one," Minka said at last. "West, then, into them beautiful colors of the sun." She shrugged mightily. "We'll make Kingston-upon-Hull before full dark. Why not?"

"Why not, indeed," said Bilious. With that, Pip wiggled out of his bag and to the ground, and in two hops he had settled himself on the beggar's shoulder.

Urchin opened both eyes wide, and grinned.

"But first," said Minka, eyeing Urchin up and down, "a meal," at which word Urchin brightened, "and a good scrubbing," at which word Urchin disappeared inside her blanket.

"To the river!" Bilious said.

"No, not the river" came a muffled groan. Urchin peeked out from the blanket's disgusting folds, with the squirrel's face tilted pitifully beside hers. "I'm not able to swim, not a bit of it, and I am sore afraid of the water! It'll pull me to the millrace, and I'll be kilt!"

But Bilious and Minka would not be moved. They pushed Urchin to the riverbank, and Minka went to strip her of her awful clothing, while Bilious looked for soap in his cart.

"You'll leave behind this horrid covering," Minka muttered, pinching the blanket with the tiniest portion of one finger and thumb and dropping it on the bank. Then: "Ohhh!" Minka wailed. "First a squirrel, now a rat! A rat!"

Bilious called, "Well, beat it back, then, woman, and bathe the girl quick!"

Urchin held up a filthy hank of matted and twisted hair that did look much like a rat. "This?" she said. She clutched it in her scrawny arms as she would a pretty doll. "It's for luck," she said.

"For luck, is it?" Minka laughed unmerrily. "Bad luck is your lot, same as me. Pitch it away, I say. A more disgusting thing I've never seen, and me a nurse, years ago. Disgusting things is what made me quit the business!"

Urchin pressed the hank of braid to her cheek, causing Minka to grimace and turn away. "Ugh! You'll toss it, or I'll beat you with a stick!"

Urchin shook her head meaningfully, and Pip ducked.

"On pain of death," said Minka, with menace in her voice, "you will throw that ratted, flea-infested hair upon the ash heap."

Bilious could be heard laughing quietly from his post farther up the bank. Minka sighed. "Keep it, then," she said. "By God, I command you to keep it!"

Urchin grinned. "I obey," she said, waving the repugnant hair over her head in triumph.

Minka smiled wide, and then without another word she pushed Urchin into the river, clothes and all.

"You wouldn't drown a poor squirrel!" Urchin cried.

"If only, but seeing as how he clings to the little beggar, I expect I'm stuck with the pair," Minka muttered over the sound of splashing.

Bilious tossed Minka a cake of soap. It was a brisk and thorough washing for girl and squirrel both, and shortly Urchin was clean and fed and dressed in a fresh grain sack from the wagon.

"Lovely," said Bilious.

"Lovely is as lovely does," growled Minka.

And as the orange yolk of the sun dropped behind the hilltop, the cart rolled west to Kingston-upon-Hull, bearing Bilious and Minka, and Urchin between them. Before long, Pip perched on Urchin's shoulder, wound his tail around her neck, and went to sleep.

Ghosts and Folderol!

In the morning, Bertram and Margaret stood in the back of the great wide nave and spoke quietly with Brother Henry while they waited for the holy mass to begin. By luck and stealth they'd managed to exit the castle (a place far easier to get out of than in), slip by the curfew guards, and make their way to the chapel in the night. When they'd told the friar about their encounter with the princess, he'd wisely asked no questions regarding how they had gained entry and exit and simply advised caution.

Father Sebastian approached, swinging a thurible of incense. He swung the smoking vessel on its chains in three directions as with purposeful strides he blessed (and veiled the stink of) the unwashed.

As the fragrant smoke wafted over Brother Henry, he bowed his head in prayer. Every step of his pilgrimage was another he must take to atone for his sins. Would a lifetime be enough? He gazed at the stained-glass windows of the cathedral and saw not their story, but his own darkest day.

Henry saw again the thundering hooves, the lifeless man, the riverbank, the town of no significance. The ring, and the vow. After all this, could he carry on with his charge to bring the package to the queen? If she got it, if it helped, then perhaps it would lessen his guilt. His vision of the captive crone urged him: *She needs me!* On he rode. But before he reached Knightsbridge, word came that the queen had died. And so he had failed. Failed his God and his queen *and* the crone. He collapsed in despair. There was a woman—he remembered her ready laughter, like the bray of Bertram's bagpipes— who nursed him back to health, but his was sickness of the heart, not of the body. So he shed his armor and left her with all his possessions, even the linen-wrapped package, and never returned to court.

He sold Gilly—magnificent Gilly—and brought the money in offering to the friary in Dale's End. And when they took him in, weak and undeserving, he fell to his knees and wept.

Now, in the cathedral, he prayed, "God, deliver my soul."

Wraithlike curls of aromatic smoke licked Margaret's cheek too. A priest went to light the tallow tapers of a candelabrum beside her—each flame for a departed soul, paid for by living loved ones—and she staggered back as if scorched by the fire. Like Beady Bone in her nightmares, Margaret had no one who would light a candle for her. The candles reminded her of who she was: a foundling with no mother or father, rejected by all, even by Minka, who'd aimed to be rid of her by marrying her off to a hunchback. She sniffed and drew her sleeve across her nose. No one gains from wallowing, she thought, save the pigs.

❧

Smoke from the incense reached Bertram's nose, and he prayed for guidance. How might he serve? How must he live? He could not follow Cousin Henry forever; eventually he must be a man and set upon his own path. He breathed in deeply, and gave a wry smile to think his breath so far had been good only for the bagpipe, and not so much even for that.

❧

Sebastian moved away down the nave, swinging the thurible, and Bertram gestured to Margaret. They left

Brother Henry with his head bowed in prayer and went out onto the cobbles of Church Street.

"What do you want to do, then?" Bertram asked when they were outside. The quiet of the cathedral was overtaken by shouts and murmurs of people moving in a strong current toward the center of the city. "Shall we go back and visit the Princess Putrid?"

Margaret tried to smile. The princess. A strange interlude indeed. Petronilla had refused her and pulled her hair and talked of death and stuffed her under the bed. No, she would not pursue the princess today, despite the odd coincidence of their like appearance.

"Today," she insisted, "we search for the wild-eyed man. After all, the soothsayer's prophecy said nothing of a look-alike girl, but spoke of the man in the glass."

"And the danger surrounding him," added Bertram. "Don't forget the danger part. And the death."

Margaret sighed and rested her chin on her crutch. In this vast city, the hope of finding the wild-eyed man seemed thin as gruel, the magic distant as a dream. She began to doubt she'd seen him at all. If she had, his chamber must be located west of the cathedral, to have gained the view of the rose window. Was there a village west of the city? If only she could gaze into the magic mirror again and learn something more.

"Come on, then," said Bertram. "Here's coin in my pocket; let's have some proper breakfast and think on it. Father Sebastian is very kind, but his dry rye, dried apple, and dry ale will not hold me."

They stepped inside a tavern and found two empty seats at the table. A serving girl brought hard-cooked eggs and herring pie, and then poured ale from a pitcher. When Margaret asked what village might lie beyond the western wall, the girl pursed her lips and stood up straight with a vigor that bumped the table and sent Bertram's egg rolling.

The serving girl looked around the suddenly silent table. "Nowt but Knightsbridge Wood," she said.

Margaret swallowed. Why was everyone stopped, mid-chew, and staring straight at her? "No village?" she said. "No . . . township?" She gave Bertram a sidelong glance.

"Nothing," said the serving girl. "Nary even a way in nor out, to the west. Only the wood, and you'll not dip a toe there," she added, "not if you value life and limb, and not if you value all what's holy."

Bertram's eyes, big as saucers, were fixed on the serving girl, his fork hovering above his herring pie. "What has you so afraid?" he said in a whisper.

As if a plug had been pulled on a keg, words came pouring all at once from all around the table.

"Ghosts!"

"Haints!"

"Eerie moans and wailing!"

"Strange blue smoke in the night—smoke but no fire!"

The serving girl raised a spoon to silence the table. "Once, my man dared me to go to the wood at night," she began, "but I wouldn't, not ever." She took a cup, filled it with ale, and swigged. "Imagine!" she said. "Me, go out to the wood at night? Even if I could scoff at curfew, which I could not. Imagine!" she said again, and filled her cup once more. "Being caught outside the gates all night with the ghosts? No thanks, I says to him." She shook her head with a vehemence that made her hair bounce. "No thank you at all."

"I seen them, the ghosts," said an old man in a large felt hat. "A pair of haints, floating four feet from the ground at the edge of the trees."

"I smelt the brimstone!" said another.

"I heard the moaning, like the Devil's own bellows!"

The patrons fell into conversations, and Bertram and Margaret hurriedly forced down their boiled eggs and herring pie.

Outside the tavern, Margaret put her hand on Bertram's arm. "I want to go to the wood," she said.

Bertram sputtered and shook off her hand. "Did you not hear those good folk? Do you not fear the ghosts?

Margaret frowned. "There won't be ghosts in the daytime."

"You don't know that. Danger and death, the prophecy said!" Bertram added.

"'Just because you limp doesn't mean you can't heal,' he said too," Margaret countered. "Mayhap at the hands of the wild-eyed man!" But then she softened. "Let's walk along just inside the western wall and see if anyplace might afford the view I saw in the mirror."

To that Bertram agreed. The city streets rambled here and there, without order, and there were many sharp turns and dead ends. Were they still traveling west? Margaret wasn't sure. When after a time they came to the North Gate, they knew they'd wandered far enough. They made their way again toward the center of the city.

"Folderol!" came a cry, and Margaret turned sharply. A jester approached, juggling three colorful stitched-leather balls, tossing and catching and pushing them around so fast the colors blended in the air. Bertram wondered aloud if the jester was the baker's wife's sister's husband's brother, and Margaret laughed. The fellow's cap was split on top into what looked like a pair of horns, one red, the other yellow. His tunic, too, was divided into red and yellow sides, from his throat to the tip of his long, pointed shoes.

"You admire my juggling skills," the jester said to Margaret. His voice rang out, high and singsongy. "You approve my garb?"

Margaret nodded.

"The jester wears two colors to mark the nature of life," he went on. "All in life is both good and bad," he said, juggling all the while, "just as every coin has two sides. And so drop a penny in my cup, for luck!" When Margaret said she had no coin, he cackled and moved away, the balls still circling madly over his head.

Margaret thought of Minka and her bad-luck coin.

"Psssst. Psssssssst!"

Margaret and Bertram turned. A girl was beckoning to them. She wore a too-large cloak that dragged in the dust, a dingy wimple topped by a cone-shaped hat, and on her feet a pair of shoes that made Margaret stare, for they were sewn of finest leather and dotted with silver pieces.

Petronilla?

"Quickly," the girl whispered, and led Margaret and Bertram through a narrow alleyway to a spot that housed a row of fat barrels and squat crates. Then she turned to face Margaret. It *was* the princess. "I knew you by your lurching gait, no offense."

Margaret waved her hand: *None taken.*

"I don't have the answers. My questions number even more than yours, I'll wager." She stopped speaking, and took a deep breath. "But I believe that we two, that is to say . . . Here." She indicated a large crate. "Sit, and I will tell all."

The princess told the tale they already knew: the story of the two half-sisters, and the wall, and the river, and the grief.

"You must be Beatrice." Petronilla's voice was quiet. "Must be!"

"Aha!" said Bertram. The ever-present bagpipes across his shoulder wiggled in accord. "I *knew* it! Didn't I say so, Maggie; didn't I tell Henry?"

Margaret, stunned, sat in silence many long moments. Finally she asked, "What makes you believe it?"

"We could not look more alike," said Petra, "excepting that you are in grave need of a thorough washing and some scented clothing to wear. No offense!"

Bertram jumped in. "Was your half-sister born with a twisted leg?" he asked.

"No," admitted Petronilla, glancing from him to Margaret, "but the leg further aids in your identity. Though you did not perish as . . ." Petra paused, looking sideways and swallowing. "As long believed, such a fall . . . could hardly have been without consequence."

"True," Bertram agreed, setting his bagpipes on the ground. He took up Margaret's crutch and picked up where he'd left off whittling.

"But would you not agree it is far better to walk with a limp all your life," Petronilla said, her voice gaining speed and volume, "than to have no life at all?" She leaned forward, lips parted, and all but begged an answer.

"Yes, of course," said Margaret. "Of course it is."

"Especially when a body has so fine a crutch," said Bertram, holding out for appraisal the wood with the designs he'd been working, and ogling the crutch from one side and another. The two girls turned blankly to him. "Not, of course, that that's what's important right now," he said.

"They won't let me remember anything about you," Petronilla said, turning back to Margaret, "nothing except . . ." She glanced away, folding slightly at the middle like a wilted bloom. She took a deep breath. "To protect me, you see. To keep me from sadness as a child, the loss of my sister and then the loss of my—of our—dear mother."

Margaret put her hand out uncertainly, and Petra took it.

"When I saw you in my chamber," Petra went on, touching Margaret's hair, "it was the comb that brought me to my senses."

Margaret allowed Petra to slide the carved ornament from her hair. Then Petra pulled a comb from her pocket and held the two side by side. The same grain to the horn, the same delicate carving, the curved design of one finished by the opposite curve of the other. A matched set. "They belonged to Mother. To *our* mother."

Margaret's heart beat fast. She knew the similarity of their appearance, however striking, could still be chance. But the combs . . .

"Mother would be overjoyed to know that you survived."

"How did I come to such a fall?" Margaret asked.

Petronilla looked away. "My father said that you were playing—you and I were playing together—and you . . .

and you simply tumbled from the wall." She crossed her arms over her chest.

Margaret sat very still. She had no memory of a terrible fall, no memory at all of a sister, of royal birth. But she had been found in a velvet dress too fine for common folk. Could it be true? Could any of it be true? Had she once walked straight and without pain? Her twisted leg ached and throbbed, as with fresh injury.

"Sister?" she said, tentatively.

Petra nodded. "My *elder* sister. And, as such, heir to the kingdom—future queen."

Margaret looked at Bertram, whose mouth had fallen slightly open, and back to Petronilla. A sudden rush of sound filled her ears, as if all clarity and reason had turned to rockfall, or furious wings.

Margaret gulped. "No," she said, over the noise inside her ears. She shook her head. "No, that can't be. I've no wish to take from you. I . . ." Again she glanced helplessly at Bertram.

Petra grinned, shaking off the gloom that had seemed to engulf her moments before. "Oh, you'll find there are a few thorns in the royal bed of roses—it's not such a loss for me."

"But . . . truly?"

"Yes. Father—"

"I must meet him!" cried Margaret.

"He is gone this day to Minster City, to arrange a wedding on my name saint's day. I am betrothed to a fat toad. I mean, to a well-positioned duke. But your arrival changes everything, and now I—I don't know, but perhaps it shall be you who kisses the toad and makes him a king."

At this, the rushing and roaring in Margaret's ears grew, insistent as Bertram's bagpipes. She stood and reached for her crutch as if to make haste away. Bertram was at her side in an instant.

Petra, too, rose from her crate. "You dislike the notion?"

Margaret's face went hot. She lost all sense of reserve, and fairly yelled over the sound of her own thoughts. "Queen?" she said. "It cannot be. I think—I must think—" She sputtered and looked pointedly at Petra. "You say I fell from the castle wall. How did I not return, then, to the castle? How is it I came to be found in the churchyard of Lesser Dorste?"

Petronilla crumpled. "I don't know!" she said, her voice shrill. She turned to the side, slid a small bottle from her purse, and went to take a sip but seemed to think better of it, for she returned the bottle to her purse, unopened.

"They didn't say," Petra said, and shivered visibly. "By the saints, I know nothing more! And what of you?" Petra demanded of Margaret. "Do you remember nothing of me, of time spent together when we were very young?" Petra narrowed her eyes. "I was but three years old, and you not yet four."

Margaret took a step back. "I remember nothing. Nothing at all." Petronilla's changeable manner—joyful, indifferent, angry—made Margaret feel as if she'd swallowed the pit with the fruit. She looked down at the ground, uncertainty returning. To Bertram she said, "If what she says is true, and we are sisters, then I wonder that nothing was spoken of it in the soothsayer's prophecy."

"What prophecy?"

"And I wonder that nothing was seen of it in the magic mirror."

"What magic mirror?" Petra stomped her slippered foot. "I demand you tell me this instant!"

All three sat down once more on the ring of crates, and Margaret told Petra everything, about the soothsayer at Grimsby—

"Don't leave out the part about the danger and the death," said Bertram.

—and the peddler Bilious's gift of the magic mirror, and how she'd seen a strange man in it—

"A man who is surrounded by death," said Bertram solemnly, "and danger."

—and how she could see, as well, visions belonging to other people, not only her own.

"And now I do not have the mirror. I'd hardly gained its power when"—she shook her head—"I lost it." She roused herself. Once more she wondered why she'd not seen Petronilla in the glass. "But the man I saw," she said, putting up a hand to Bertram to stop him from speaking again of the death and danger, "with fair hair and green eyes. Do you know such a man?"

Petra shrugged. "Many a man answers to that description."

"Does your father, Lord Geoffrey?"

"Certainly not. Father is balding, and beak-nosed, and beady-eyed on his best days." Petra frowned. "Best not to mention the mirror to him. He's a fiend for his own reflection. The man has fifty mirrors if he has a single one; they line the walls of his chamber."

"There was something else," Margaret said. "In the mirror, I could see out of a window in the man's chamber. I saw the cathedral, and the rose window in the distance. That is how I thought to come here. What village lies to the west of the cathedral?"

Petra's brow knotted. "There is no village beyond the west wall, only Knightsbridge Wood, and none go there, for it's riddled with outlaws and ruffians and thieves and ghosts. Not even a road dares pass through it."

"But I swear I saw the rose window from that direction," Margaret mused.

"Perhaps the magic mirror doesn't show everything true."

Margaret pulled at her lower lip. She had to conclude that she didn't know how the magic worked, or whether the visions it showed were true scenes or dreamlike enactments. Why hold closer to the tales shown there than to the truth in front of her?

Petra squinted at Margaret and tipped her head slightly. "Nothing of our childhood in the mirror, then," Petra said, taking Margaret's hand. "We were little lambs, I suppose, too young to remember."

"You'll begin now to make memories," said Bertram.

The two girls grinned, and when Petra opened her arms, Margaret gratefully stepped into her embrace.

A Pup for Petronilla

"Do you play," Petronilla asked Bertram, with a nod at his bagpipes, "or merely carry the pipes here and there like a coddled pet?"

Bertram's shoulders sagged. "I play," he said, and glanced apologetically at Margaret.

They walked the city end to end, and in their gladness everything seemed brighter, laughter louder, smells sweeter. They passed by the baker's stall and heard his wife calling out, "Petronilla pies! Hot pies!"

Bertram and Margaret exchanged a look, and Petra pressed them for the reason.

"Well, er, those two seemed to think . . ." Bertram

scratched his head. "But then, they've never even met you; let's just—"

"What is it they said?" Petra demanded, her voice rising.

"Well, they said, begging your pardon, they seemed to suggest that Your Royal Highness is, um . . . a bit . . . touched. . . ." Bertram tapped his temple.

Petra's face reddened. "They call me the Princess of Hearts," she whispered. "I think they fear I *have* no heart." Then she smiled. "But never mind," she said breezily. "Nothing matters now that we've discovered each other."

They walked along Cloth Street, and Margaret talked of Minka and of Hugo the woolmonger.

"Our lives are not so different, then. You a hunch and me a toad," Petra said over her shoulder as they worked their way through a narrow slot alongside a passing horse and cart. "They say Lord de Vere is an idiot. Father chose him so that he could hold on to his power, even I can see that." She turned around and ran smack into the broad chest of a liveried guard.

"Mind your step!" he said gruffly, pushing her aside without so much as a glance.

Petra dropped her head and shrank within her cloak. Margaret and Bertram, sensing her alarm, melted into the crowd. Moments later they met up again.

Petra pulled them both near. "The man with the gut like a barrel is my father's trusted guard." To their surprise, she giggled. "I wonder what he's up to, in Father's absence. Indulging in port wine and sweetmeats, no doubt. I've a mind to make sport and follow him!"

Petra ran off after the guard, dragging the hem of her cloak in the mud, and Margaret and Bertram hurried to keep her in sight.

But when they came upon him and hid behind a nearby stall, the guard was not seeking port or sweetmeats or any such luxuries. Instead he stepped to a stall where a woman was selling small and exotic animals. Strange furry piglets, colorful birds in cages, kittens and pups and scale-plated reptiles.

"I am in need of a new pet for the Princess Petronilla," said the guard to the merchant.

Margaret remembered the rabbit nibbling bits of vegetable in the pretty hutch in Petra's chamber. "A thoughtful gift!" she whispered in Petra's ear.

But Petra had gone pale, all trace of good humor drained from her face. She stood hunched, clutching her hands, and making small, mewling noises. She reached into her purse as she'd done before, and withdrew a little vial.

"I . . . I have stayed away too long," she said to Margaret in a low voice. "I should never have—"

"Petra, what—"

"Shhh," Petra hissed. "Please. I dare not. . . . It's not safe." She backed away and disappeared into the crowd.

Margaret and Bertram stood dumbly by the stall, where, unnoticed, they overheard the guard's request.

"A pup. A good and loyal pet for the Princess of Hearts."

The merchant glanced at the little brown spotted dog and bit her lip. Then, peering up from under her cap, she said, "Begging your pardon, but I've heard that she, that her pets, that is . . . Might she prefer"—her gaze cast about the stall—"a turtle? A lizard? Something, er, not so soft and gentle?"

"Not at all. The Princess Petronilla loves her pets," said the guard. "She loves them to bits."

The merchant winced, held the pup to her cheek, then handed him over to the guard, fear in her eyes. "Good health to the Princess Petronilla," she said, voice hoarse. Then she bobbed her head and turned away.

Margaret watched the guard depart with the wriggling puppy and wondered what the merchant was afraid of.

And what Petronilla was afraid of.

Fortunes and Letters

Twice the next day, Margaret and Bertram went to the castle and waited, but the princess did not come out, and they did not try to gain entrance. Margaret wanted desperately to see her newfound sister again, but Petronilla's strange turn of mood and abrupt departure from the pet stall confused and disturbed her. What of the dark insinuations of the guard, and the strange behavior of the pet merchant? What was in the little bottle in Petra's purse? That night in the chamber, hidden under Petra's bed, she'd overheard Lord Geoffrey speak of elixirs and press a reluctant Petra to drink. Margaret heard again Petra's worrying comment: *It is not safe.*

On the second day, Petra appeared outside the cathedral. Margaret threw her arms around her sister, then stood back. "Are you well? I have so many questions, I need to—"

Petronilla held up a hand. "I know, and I'm sorry. Please." She looked beseechingly at Margaret. "I'm feeling better now. Let us put aside our worries and questions for today and enjoy each other's company."

Bertram spoke up then. "If you've something Maggie must know, then you—"

"Leave it!" Her voice was regal, and final. Bertram looked to Margaret and lifted an eyebrow. *What say you?* he seemed to ask, and *I will follow your lead.*

Margaret chewed on her lip. If only she had the magic mirror, she might see some ripple of her sister's nature and discover what troubled her. But she had no magic, and so she would have to rely on her own senses. She would have to be patient and get to know her sister's true heart in good time.

"Oh, I *am* happy to see you again," Margaret said.

"I know!" Petra said joyfully. "And I you!"

"What about me?" said Bertram, arms open wide.

"And you, of course, Master Bagpipes."

❧

With Lord Geoffrey gone, the household servants were lax, and Petra found it a simple matter to leave the castle. She wondered that she'd never wanted to escape her confines before this time. She loved the bustle of the

173

city, and the new friendship of Margaret and Bertram. They, in turn, had never been fed so royally nor had their needs so fully met. They spent their days playing with Petra's new pup, Walter—sneaked from the castle in a wriggling purse—and their nights in the lady chapel of the cathedral.

"What's he like, Lord Geoffrey?" Margaret asked one day as she strolled with Petra and Bertram through the market. Petra, as always in disguise, shook her head within her hood. "Tall, proud, and utterly without humor." She pointed a finger in the air. "Example," she said. "At Christmas ofttimes the household roles are reversed, for sport. A telling jest, I'd say, and one year Miriam the kitchen maid was set up to be the lord. Father didn't like it one bit, and bade them all stop at once. He prefers the wheel of fortune with himself at the top."

Just then Petra spied a brightly colored tent. "Ooh, let us to the fortune-teller's tent!" So one by one they went into the tent. When they compared their fortunes afterward, Petra declared the soothsayer a fraud, for the girls' fortunes were well-nigh the same.

"Say it again," asked Bertram, fingering the holes of his bagpipes. The three had walked to a quiet spot just outside Isobel's Gate and off the road, sparse of tree and travelers, for those approaching hurried on, eager to reach their destination.

Petra rolled her eyes. "'The truth shall set you free,'"

she said, tossing a pebble. "It isn't even a proper fortune. We'd have gained more by eating our halfpennies."

Margaret smiled and nodded, but her brow knotted, for her fortune had, in fact, *not* been the same. Not quite. *You shall set the truth free,* the seer had told her.

"And what of you, Bertie?" Petra asked, interrupting Margaret's thoughts. "What does your future hold?"

"Bagpipes," said Bertram, adjusting the pipes across his shoulder. "I am to practice with the faith of St. Patrick, and all will be well, I'm told."

"Oh, horrid vision," said Margaret, covering her ears, yet smiling.

Bertram chuckled good-naturedly, and set aside his bagpipes. He sat upon a stump and picked up Margaret's crutch. He'd been continuing to whittle on it, evenings at the cathedral, carving intricate patterns of blossoms, vines, and water droplets.

"Bertie," Margaret said, "what is this mark here?" She pointed to a jagged line near the top. It seemed out of place, and not as pretty as the rest. She glanced at Bertram, afraid she had betrayed disappointment with the carving, but an expression so intense overcame his face that her smile slipped.

Then Bertram sprang to his feet and pointed his knife at Margaret.

"Bertie!" she cried, pulling back into Petra's protective embrace.

"Em!" he uttered, and drove the knifepoint into the

tree stump. He held both hands out toward Margaret. "The letter *M*! And you, my Maggie, must learn to read and write!"

Petra released Margaret, and clapped. "A worthy project! Let's begin." She smoothed a spot in the dirt, and Bertram yanked his knife from the stump and began to scratch out marks on the ground.

"*A* is for *apple, ale, apostle*," he intoned.

Margaret scowled. "I don't want to know letters. I want to know words! Poems! Songs!"

"But the letters go together to make the words," said Petra. "That's where you must begin!"

"All right," Margaret said, her voice dejected. All she'd been taught in formal education had come from the parish priest: weekly lessons about the seven deadly sins.

"*A* is for *apple*, then," Bertram continued. "*B* is for *barley, barrel*, and *bog*. *C* for *clodpole, cake*, and *cow*. *D* for Saints *Denis, Damien*, and *Dogfan*."

"And *dung*." Margaret sighed.

"Oh, I wonder if I vexed my tutor so!" said Petra. "I expect I did. I suppose we might put a few letters together this minute for you. What is the word you most want to know?"

Margaret thought a moment. How much her life and fortune had changed in so short a time, how happy it made her to know who she was. "*Sister*," she said.

Petra paused. "All right." She spoke the letters aloud,

and Bertram scratched them into the earth. "S-I-S-T-E-R. *Sister.*"

Sister. She could see each letter. She could read the word. Margaret's skin tingled with warmth, and a bubble high in her chest threatened to burst into laughter or tears. She leaned forward on her knees. S-I-S-T-E-R. Those were the letters that made the word that told who she was in the world. There it was for anybody to see, including herself!

But poor Bertram, she remembered with a start. Was he thinking of Taggot? She looked at him, the thought of his sorrow dampening her gladness. But he wore a small smile, and was busily scratching his knifepoint into the ground.

M-A-R-G-A-R-E-T
G-I-R-L
B-A-G-P-I-P-E
B-E-R-T-R-A-M
P-E-T-R-A
H-A-P-P-Y

She could not speak the words to name what she was feeling. A dung beetle crawled over the top of the letter *I* in G-I-R-L, and crossed it into a *T*. She watched the beetle pattern the dirt, and then all at once its hard-glossed shell split apart, and it lifted high on quick wings. Margaret turned her face to the sky, watching the beetle go, and she gripped her elbows to hug herself.

Even the lowly beetle was overcome, surely, when first its shell hinged and took wing. Surely even the beetle felt wonder.

Later, when Margaret and Bertram walked back to their lodgings in the church, Margaret saw everything with new interest. They walked slowly, stopping often, and as she pointed at all and sundry—the city wall, the statue of the old king, a squealing pig, a boy and a bucket, bushel and pole and ale—patiently, tenderly, Bertram's fingertip drew each word in the palm of her hand. And so the thrill of knowing was not limited to new words but encompassed new feelings, as well.

In the evening, at the cathedral, Margaret sat shoulder to shoulder with Brother Henry, and he ran his finger beneath the lines of verses in his holy manuscript. They sat where the light was best, and when the light failed, Henry lit a candle. The vellum glowed gold, with pictures inked in jeweled hues. Henry turned pages to select passages from here and there. He spoke softly and carefully, and Margaret mouthed the words. She felt dizzy with it, and every psalm and chapter seemed meant for her this night.

"'Just as water mirrors your face,'" Henry read, "'so your face mirrors your heart.'"

And: "'For now we see only a reflection as in a mirror; then we shall see face to face.'"

And then: "'Behold, all things are become new.'" Margaret stole a glance at Bertram and caught him looking at her. Both of them flushed hot and looked down and away.

And: "'Ye shall know the truth, and the truth shall make you free.'"

And when the candle was spent and Henry urged her to sleep, still Margaret lay awake on her pallet, staring wide-eyed into the dark of the lady chapel, as letter by letter, over and over, she traced the words on her skin. *Truth. Mirror. Heart. Behold.* It was like-enough to magic that she shivered.

A Sad Goodbye

Two more days, and countless more words, but the magic didn't last.

After spending more than a week in Knightsbridge, the pilgrim party was moving on to Holywell, there to visit St. Winifred's Well.

"Please come, Maggie," Bertram said. "Come with us—we're not far now, three days' travel, and you could ride the horse! Henry's borrowed a fat pony called Gertrude."

Margaret's fingers tightened around her crutch. "I can't, Bertie," she said. "I can't, but . . . but do you have to go?" Bertram began to speak, but she didn't hear him.

"You could stay in Knightsbridge a time, and find work at the abbey, or in the field—"

"Maggie—"

"Bertie!" She didn't know why she shouted and stamped her foot, and then she felt foolish. But why? Why was he going away? "I know we haven't known each other long, but I—well, I've grown used to . . ." She shrugged. "Your face, I suppose, and even your piping." She glanced at Bertram. "But I suppose if you must go, then you must go." She frowned and dug her heel into the dirt.

Bertram smiled. "It's Brother Henry must go, and so must I follow. I'm bound to him in servitude. But I've grown"—he swallowed—"used to you, too, Maggie. I've grown very used to you."

Margaret moved her finger over the carvings Bertram had made upon her crutch, felt the letter *M* cut deep.

"Mayhap we'll meet again. I hope so." Bertie pretended a casual manner. "When next I pass this way, you'll likely have wed the Toad, and you won't even see me from way up in your castle window."

Margaret swallowed at the tightness in her throat.

"Petra speaks as if it would be so. She eagerly awaits her father so that he can announce my return; I dread his arrival, as I fear he'll prove me an imposter."

"But . . ."

"Either way, I must know. I must stay. You understand, don't you?"

"Yes," said Bertram, his voice quiet. "Of course."

"I would see you, Bertie. From the height of a castle tower or from down in a ditch. And I will miss you," she said. "Thank you for my beautiful crutch." Again she ran her fingertips over the carvings, the leaves and apple blossoms, the small droplets that spiraled round the stick.

"It's the rain, what I've carved."

"Yes, I know," she said, smiling. Oh, Bertie.

"You like the rain," he said.

Margaret nodded. "That I do." Don't go.

"I won't forget what you told me that day, about hearing Taggot's name on the rain." Bertram nodded gravely. "It's a comfort, and I thank you for it."

Margaret wanted to thank him for freeing her from John Book's camp. For finding a way inside the castle and Petra's chamber. For teaching her the letters. For being her friend. But all at once she could not trust her voice to speak.

Without thinking, she took up his hand and held it to her cheek. In the next moment she turned Bertram's hand and kissed the palm of it; then, realizing what she'd done, she spun round and ran—*clump-slide, clump-slide*—as fast as her legs would go, and never dared look back.

If she had done, she'd have seen Bertram staring after her, slack-jawed, and holding her kiss in his hand.

Lord Geoffrey Returns

Petronilla spotted the flags of her father's contingent, and so she ran down the stone steps of the tower, across the castle yard, and out to the gate, and she would have thrown herself in her father's arms, but he did not dismount.

"Father, you'll never believe it!" Petra shouted up to him, atop his fine horse.

"Believe what?" Lord Geoffrey's sharp eyes took in his daughter's eager face. She looked . . . well.

"My sister is not dead!" Petra cried, her voice filled with joy. "She is here! Here, in Knightsbridge! She came and found me and stayed in the lady chapel but now she's—"

"Petronilla!" Geoffrey boomed. His heels dug into the horse's sides, and the horse reared and sidled in confusion, while Geoffrey's expression changed as rapidly and dramatically as the clouds passing overhead.

"Petronilla," he said again, glancing all round at the riders, "your nerves play cruel tricks." He swung his leg over his mount and dropped to the ground, slapping the horse's rump and tossing the reins to a squire. He bent his head as to kiss his daughter, but hissed in her ear instead. "Inside, Petra," he said, guiding her into the palace. "We'll discuss this in private."

"Yes, let's!" said Petra, smiling broadly at her father. "And how do you find the Toad?" she asked sweetly. "Is he well?"

"Petra!" chided Geoffrey. "If you must know, I never met him—he was evidently ill and thus in seclusion—but never mind that."

"We'll soon brew the bride ale for Maggie and not me, I wager!" Petra said.

Geoffrey stopped and pointed. "Go wait in my chambers while I catch my breath."

Geoffrey walked slowly, removing his riding gloves finger by finger. Petronilla's greeting was outrageous! Beatrice, alive? Impossible. Here in the royal city? Inconceivable. He ripped the gloves from his hands and bit the leather between his teeth.

He had been sure . . . He had ensured . . .

Cursing now the saints, the River Severn, and his

trust in the thief John Book, Geoffrey slapped his riding gloves against his thigh. Then he went to meet with his daughter.

🌿

"Petra, how can you be sure this girl is not a fraud?"

Father and daughter faced each other across the room, their figures reflected many times over, for there were mirrors everywhere. Mirrors hung on iron hooks mortared in the stone, on pegs and in corners; they rested flat on the table and bench.

Petra pointed to one of the mirrors on the wall. "She is my likeness, Father—a more precise reflection one could not imagine—and she wears a comb of Mother's, the mate of mine. She could be no other, of that I am certain."

A new puppy pranced at Petra's heel, and she bent to scoop it up. "Besides," she added, smiling, "a soothsayer read our palms and divined for each of us the same!"

A fortune-teller? A comb? Geoffrey would not be undone by trifles. He frowned at the absurd bow around the dog's neck as Petra stroked its head. Another pet to go the way of the others, mayhap by means of that ribbon—*that* would bring her back to earth, for the girl was fairly floating. Look at her. Face pinked with enthusiasm, her smile easy, and the way she stood there, regal and possessed of herself. In his absence had she not been given the elixirs? She was changed. He didn't like it.

Geoffrey cleared his throat, poured a glass of red wine, and drank it down. With a careful mixture of opium and mandrake he'd dandled her tempers like a puppet master. He'd grown fond of ruling alone. Now that she was old enough to wed, he'd settled her marriage to a duke he'd been assured was a drooling idiot, thus increasing Geoffrey's holdings threefold and securing his position of control as regent. What now? he thought. What now?

Schooling his expression, Geoffrey turned to Petra and opened wide his arms. "Bring her to me at once!" he said, putting on a merry voice.

"Yes, Father, I will, without delay!" She went to leave the chamber, but turned. "I beg of you, Father, one thing. Margaret—let us call her Margaret, for that is how she knows herself—she is lame, surely caused by . . . by my . . ." Petra set the pup down to cover her trembling. "I beg you, do not tell her that I am the cause. She and I love each other as sisters."

Geoffrey looked at Petronilla—those eyes, so like her mother's. He stretched his lips into a smile. "Have I not made to you my solemn vow?"

Petra ran to him and embraced him.

"Thank you, Father," she whispered. "Thank you."

An Oath

Lord Geoffrey called everyone to the castle for a feast of four courses. The soaring walls of the great hall were hung with banners and coats of arms, and as light faded in the tall windows, the torches were lit along the walls, and there were candles on every table, as well. Margaret, beside Geoffrey at the high table, was seated on a grand but uncomfortable chair. The table groaned with food, the likes of which Margaret had never seen nor imagined. First came the potted meats and the cheese, then ground beef in spiced wine, a leg of pork, and a black swan—plucked, roasted, and covered over again with its own feathers. The servants had outdone themselves, and on one day's notice, too. The linen-draped table was finer dressed than Margaret herself had ever been up till the evening before.

Margaret barely needed to chew the soft bread, a spoonful of orange conserve on top, and she savored every bite of food on the trencher she shared with Petra, though at the same time her heart squeezed: everything was so strange and new; she would have taken a kind of comfort in choking down the old familiar tough brown rye. She swallowed the bread, fed morsels to Walter under the table, and studied Lord Geoffrey from the side.

The meeting in Geoffrey's chamber had been quick. "The prodigal daughter has returned," he said softly, and then embraced her, though scarcely touching her. "Stepdaughter, I should say. Half-sister, I should say, though"—he waved his hand dismissively—"it matters not. Dear Beatrice. How we all doted on you!"

He'd motioned for her to turn round, and like a squab on a spit she had done so, and he observed her twisted leg and then moved behind her and lifted her hair from her neck. He paused, and Margaret thought she heard a sharp intake of breath before he bent to kiss her nape and let the hair fall.

Margaret submitted to his scrutiny with the confidence of one just washed. He'd find no pests on her this day! She had bathed in hot water, and Petra's maid, Emma, had scrubbed her raw and washed her hair with scented oil, and picked out every louse and nit; she'd never been so clean in all her life.

Now Geoffrey, dressed in a fine quilted doublet, rose from his ornate chair and lifted high his goblet. Petra wore a gown of deep crimson silk, and Margaret was dressed in a rich green velvet that, by its similarity to her cherished velvet scrap, gave comfort. Its beaded bodice made lovely tinkling noises when she moved. The castle's great hall went quiet. Margaret dared not breathe lest her dress interrupt. She stifled a snort. If Bertie could see her! Would he know her? She hardly knew herself.

"God's mercy has shone upon us this day, and our family's tragic story has been turned upon its head! Let the celebration ale flow! Let the people rejoice! To Beatrice!"

"To Beatrice!" came the response from all the great hall.

Below them, less important people ate bread that was not white, but it was still fine wheat bread, and farther down the line there was coarser cocket-bread, and finally, away at the far end of the great hall, was served the rough brown rye.

It was lowly bread, for lowly folk, and as the smells of rich food not meant for them reached their noses, the people in the hall remembered the sad story of the lost girl, and the queen who died of grief. And they rejoiced at the sight of Isobel's true heir, returned to them by God's own grace.

"What joy!" said a slender man seated between his portly wife and a neighbor who had not bathed. "The elder one is come back, never dead at all, but found by a good soul and raised in all innocence of her true identity." The man had bought a pair of new shoes fit for the fine occasion. "Imagine!"

"It's a shame about that one," said a wizened old lady sitting farther from the nobility. She pointed to Petra and then tapped a finger to her temple. "Touched in the head. Right good she won't be queen."

"Now we got a cripple, we're better off, eh?" said her companion, whistling through a gap in his teeth. He took a great pull of ale, then dragged his sleeve across his mouth, and belched.

❧

It was near dawn when the last revelers left the great hall and the kitchen went quiet and the dogs quit nosing the rushes for scraps and bones, and Margaret and Petronilla, stuffed and woolly-headed, flopped into bed at last and whispered.

"Of course it's a shame you must wed him, Margaret, but how much better to wed a duke than a woolmonger!"

"If neither be for love, then I agree," said Margaret, biting her lower lip. "But why *not* for love?" Much to Margaret's surprise, Lord Geoffrey had seemed to agree that she and not Petra should marry the Toad.

"Pshaw. Love's not a promise anyway. My maid Emma wed for love. She wed for love three times, and buried two out of three!"

"That's horrible," said Margaret.

"Her men were horrible," said Petra, patting the bed to encourage Walter to hop up. "Emma chose for herself and chose unwisely, for each among them beat her black and blue." She shook her head and frowned, freshly tying the dog's purple ribbon in a great looping bow. "Though I'm sure I'd judge more fair than Emma, had I her freedom." Walter sighed and put his head down on his paws.

Margaret went up on her elbows. "What would he be like, then, your husband?"

"Good and kind and true, certainly, and with a playful spirit. One who'd make me laugh."

A picture crossed Margaret's mind's eye. Black hair glossy as a crow's wing, head bent over a whittling knife, a wink in the glow of a fire's embers, a song, a kiss on the ha—

"And what of your husband?" Petra asked.

Margaret flushed and plucked at a gold thread gone loose on her pillow. "None would have me," she said. She rolled onto her back and stared up at the canopy. "The Toad will be sore disappointed when we meet."

Petra just laughed. "Oh, we'll have such fun tormenting him. And you'll have hardly any business with him at all, you'll see." She flopped beside Margaret. "All will be well, Sister. I shall never leave your side, nor shall you leave mine." Her face sobered, and light from the candle flickered across it. "An oath!" she cried, sitting up. Her movement caused the flame to flutter and dance, and for a moment sooty smoke clouded Margaret's eyes. "As the knights take their oath to God, so shall we to each other. An oath of fealty!"

She flew to her little table and from her basket produced a sewing needle; then she dashed back to the bed, grabbed the astonished Margaret by the wrist, and pricked her thumb.

"Ow!" said Margaret, and stared at the little ball of blood that formed, ruby-like, on the skin. "Does a knight bleed his thumb before God?"

"No, but we are ladies. You'd rather the clout of a sword hilt?"

In the next instant Petra pricked her own thumb and pressed it to Margaret's.

Petra spoke quickly. "I promise that from this day forward I will be faithful to my sister, never cause her harm, and protect her from all others in good faith and"—Petra swallowed—"and without deceit." She glanced away. "Now you, Margaret."

"I promise . . ."

"That from this day forward—"

"That from this day forward I will be faithful to my sister, never cause her harm, and will protect her from all others—"

"In good faith—"

"In good faith and without deceit." She finished the pledge in a rush.

The two girls smiled furiously at one another, proud and glad and bold. Then they pulled their thumbs away and stuck them in their mouths like grinning gargoyles.

"That thtung," said Margaret, around her hand.

"Yes, but now we are forever bonded, no matter what."

Margaret smiled at Petra, and her heart felt big in her chest. "No matter what."

Walter sneezed in his sleep.

Bertram at the Well

After three days' travel, Bertram and Brother Henry had come to St. Winifred's Well. A crypt built into a hillside protected the clear waters of the holy spring, which continuously filled a basin shaped by eight points of a star. Near to the crypt stood colorful tents where pilgrims might remove their traveling clothes, to then take their illnesses to the healing waters of the well. Henry and Bertram sat apart from their companions on the grassy bank beyond the wall that enclosed the crypt.

Henry was pleased with the journey. "I feel at peace, Bertie," he said.

Bertram sat unusually silent.

"No singing today, then, Bertie? No tune on the bladderpipe?" the friar asked.

Bertram shook his head, glancing at the bagpipe beside him on the embankment, and said nothing.

"Bertram," Henry said, "do you remember how you came to be in my employ?"

"Of course," Bertram replied. "Mother and Father died of the pestilence and Taggot drownt and I alone was spared."

"Yes, yes, but why came you to *me*, I mean, that day in Minster City, at St. Paul's? 'Twas God's hand at work. A miracle you found me."

Bertram looked up at Henry. "I knew your broken nose. I saw your profile at prayer, and ran to you like a calf to its mother."

"Thanks to God I am not handsome," said Henry.

Bertram smiled. "You said a cheerful lad would be a good companion, as a squire to a knight. But I was never any squire, and you—why did you give up your knighthood, Cousin? You never said. I never questioned, but often wondered."

"And why did you never question?"

"Because I was afraid."

"Afraid of what?"

"That if I questioned, if I failed to entertain, to serve, I would be turned away."

"Have we no trust between us, then, after these many years?"

Bertram looked away and tugged on a blade of grass. "Well, after a time I thought . . . you would confide in me if you truly trusted me. . . ."

"Let me tell you something, Bertram. A finer son I could not have had. I think of us not as master and servant, but as father and son."

Bertram looked up.

"And you are free to go at any time."

Bertram's lips parted, and he tipped his head slightly. "But I have pledged to serve you."

"No more, Bertie. I release you. I always thought to release you when you were ready. It is time."

Bertram was silent; frowning, he studied his feet.

"Is there not somewhere you would go, then, Bertie?"

"Cousin. I belong with you."

"You have belonged with me, Bertie. But you will find your own place—find it, mayhap, more than once."

"I don't understand. When I alone of my family was spared . . ." He swallowed, and when Henry reached a hand to clasp his shoulder, Bertram turned to him. "I expect God in his wisdom meant to strike me. Taggot was in my care, and I failed. I let go. In the river, I let go. And she died."

"Taggot's life was not yours to claim, no more than any man's. You did not fail her, but did your best. And you were a child yourself. Had you held on, you too would have perished in the water, and I would not have carried on."

A frown of confusion creased Bertram's brow. "What do you mean, you would not have carried on?"

"God gave me charge of you, a duty. And I allowed you to believe you were indebted to me, when it is I who owe my life to you. Had I not been trusted with your care, I would not have cared for myself enough to live or die. Like you, I was afraid. Afraid I'd lost my soul by my wrongdoings."

"If I could have offered my life instead, Henry, I—"

"It is not our place to bargain with God, Bertram, noble though your thoughts be. And sincere, I know."

They both sat quiet, and the water gurgled mysteriously. Bertram picked up his bagpipe, absently twiddling the tuning pegs, and wondered what the water could be saying. Surely Maggie would know. He listened hard, but heard no words.

"I continue on pilgrimage," Henry said, "for I believe God is not yet through with me, and I have much to learn along the path. Might God have something else in store for you, Bertram? Might that be why he spared you?"

"To do what?"

Henry shrugged. "Things are not always as they appear; that is what I know of truth."

Bertram rolled his eyes. "Must you speak in riddles?"

"All of life is a riddle."

"No, it isn't," Bertram said, and stood abruptly. "It isn't any riddle at all. It's simply one step beyond the other, in a chosen direction."

"Hmm." Henry rose and started toward the well. "And what, then, is your chosen direction?"

Bertram looked quizzically at the monk. "I have always followed. I have followed you these last seven years."

Henry nodded. "And now I believe that I shall follow you."

Bertram shifted his weight side to side and scratched his chin. He swallowed. "I—I choose to go back to Knightsbridge."

"Ah," said Brother Henry, his smile knowing. "I see."

"See *what*, Cousin? I—"

"Bertie." Brother Henry smiled gently. "After these many years, do you not believe I know your heart?"

Bertram flushed. Then he looked to St. Winifred's Well. "There is something I may give Maggie yet."

A Dark Visit

cAfter the grand feast presenting Margaret to all of Knightsbridge, the next days passed in a flurry of lessons: Margaret would learn to be a lady. She learned that embroidery called for the patience of St. Simon and the eyesight of St. Lucy, that flowers spoke in language both foolish and lovely, and that of all the herbal remedies—oil of violet, water of rosemary, henbane, calamus, and clove—none accomplished forgetting. She would gladly forget her betrothal to the Toad. She might forget Bertram, too, for to think of him caused her a new kind of sorrow. If she held the magic mirror in her hands now, would it be Bertram she'd see in the glass, and not the wild-eyed man? Oh, those haunted eyes! She remembered him now with a pang, for she'd left her quest unfinished. And what of Minka? She could not forget her, either.

"This needlework is driving me mad," Margaret fumed one afternoon. The chamber had grown stuffy, and her mood was pricked with annoyance.

"If a bit of colored thread's enough to drive you mad, then you're made of weaker stuff than I believed," Petra said crossly.

Margaret plopped her linen to her lap. "I swear it's some kind of torture," she muttered.

"Ha, torture, you say," said Petra, but in a tone that did not suggest alliance. A strange light burned in her eyes, and her skin appeared damp, perhaps with fever. Margaret put her palm to Petra's forehead, and Petra jerked away.

"You seem . . . ill at ease," Margaret said. "Are you well?"

"I'm very well," Petra snapped. "You've soured me on embroidery, is all." Abruptly, she stood. "Come"— Walter leaped to her side—"I want to show you something," she said, and turned away without waiting for Margaret to answer.

Margaret followed Petra out of the room and down the hall, the sounds of Emma's protestations fading behind them, Margaret's crutch thudding dully upon each stone stair as down they went, and down, and down again, past the weapons room, past the watchman, until they were underneath the working quarters of the palace. Margaret's sleeve brushed against slimed stone, and she pulled her elbows in. Walter snuffled the musty rushes strewn across the floor. Scuttling and scrabbling sounded from dark corners. And the smell. This was no place for the living.

"Why have you brought me here?" she asked Petra.

Torchlight crossed Petra's damp cheeks and brow, and for a moment Margaret felt caught in her fierce gaze. What *was* it in Petra's eyes? Fear and . . . challenge? Then Petra shrugged, and her eyes dulled. "Father used to bring me here," she said, turning to move ahead. The torches set high in the stone cast but sputtering light alongside a grid of iron bars. "When I . . . misbehaved."

Margaret heard moaning from inside the first in the line of cells. Shuddering, she hurried along, glancing left and right and behind, until she bumped up against Petra.

"Look there," Petra whispered.

An old woman sat propped against the wall in the second cell. Gray hair a filthy cloud. Colorless clothing— rags, more like. Legs scaly sticks, like a chicken's. Bare, roughened feet. And the toes . . .

Suddenly the crone tipped her head and fixed Margaret with a stare. Margaret jumped. Small, dark eyes peered from a face like a shrunken apple. Her gaze—keen for one so wretched—passed slowly over

Margaret, from her crutch to her face and back again. Margaret stepped back, pressing her velvet scrap to her nose. The dank air moved; the torch flared. Alert, the prisoner peered more closely still, and then, as if pulled by a string Margaret unwittingly controlled, rose nimbly to her feet.

Petra grabbed Margaret's arm. "Come away," she gasped, but Margaret, in the grip of the old woman's stare, didn't move, nor did the crone turn at Petra's voice. She squinted at Margaret, her gray head tipped to one side, fingers touching parted lips through which came a sharp hiss of breath.

Margaret blinked. The poor woman, surely unaccustomed to visitors—how she gawped! The prisoner's fevered curiosity drew Margaret as forcefully as the unfortunate filth repelled her. But those *eyes* . . . She didn't look mad so much as . . . haunted.

Again Petra urged, "Come away!"

"Stay!" cawed the old woman, reaching a hand through the bars toward Margaret, and then, in a whisper: "Is it you?" Now her hands flew to her cheeks.

"Yes, it's my sister!" Petra blurted. "See? She's not dead at all. She's come back!"

The old woman glanced at Petra, then back to Margaret. "By the saints and holy martyrs," she whispered, still staring at Margaret, "I've a feeling . . ."

"Madwoman!" Petra barked. Then she turned and ran away in a swish of silk.

Margaret looked once more at the old woman—those searching eyes, the clawlike hands that clutched the iron bars—then turned and followed Petra as quickly as her crutch allowed.

❧

"What was that about?" Margaret asked when later, breathless from the climb, she joined Petra in the great hall. "What has the poor woman done?"

"She's mad, that's all," said Petra, looking pointedly at Margaret. "She's a madwoman, and she . . . she frightens me."

"If she frightens you so, then why did you take me to see her?" Margaret gave a shudder.

"I . . . I don't know." Petra wound her hands around each other. She wanted to keep her true nature—was she mad like the crone, as Father said?—a secret from Maggie, but at the same time and just as strongly, she wanted her sister to *know* her. Know her and yet still love her.

"I didn't like it," said Margaret. "That pathetic creature! That miserable place!"

"I'm sorry, Maggie. I am." Petra reached out her hands. "Forgive me."

Margaret smiled tenderly. "There's nothing to forgive," she said.

Petra felt sudden tears, and squeezed them back.

"But why—" Margaret began.

"*There* you are," said Emma, bustling into the hall.

Petra dabbed her eyes, then smiled. "Embroidery awaits," she said.

꧁

The castle was growing quiet after supper that night, as the sisters played a game of checkers on the feather bed.

"Stop! Walter!" Petra screamed in mock anger as the dog put his front paws on the bed and scattered the checkers. "I'll take away your handsome ribbons, and then won't you be sorry."

Margaret snorted. "Handsome! Humbling, more like." She rubbed the dog's velvety ears. "Poor beribboned Wal—"

The door burst open, and Geoffrey strode into the chamber. Both girls stood at attention, Walter at Petra's side.

"Margaret," Geoffrey began, "you will not wed Lord de Vere."

Margaret thought to clap and shout with joy and relief, but something in her stepfather's tone made her know he would say more. Petra scooped up handfuls of checkers and tossed them high, dancing about the room. But Margaret waited.

Geoffrey smoothed the front of his red tunic and cleared his throat, twice. "It has been decided that I, and not de Vere, shall wed Margaret."

Petra froze mid-jig.

"My—my lord?" Margaret stammered.

Petra stomped a slippered foot. "Father! You make no sense. Margaret is your daughter!"

"No, Petra," Geoffrey said smoothly, "Margaret is your half-sister, but no such relation to me."

The silence stretched long. Margaret's stomach roiled. The joyful discovery of a sister, the past days spent in happy company, the soft bed and rich meat and white bread—all of it deception, just as good oats atop the vendor's sack hide a spoiled and rotten bulk.

Petra paced around the room, sputtering and flapping her arms in distress.

"No," said Margaret in a quiet voice.

Petra stopped, and stood still. Geoffrey stared at Margaret.

"Excuse me?" he said coldly.

Margaret swallowed the lump of bile at the back of her throat.

"I don't want to be queen. I'll leave."

"Leave? Forsake your duty? Never see your sister again?"

Margaret blinked. "Never . . . ?"

"I can assure you, your banishment would be quick and permanent."

Margaret breathed deeply, squared her shoulders, and looked straight into Geoffrey's eyes. "Better yet, I will be queen without a king," she said.

Strange, she thought, that Lord Geoffrey's eyes—had

she really looked into them before?—were cold and flat. And yet the wild-eyed man? Though seen only in glass, his eyes were clear and deep and full of life as the flowing river. She didn't like Lord Geoffrey. She didn't trust his eyes.

Geoffrey held her gaze a moment, then barked a laugh. "Do you have advisers?"

"I could find them," she reckoned.

"An army?"

"I'm sure I could"—she swallowed with some difficulty—"gather one."

"Is that so. And your own guards and staff? Hmm? Do you know your allies and enemies? Do you know how to protect your kingdom, your people?"

With each demand, Margaret crumpled more inside, but she wouldn't show it. She glared at her stepfather, narrowing her eyes against the onslaught of doubt and entrapment.

"I thought not." Geoffrey smiled, unfeelingly. "We will wed ten days hence, as was planned for the wedding to de Vere," he said. He turned to Petra. "And you shall wed de Vere, later this summer." Without further explanation he turned and left the chamber.

For a few long moments Petra and Margaret did not speak. The torches on the walls spat and flared. Walter whined.

"I'll not pretend I am not shocked, Margaret, for I am," said Petra. "Shocked!"

Margaret fell to the bed. Tears began to trickle down her cheeks. Whatever she had imagined when she'd longed for a family, it was not this. How selfish she'd been to run away, how stupid! If only she'd never taken that magic mirror in her hand!

"Shall we try to see some good in the match?" said Petra. "True," she said, pacing the room, "he is old, and till a moment ago you considered him a father, but . . ." She threw her hands up and then came to the bed and put her arms around Margaret. "I know it's dreadful, but . . . think of me! Now I am stuck once more with the Toad!" Petra touched Margaret's cheek. "Please laugh, Maggie. Please smile."

Margaret thought of all the turns at which she might have gone back, the ways in the road she had not taken, every choice that had brought her to this terrible place where she had no more choices. She buried her face in Petra's shoulder, and wept.

Accused

Was there nothing to be done about it? Petra wondered, after poor Maggie had fallen into a fitful sleep. She would go and speak to Father, beg release from betrothal to the Toad, and plead the case of her sister. Neither of them had any choice: marriage was not a matter of the heart but of the purse. But there were limits, surely, to what a girl must endure. Thought and feeling boiling in her stomach, Petronilla stuffed her feet into her shoes, then stormed down the dim-lit hall to her father's chamber.

When Petra came to the door, loud voices issued from within.

". . . fine fat purse, my Lord Geoffrey, but not enough.

My price is fair, considering." Hmph. Price for what? Had the Toad arrived early to renegotiate? The man's voice was deep and loud and rumbled unpleasantly like millstones.

And now her father's voice: "Considering you failed to do the job for which I paid you, you should have come to *return* my coin, not demand more."

What job? What coin?

"What matters is, all of Knightsbridge is in raptures that her little ladyship's come back. And I know what I know." He laughed, a sound that chilled Petronilla. There was mumbling, and she pressed her ear closer.

"You paid a king's ransom so that I would kill her off," the man went on. "That I did not do the job will hardly put *me* in a bad light." Now Petra's blood ran cold. "I know what I know," he said again, his voice carrying a threat.

She covered her mouth with both hands and measured her breaths to keep a steady head. Could it be true? Her father had paid . . . to have Margaret killed? Which meant . . . he knew she'd survived the fall? Now the stranger spoke again.

". . . couple of my trusty mates knows of our little arrangement, so don't go whipping out the knife you've hidden in your hose. Truly, Lord Geoff, I am handy with a falchion myself, and have had much practice slitting a throat." Silence. Mumbling. Then: "Many thanks, friend."

Heavy steps approached the door, and Petra slid

behind a tapestry that lined the dark hall. The door opened, closed. She held her breath and waited for the footsteps to pass; then she slipped out again and opened the door. The fire in the great hearth burned; darting flames reflected her father in the many mirrors about the room, as if it were a small chamber of hell and he the Devil himself.

For a moment they stared at one another.

"I know, Father," Petra whispered. "I *know all!*" she said more forcefully. Lord Geoffrey crossed the room in two strides and grabbed her arm, saying, "Shhhh, shhhh, you don't know what you're saying; you don't know anything." Then his face crumpled, and he let go her arm and Petra fell to her knees.

Petra narrowed her eyes at her father, and he turned from her and crossed the room to the trestle table, and with shaking hand he poured a draught of ale.

Petra went on in a low voice made hard by betrayal. "You let me believe I killed my own sister," she said. She shook her head so violently her hair came loose from its coils. "And all the time it was you!"

"What fresh madness is this?" Geoffrey said. "You're possessed by a fit." He drained the cup of ale and then stepped toward her, and reached a hand to help her from the floor, but Petra turned away.

"I heard, Father. I was outside the door, and I heard that man! The horrible man who calls you *friend.*" She pushed herself to her feet. "But *you* are the horrible man!" she cried. "Everything I thought was true is false. Everything—everyone—I thought was good is bad." She pointed at him, and her hand trembled. "*You* are bad! And *I*," she said, her voice breaking, hand upon her chest, "I am *not* bad! I did not kill my sister. I never did it!"

Geoffrey took her arm, but she shook him off with an angry turn of her shoulder. "And my rabbit?" she said. "My dogs?" She began to weep. "I never killed them, either! Did I?" She pounded her chest with a fist.

"Petra, calm yourself. Let me call for Emma." He turned and made for the door, but Petra ran to him and clutched at his robes.

"No!" Petra cried. "I will tell my sister everything. You'll be tossed out. You have no claim here. The manor lands are mine, through my mother," she said, "and never yours!"

Geoffrey began to speak in sweet tones as he reached for Petra, but she stood tall and straight, and her voice came strong over his. "You are no longer my father. My mother could not have loved you, for you are evil and wicked and horrid and I will . . . I will have you locked in the dungeon!"

Geoffrey drew back, and his head snapped to the side as if Petra had struck him in the face. There was a pause in which only the sound of Geoffrey's coarse breathing could be heard. His tormented image shone back from countless mirrors on the walls.

"She did love me, and I her," he said, his voice an anguished groan.

"You are not capable of love, of being a father. You're an imposter!"

And then an animal smile stretched Geoffrey's lips across his teeth, and he slowly shook his head. "Poor Petra," he whispered. "So sad. It pains me to see your mind so broken. *In parte insana,* poor dear." He crossed the room and plucked a small vial from a cupboard.

"I won't drink it!" Petra backed toward the door, but Geoffrey caught her by the lacing of her sleeve. The silk gave with an angry rip, but he held on. She began to scream and kick and claw at his face, scraping three jagged lines down his cheek.

Holding her fast, he spoke low in her ear. "*I* will not be locked in the dungeon. And *I* am not the imposter." Then he turned his bleeding cheek and yelled for the guards.

No More Pickpocketry

Minka and Bilious had traveled and searched over all of Rowne—east and north and west and south, and then round the compass again. Minka's temper was short, and Bilious had strayed so far from his route that he feared he'd lost his good custom forever; each had begun to fear that their zigs and zags across the country were for naught and that Margaret had met with misfortune, and they uttered their prayers with more vigor than ever.

One morning on the road heading west again, their cart was overtaken by a party traveling at a clip Old Penelope could never match.

"Where are you going in such a hurry?" Bilious called to the driver of the cart, a bent and skinny fellow whose kneecaps poked from holes in his hose. Minka fanned away the dust kicked up from the road as the cart passed.

"Haven't you heard?" replied the driver, over his shoulder. "There's to be a royal wedding in Knightsbridge, come St. Petronilla's Day."

Minka counted on her fingers. "That's but five days hence," she said. "Go faster, Bilious!"

"You'd best hurry along," called the knobby-kneed driver, as he pulled farther ahead, "if you're to arrive in time with that old nag!"

Urchin snorted.

"It isn't *me* he means," said Minka, puffing up.

"I should say not," said Bilious, with a wink at Urchin. "Besides, we're but a day away from Knightsbridge."

Before long they came upon a village and pulled to a stop to sup and rest Penelope. Urchin, dressed in her grain sack with a clean blanket wrapped around her like a cape, began to cavort about, hopping and leaping left and right and back and forth.

Bilious glanced up from the pan of sausages grilling on the fire. He broke off a bit and fed it to Pip, who nibbled it eagerly.

"Got a flair for the dramatic, that one," Bilious said.

Minka grunted her agreement.

Before long, a crowd of ten or twelve had gathered to

watch Urchin's odd dance, some pointing and nodding, others laughing. After a while, she stopped jigging about and stood still, chin raised, posture straight as a candle. She pulled the blanket tight around her, and looked down her nose at the people.

Minka elbowed Bilious. "What is she up to?"

Bilious shrugged and speared a sausage in reply.

"Loyal subjects," Urchin began in a loud voice that carried like a crow's caw, "I, Your Royal Highness Queen Urchin, do you the honor of greeting you!"

She tipped her head slightly and circled her hand from the wrist. "Ladies and lords, I need hardly say how distinguishable I am, how very popular I am, and I can only say I will die afore I yield to, to . . . to the enemy!" She raised a fist in the air. "Yes, every last one of my knights"—she gestured to Bilious, who, mouth full of grilled sausage, cheerfully waved his spoon in the air— "will take to their fine mounts"—she swept an arm toward Old Penelope, who passed wind as if on cue— "to defend the hills, the rivers, the cities, the villages and *allllll* the people in them, to fight off . . . the evil, ugly, enemy horde." Here she pointed at Minka, who growled, seemingly accommodatingly. "The ugly horde," Urchin repeated, "that even now rumbles at our gates!"

As Urchin's royal rallying speech gathered speed, the people were chuckling more and more loudly, welcoming the surprise of entertainment from an unexpected source. Urchin paused to breathe.

"History," her speech continued, "tradition, pomp, duty, golden crowns, and so on and so forth. Free bread and blankets! So that wolves do not invade the kingdom and its flock!" Urchin finished strong and shook her royal hempen garb.

"Huzzah!" A cheer went up and was echoed by three or four members of the crowd. Urchin tipped her head in gracious appreciation.

"In conclusion, I thank me for honoring you in this way, and remind you that none of this business of good rulership can be kept up without you pay your taxes, withal." With that, Urchin whipped the hat from Minka's head and passed it around, and several amused folk tossed in coins, so that some merry clinking could be heard above the laughter.

$$\cdot\!\!\!\int_{\!\!\!\!-}$$

Later, Urchin counted the coins as they rode west toward Knightsbridge. In among them were a spoon, a thimble, two walnuts, and a pin.

"Where did you come by those items?" Minka demanded.

"Pip," Urchin replied. "He's a clever one, even for a squirrel."

Minka gasped and put her hand to her bosom. "Bilious!" she barked, shifting on the wagon seat to fix her eye on him.

"Ye-es?" Bilious stared straight ahead, eyes upon the road.

"I insist you reform that rodent," Minka said, eyeing the squirrel around Urchin's neck. "No more pickpocketry! I'll not attach myself to a life of thieving."

"Attached!" Bilious looked at her now, and held back a grin. "Attached, are we?"

Minka humphed. "Attached is a bunion to my sore left foot, that's what," she said, and crossed her arms.

Bilious chuckled and jiggled the reins. "Heeya, Penelope! Onward to the royal city, and rich as royals we are," he said, "rich as royals!"

Get Her Get Her Get Her

"Where is she?" Margaret whispered.

"I've sent her to the countryside," said Lord Geoffrey. "For her own protection, and yours, my dear. Who knows what she is capable of? I am sorry you had to learn the truth this way. I have tried to shield you, to shield everyone, from Petra's true nature."

Margaret stared into the cold hearth. The horrible things he had told her! *In parte insana?* The words of their oath of fealty in the dark of night came to her. Her thumb throbbed like the devil, as if to needle her with doubt. *Was* Petra mad, as Geoffrey claimed? *Could* Petra have pushed her from the wall, those years ago, and set in motion the life Margaret had led? She pictured the fevered way Petra had thrown her out the day they met. The strange turn of mood and abrupt departure from the pet stall in the marketplace. The insinuations of the baker and his wife and their bitter Petronilla pies. The elixirs. *Could* she have strangled her pets, the sweet rabbit in the hutch?

The puppy, Walter, whimpered at Margaret's feet, and she reached to pick him up and hug him close. The ribbon bow around his neck brushed her chin. Might Petra have later used the ribbon to—to—oh, she couldn't even think it.

"The poor lamb," Emma said, "never quite right in the head, though I love her still, I do!" The maidservant wiped at her red-rimmed eyes with a handkerchief, and then blew her nose loudly. "She cannot help it and never could." With feeling she picked up a mending basket and bustled out of the chamber, shaking her head all the while.

"I want to go to her." Margaret rose from her chair. She had to see her. She had to look into her eyes. "Please."

Lord Geoffrey came and patted Margaret's shoulder, pressing her back into the chair. She tensed and rubbed Walter's ears for comfort. She wished Emma had not left her alone with Geoffrey.

"I dare not. . . ." Geoffrey gave a deep sigh. "Dear Margaret. I worry that seeing you—her own face upon you—is the very thing that has sent her deeper into madness."

Margaret let the puppy to the floor. "Then I must go

from this place, for this is *her* home. If it be I that make her ill, then I will go."

"Ah, but what a bind we find ourselves in," Geoffrey said with a prim smile. "You must know, surely, that it is also you who gives her a reason to come back from that madness." He clasped his hands and bent his head, as in prayer. "She must be away from us, for now, until she is well, until after our marriage is"—he waved a hand absently in the air—"accomplished."

"And if I refuse to marry?" Her mouth was dry; all that she could manage was a whisper.

Geoffrey's glare touched Margaret like a chill wind. Then he gave a shrug that lifted the hem of his robe from the floor. "The choice to wed is simply not yours to make," he said, walking closer, "nor so the choice to come and go." In no hurry, his voice soft and menacing, he added, "Nor to rise from bed or return to it, to eat, to drink . . ." His cool gaze traveled to her twisted leg, and his lip curled and his voice stabbed: "Nor to hobble here, or to lurch and stagger there." He touched one finger to her cheek, and she pulled back and stared at the red lines scratched upon his. Then he turned and strode from the room in a swirl of red cloth.

Margaret's skin went cold, and her head felt heavy, too heavy to hold up. For all the comforts she'd had here, she was as good as locked in prison.

Emma quietly entered the room. "Are you all right, Highness?"

Margaret reached for Walter again, and she plumped the bow round his neck, for Petra's sake. "Is she frightened, Emma? Do you know? Is she safe?"

When Emma did not answer, Margaret rose from her chair. "Emma?" Walter looked from one to the other, alert.

Emma did not meet Margaret's gaze. "I don't know." Then she picked up the sewing basket and brought it to Margaret's chair beside the cold hearth. "Let's busy ourselves with our embroidery, eh?" she said.

Margaret was silent.

Then: "No," she said after a moment. "He can separate me from my sister. He can mock me, and frighten me, and force me to wed, and lock me in this room for all eternity, Emma, but . . . there will be no more embroidery."

Emma stared in surprise at Margaret. Margaret was the first to laugh, then Emma joined her, and then, overcome, they both wept.

❧

A storm attacked the castle in the night. A violent crack shook Geoffrey's bed, and he woke with a gasp: Damn the glazier.

Geoffrey stared up into darkness rent by lightning. That evening years past, in the cathedral, when he'd gazed into the magic mirror, it was himself

he'd seen: an old king, with Isobel by his side looking lovingly—adoringly!—up at him, her pale hand
upon his chest. He'd seen everything he wanted in the
glass. Everything he deserved, everything he'd done
to get it.

Of course, he'd made demands—strong demands—
upon the glazier. The man had gone mute, not a word
in years. And no new magic mirror.

But—he plumped his pillow and rolled over—he'd
managed to make his own magic yet again.

🎵

Another crack of thunder, and Emma's eyes flew open,
in the servants' quarters. Where *had* Lord Geoffrey sent
Princess Petronilla off to, dear lamb? Was she frightened by the same storm, this night? Was she taking
her elixirs? She didn't like to swallow down the icky
liquids, but without them could she find peace? Could
she sleep? *Elixir . . . elixir . . .* funny word, that. Emma
yawned, *elixir,* and fell back to sleep.

🎵

A boom and rumble found Walter shivering and whim-
pering in the dungeon stairwell. "What're you doing
roaming about down here, little fellow?" said the night
watch. "Lost, are you? You do wander round the castle,

don't you, pup." He fed the dog a bit of chicken from his supper, and stroked his brown spotted fur. "There's a good dog. Good dog."

⁂

Margaret shivered beneath her coverlet and turned over in sleep. The storms of the day had tossed her plenty. She did not wake.

⁂

Days passed numbly. Margaret was allowed to venture out only to attend mass, and then always in the company of a guard. Father Sebastian kindly let her help him in the almonry annexed to the nave, where sorting food and blankets for the poor helped take her mind off her troubles. During these times, whatever guard was on duty stole the opportunity to snooze or socialize or pray, depending on his nature, for the almonry room was small and secure, its street door locked against thievery, and the trusted Father Sebastian had the only key.

At night, she dreamed of Beady Bone, in search of the truth.

Sweating and with pounding heart, Margaret woke from such a dream one night, rose, and lit a candle. Rain fell outside the open window, and she limped over, breathing in the damp air. She saw her face in a pane of glass, and thought of the magic mirror.

It all seemed a distant season, a different life. Could it have been only a month ago?

She'd longed for so much. Now she only longed to know the truth. Had Petra pushed Margaret from the wall? What was she to do? And where was Petra being held? Margaret had begged Geoffrey to tell her where she was and how she was, but he would only say she was in the country and that she would be fine, in time. Emma was no help: "How I miss my dear lamb," she'd say, and turn away.

Walter lifted his head from the foot of the bed where he'd been snoring, jumped down, and padded to Margaret at the window. He'd grown so big, she hardly had to reach at all to stroke his back. The bright ribbon was gone now, of course, without Petra's attentions. She should replace the bow, for Petra's sake. Margaret dug her fingers into his fur and scratched, and—she paused—her fingers found a thin cord, tied deep in the ruff of Walter's neck. She bent to untie the complicated knot and pulled the lacing free. Thoughtfully, she wound it round her hand. Emma, she thought. Emma loved Petra this much. But Margaret could do better than a plain sleeve lace!

She moved to the room's small table, where Petra kept ribbons and laces, jewels and ornaments, and writing tools—pots of ink, powder for drying, a knife for sharp-ening and for scratching out errors. First she found a pretty purple ribbon and tied it in a bow round patient Walter's neck. Then, curious, she pulled out the stack of softened vellum and riffled through the sheets. Margaret brought the candle closer and bent her head to the pages; Petra's hand was clear and sure.

mother
sister
heart
bunny
fear my soul lost

She did not know all the words, but was pleased that she could read many, and said a silent thanks to her teachers, her friends.

And then, on a skin at the bottom of the stack, she came upon a drawing—two small girls holding hands, the aged parchment inked some years past, and with a youthful hand. The picture showed Petra's heart's true nature, sure as any magic mirror. Margaret took out Petra's goose feather and inked across the bottom of the parchment the first word she'd learned by heart. *Sister.*

Margaret stacked the skins, her pulse quickening, and laid her hands upon them, and with a certainty sudden and sharp as the pricking of her thumb, she knew that whatever had happened in the past—if she had been pushed from the castle wall—was not by Petra's will.

These were not the words and pictures of the insane. These pages bore the love of a sister. A sister who laughed with her, who taught her the letters, who welcomed her even though Margaret's arrival meant Petra would not wear her mother's crown.

Geoffrey was lying. How had she not known it before?

Rain began to fall in earnest.

Get her get her get her get her.

Sommat's Amiss

"Have you seen, come through here, a girl with a crooked leg?"

Minka and Bilious and Urchin stood before a grand gatehouse and plugged their noses against the stench of the disgusting river that ran beneath the bridge they had just crossed. The spires of the cathedral towered above the high, imposing walls.

The guard smirked at Minka. "Have I seen a girl with a crooked leg, you ask, missus? Was she fair, but not washed nor et in many days, and leaning on a crutch?"

"Yes, likely!"

The guard laughed, showing blunt teeth. "I seen her by the dozens," he said.

Minka growled at the guard, and she and Bilious and Urchin passed through the gates into the city.

With them were all the makings of a fair—mummers and musicians and jugglers and all manner of folk—for people were arriving in droves in anticipation of the rumored royal wedding.

Late in the day they entered Knightsbridge Cathedral, Bilious to light a candle for his dead wife, Minka to give God a piece of her mind, and Urchin to spy for offerings she might pilfer. The great nave was shot through with color as afternoon light streamed through the glorious glass window.

Minka spied a young woman dressed in a fine gown, her shining hair coiled into ramshorns above her ears, and wearing delicate shoes. The fine lady's head was bowed in prayer, and Minka gave her wide berth, the respect due nobility. The sun moved, casting colored light upon something resting on the floor beside the lady: a crutch.

Minka's gaze shot to the lady's face again, and then she shook her head as if to regain sense after taking a blow.

"Bilioussss!" she hissed, never taking her eyes from the young woman kneeling in prayer. When Bilious saw Minka's frantic beckoning, he came hopping to her side.

"Look there!" Minka said, jutting her chin at the young lady: the bowed head, the delicate shoes, the left foot wrong, and the carved crutch.

Bilious swallowed, glanced at Minka, and loudly whispered, "Maggie?"

The lady turned.

Minka, seeing that it *was* Mags, began to advance upon her, but Margaret, to Minka's annoyance, disappointment, and outright anger, put up a dainty—dainty!—hand to indicate she should stop. Minka did. Margaret's face was stiff with concealed recognition and astonishment, and she was cutting her gaze left-right-left as though she had a tic, and waving that hand to mean *some*thing, but—

Bilious bent to Minka's ear and whispered, "Sommat's amiss. Wait. Watch."

Margaret dropped her head again, as if in prayer, and remained that way a few moments. Then she rose, and crossed, *clump-slide,* to a man in the garb of a soldier and spoke with him. He nodded and then sauntered several paces away, stood by the west porch door of the cathedral, and joined another man in conversation.

With a glance at Minka, Margaret made her way along the length of the cathedral to a small door on the south wall of the nave, and after another meaningful glance at Minka, passed through the doorway.

"I'll go first," Minka said to Bilious.

"Slowly, now," he said, "slowly."

As Bilious watched, Minka traversed the nave, looked wonderingly at the great rose window, took a few steps backward, knelt for a moment in prayer, then crossed the nave at an angle so sharp as to attract attention from three different worshippers, but, Bilious marveled, she drew not even a glance from the soldier at the door. Then Minka was at the small door to the annex that was the almonry, and disappeared within.

Inside, Minka saw Margaret waiting eagerly for her. Minka crossed the room in two long strides, fell to her knees before Margaret, declared it a minor miracle, and then stood and hit her with her hat.

"Have you any thought to what I've been through, looking all over God's creation for you?"

Then Minka surprised herself by tossing aside the hat and throwing her arms around Margaret. "Oh, Mags!" she cried. "Oh, my girl."

And Margaret held to Minka as for dear life, and so they remained many long moments, both of them weeping, until Bilious entered the room, looked around the series of low vaults and thick columns, saw the annex was empty save Maggie and Minka, and cleared his throat. "Is it safe?"

Margaret nodded, wiping at her cheeks. "The guard doesn't follow me into the almonry, and the priests are at vespers. How is it you are here? I am so happy to see you, and you, too, Bilious," she added, looking curiously at the peddler, then at Minka, and back again.

"I?" said Minka. "How is it that *I* am here? Why, I'm here to visit the bones of St. Sincere, I am." She turned to Bilious and elbowed him.

Margaret, distracted by a grubbily clad girl slipping

in the door, said, "I'm sorry, it isn't time." She pointed to a padlocked door on the opposite wall. "Come round midday tomorrow, along to the churchyard door."

"Never mind her; she's with us," Minka said, then she popped Margaret on the head. "*I* came looking for the magic mirror," she said. "And truth be known, I came looking for you, Mags! Why else?"

"You—you left the house for me? You risked the bad luck of the world?"

"Found plenty of it, I might add," Minka said, "and I picked up this lot, for my trouble." She jerked a thumb at Bilious and then noticed Urchin sidling toward a collection plate. "Tsssst! Have off!" she hissed, waving the girl away.

"But I'm as poor as any," Urchin reasoned loudly.

"Poorer than many, by any measure of morals," Minka said. She turned to Margaret. "And now you've met our Urchin," she said, and, shaking her head, rolled her eyes heavenward.

The two girls looked at each other. Margaret smiled, and Urchin made an elaborate curtsy that threatened the floor with her nose. A little russet squirrel peeped out from the girl's pocket, and Margaret startled.

"Don't ask," said Minka. "A most disreputable pet, that rodent. He'll go in anybody's purse or pocket and take whatever shines."

"And if he finds nothing shiny," Bilious explained, "he makes himself at home."

"Nods off," Urchin agreed.

"Bit dull, in fact," said Bilious, scratching his ear.

Minka sighed deeply. "Such is the wisdom and value of your trades, Bilious." She was still bitter about the cup made of a coconut. "But here is our Mags," Minka went on, looking Margaret up and down. She was overawed and put out and blustering and loving, but what came out was huff and vinegar. "Here she is, all cleaned and polished, and here I come all this way to rescue her and what's clear as day is I'm not needed. And look at that crutch, would you, carved up so pretty? She doesn't need this one, now, does she," she said, jerking her head at Bilious, who leaned upon Margaret's old crutch of rubbed ash. "*You've* the skill to make a trade, I'd say, Mags," she muttered with another glance at Bilious. "Traded up quite fancy, by my eyes." She looked at Margaret, and her eyes welled with tears. "You might have said sommat," she said. "You might've said goodbye."

"Oh, Minka." Margaret's chin crumpled, and she thought of the night she left Minka snoring at the house in Lesser Dorste. Though quick with the sharp tongue and the willow switch, Minka had been the only mother Margaret had ever known. "I am sorry," she said. "I have so much to tell you. I don't know where to begin."

Bilious said, "At the beginning. No use starting in the middle, and we've never come upon the end, as long as we're alive."

"Begin with the mirror!" Minka's words burst forth,

and she began to pat Margaret roughly about the hips to discover a hiding place. "Where is it?"

"I don't have it," Margaret said, miserably, batting away Minka's seeking hands.

"Don't have it?" Minka was flabbergasted. "Don't have it! All my trouble coming after you, and you don't have it!"

Bilious stroked Minka's arm and made soothing noises in the manner of speaking to his mare, Old Penelope, and as he did, the almonry door cracked open. Margaret glanced up in alarm, but no one entered, and the door closed again.

"Come around here," Margaret said, and led them to a bench concealed by a great wooden coffer bound with iron. There they sat, and she told them everything. At first Minka interrupted, but Bilious bade her keep her mouth shut. Minka had to settle for gasping and clenching her fists while Margaret spoke at length. She began with seeing the wild-eyed man in the mirror, and how such a longing was stirred in her to find him. How she dreaded a wedding to Hugo the hunchback, how she ran afoul of John Book and lost the magic mirror, how she took company with Bertram and Brother Henry and the pilgrims. And then she told of finding Petronilla, her own sister, discovering her true identity as a princess, and being betrothed first to the Toad and then to her own stepfather, Lord Geoffrey, and—

"And that's not all," Margaret said.

"Is that not enough?" cried Minka. Bilious patted Minka's shoulder comfortingly. Urchin picked her teeth with a straw.

"Petra has been accused of trying to kill me. Lord Geoffrey says she is sick in the mind, and he has sent her away, I know not where. But I don't believe it! Any of it! Petra is kind and good and spirited. I must go and get her. I"—Margaret looked sheepish—"I heard it on the rain!"

"Heard it on the rain? Heard it on the rain . . . now who's ill in the head," said Minka, raising an eyebrow at Bilious and tapping her temple. "Mayhap she does need my help, then, and just in time I'd say," Minka said in Bilious's direction. Turning to Margaret, she straightened her wimple and settled her hands on her hips. "Hugo the woolmonger looks a fair bargain now, eh?" she said. "I'd suppose the hump doesn't appear so pronounced from this distance!"

"If only I had the magic mirror," Margaret said, ignoring Minka, "then I might somehow know what next to do."

"But we don't have the mirror, do we," said Minka. "Come away, now, Mags." She leaned in toward Margaret and spoke in urgent tones. "Whether Lord Geoffrey speaks truth or lies, neither bodes well for you. You know not where Petronilla is, and there's naught to be done for her from your present position. So let's get you away—"

All turned—froze—at the sound of jingling and footsteps approaching. Through the door strode a figure clothed in black.

"It's good to see you, Father Sebastian," said Margaret.

"Won't you introduce me to your friends?" the priest replied.

❧

The sun was gone, and the day's warmth gave way to the chill of night. Light from within taverns and houses lit up the twisting alleys and streets they followed toward the city wall, which would lead them to Isobel's Gate.

How it happened that Margaret was huddled beside Urchin in the back of Bilious's cart was this: Father Sebastian let Minka, Bilious, and Urchin out the almonry door onto the street known as St. Mary's Churchyard and bade them return with their cart. Then he called the soldier in and begged to keep Margaret longer at her work; the recent storms had left many cold and wet and in need of warm blankets. The soldier allowed it.

Father Sebastian drew up the jingling rope at his waist, removed from it a single key, and pressed it into Margaret's palm. He nodded at the almonry door to the street. "Let yourself out when your friends return," he told her, "and I will go and make myself conspicuous outside."

Now, as they drove away, Margaret spied the maidservant, Emma, in animated conversation with the guard at the door of the cathedral. As the cart rolled past, Margaret thought Emma might have seen her. "Hurry, we haven't much time."

Bilious urged Old Penelope as hard as he dared, and at last they reached the gate.

Only a few more rolls of the cartwheels and she'd be free, Margaret thought. She pulled her hood to better hide her face.

The church bells began to ring. As Bilious drove his wagon directly toward the gate, a soldier raised a burning rush and approached. "Do you wish to leave the city?" he called.

Yes, Margaret thought, she wished to leave the city; yes, she wished to be free of wicked Geoffrey, to leave this place and never look back. And Petra? Emma loved her, and she would take care of her dear lamb somehow. Margaret never had asked the maidservant why she'd replaced the ribbon around Walter's neck with a lacing.

"You may pass," said the soldier, waving the wagon through.

A lacing like the ones Petra favored in her sleeves. Margaret's lips parted with a sharp breath of revelation. Petra? Not Emma, but Petra? *Petra, in the castle?*

"I was hoping we'd've been caught," Urchin said with a grin. "I'd have liked to seen the dungeon."

The dungeon! Margaret pulled her hood deeper over

her head, shadowing her face as the wagon rolled past the soldiers. A cold mist worked its way inside the folds of the cloak, and she shivered. This was her chance to slip away forever, to escape. And she could not take it.

The heavy doors groaned on iron hinges, and the soldiers' broadswords clanked as they grunted with the effort of swinging them shut.

"Heeya." Bilious encouraged his mare to lumber through, and with him the last folk departing the city for the night. Margaret pulled Urchin against her and leaned to her ear.

"Find me at the almonry," she whispered. She whirled away from Urchin's grasp, fell stumbling from the rolling wagon, and made herself small and her hood deep, moving slowly backward against the flow of exiting people. And the great gates closed between her and Minka once more.

Another Rescue

"Curfew is nigh! Take to your houses!"

Margaret found the shadows. She humped her shoulders and hurried away. At the sound of stomping feet behind her, she turned quickly. A band of armed soldiers was marching down the street. She ducked into an alleyway, and all went dark—someone had just closed the shutters for the night. The soldiers filed past the alleyway, steps from where she huddled against a wall. She murmured a prayer of thanks.

If she were to be caught on the streets past curfew, she would have too many questions to answer. Surely an alarm had gone out when she wasn't to be found at the cathedral. People would be looking for her. She had to get to the castle, had to find Petra. She dared not go by the wider roads, and stuck instead to narrow passages. She clumped down a narrow alley with walls so close she could have touched the other side if she'd reached out her crutch. She was nearly at the other end when a figure stepped toward her.

Margaret stopped, turned, and began to run. A rat scurried across the way at her feet; she startled. Her crutch slipped in a puddle of muck; she fell. Chattering erupted from her cloak, and her pulse raced till she saw a set of tiny tufted ears—Pip! She envisioned how she'd pulled Urchin to her in the cart. The squirrel must have got from Urchin's pocket to her own, and made himself at home. But now—footsteps! She scrambled to her knees quickly, heart pounding in her chest, tugged her crutch from the mud, and began to lurch away.

"Princess!" came a whispered cry.

Hearing the call in the night so frightened her, she stopped and turned around, ready to brandish her crutch.

Then the voice came again—"Princess, oh! Thanks to God"—and she realized it was Emma.

Margaret fell into the maidservant's arms, and though she didn't know if Emma would betray her, she was weary and frightened and badly in need of an ally. (Pip didn't count.)

"Emma ... did you tie a lacing around Walter's neck?"

Emma's baffled look was answer enough. Margaret took a breath—and a risk.

"Petra's in the dungeon," she said. "Geoffrey lied."

❧

Moments later, the two were hunched over cups of mead and a plate of bread and cheese in a shadowed corner of the Crown and Bean, the alehouse dim-lit and open illicitly past the hour of curfew. Emma explained how she'd come to find Margaret in the alleyway. Her interest had first been piqued when Margaret did not return to the castle before tea. Upon arriving at the cathedral, Emma peered into the almonry and saw Margaret in conversation with three strangers, and by the princess's attitude knew these folk to be friend, not foe. She then found the guard smoking a pipe outside the lesser south door of the cathedral, and announced that the princess had taken ill, and that she'd sent her to the castle with an escort, and she twisted his ear for not noticing them slip out.

"Forthwith I returned to the castle and spun Lord Geoffrey the same story, and said you'd taken supper in your chamber and then to bed."

Margaret clapped silently. "A tale more twisted than my crippled leg. Thank you, dear Emma," she said as

240

she slipped Pip a nibble of cheese. "But why would you help me?"

Emma wrapped her fingers round her cup. "Help comes when you least expect it. As for me, a rock fell unexpected from the sky onto my cursed second husband's head. As for you? I wanted you to escape."

Margaret, speechless, stared.

Emma tipped back her head, drained her cup dry, and set it with judgment on the scarred oaken table. "You are right. Geoffrey is not a good man. I seen him kick Walter in the ribs, and I need no more than that to know it," she said. She looked intently into Margaret's eyes, then pointed at Margaret's cup of mead. "Will you be finishing that?"

Margaret shook her head, and so Emma drank it down and drew her sleeve across her lips.

"I don't doubt he put her in the dungeon, the pure devil."

❧

They weaved through dark streets to the castle. Emma cajoled the gatekeeper with hot soup from the Crown and Bean, and while he slurped, Margaret sneaked. The key to the cells was kept hanging on a peg in the wall of the weapons room, guarded by a watchman. As planned, Emma lured the watchman away with a wink and a flash of ankle, but—not as planned—he locked the door of the weapons room behind him. Now what?

Emma had told her to go one flight down to the dungeon, once she had secured the key. She could see it through the barred opening in the weapons room door, but she couldn't reach it. And now she was alone and without a scheme, and Emma's amorous advances on the guard were for naught. If she went after Emma, she'd be discovered, and so would Emma's part in her deception. What should she do? Sticking her crutch through the bars, she tried to reach the key on the wall. Not quite. She leaned into the bars and stretched her crutch an inch farther. So close, but not close enough. And then she felt a small furry creature stir in her pocket.

᪥

Margaret murmured a prayer of thanks to all the saints of thieves and liars: Pip was a fine pickpocket, no matter what Minka said. Key in hand, she crept down the damp stone steps to the dungeon below, a journey no different by night than it had been by day. She thought how dreadfully the hours and months and years must pass in such a place, with no sun to bless a new day, no moon to comfort at night, only the hellish torches.

Loud, regular snores came from the first cell. Margaret passed it by. She glanced into the second cell. The madwoman was awake and watching, she realized with a start. Margaret stepped to the next cell, and saw someone lying on the floor in a heap of silk. "Petra?" she whispered. "Petra, I am come." The figure did not stir. Margaret worked the key in the lock and swung open the door.

"Petra!" she whispered, kneeling and shaking her. She leaned her cheek to Petra's parted lips and felt faint breath. Not dead, then, God be praised, but drugged, more like. Two vials lay on the floor among the dirty rushes. Margaret studied them, then put them in the purse at her waist.

The snoring from the first cell stopped abruptly; then came a snort, and the snoring resumed.

Margaret drew the prone Petra's arm across her shoulder and, with effort, rose from the floor, gripped her crutch, and began to drag Petra away. Petra roused from her stupor. "I knew you'd get my message."

Margaret grinned. "Walter made a fine messenger. But I was slow to understand."

They stumbled toward the steps, past the mad-woman's cell, where she stood gripping the iron bars. "I had a feeling," she whispered meaningfully, though Margaret couldn't fathom what she meant.

The woman coughed and tried again. "For years I could not even beg God's forgiveness," she whispered hoarsely. "It weren't my fault, but then again . . . I beg . . ." She held Margaret's gaze as if by force. "I beg of you . . ."

Those eyes . . . Margaret tore her gaze from the old

woman's, fumbled for the key. "All will be well," she said, merely to calm the poor woman and ease her way. She turned the lock and pulled open the door. She looked at the old woman and gestured *come out.* "What is your name?"

"Lucy. I—I'm Lucy."

"Hurry now, Lucy."

But the madwoman stood on the threshold, cheeks wet with tears. Then came to Margaret's mind a picture: the little family of quail on the road to Knightsbridge. "Follow me," she said.

The madwoman stepped out.

"What of the other poor creature?" said Petra.

"Leave 'im," Emma panted, arriving in a rush. "That's my third husband, may he rot."

A Feeling

The madwoman blinked in the scant light of the moon, breathing the clean night air into her lungs. She could have followed along behind the girls—wanted to very much indeed. But she didn't. Nor did she set out to find Tom the apothecary, who would surely take her in, if he yet lived. He had come to see her down there, once or twice, but he'd had no money to buy her freedom. And anyway, she'd deserved her fate.

Oh, how guards talk when they think their wards aren't human. So she'd heard that Will Glazier was being kept in the old kiln. She'd always wanted to get word to him, but never did; what she had to say couldn't be done secondhand. Face to face was how it had to be, to tell him the story of his wife, his little girl. Now—she had a feeling—there might be a new story to tell. There might.

And so she went alone to Knightsbridge Wood.

There was only one way out of the city past curfew. She found a place where the riverbank allowed, gathered her courage, and leaped into the River Severn. She swam the stinking length of it where it curved around the city. She floated with gobs of rubbish that in the dark could have been anything alive (and biting) or dead (and decaying) or worse. Though for one who had rotted in a dungeon for so long, the water was, if not refreshing, at least reviving. Along the wall she paddled, beneath the bridge, past the gatehouse. Then she dragged herself out and made for the trees.

She waited and watched until she saw the ghosts: two pale figures moving slowly in the wood. She crept closer. She listened. But they weren't ghosts. Of course not.

"If you could just make him what he wants," the large one said to the other. "He simply wants to see Isobel in the magic glass he swears you have the power to make."

The other did not speak.

"He's a man possessed. If he could see her but once, I trust he'd set you free. Don't I come and give you a bit of exercise now and then? Do I bring the right amount of wood to burn? Perhaps the wood's not dry enough.

Is there any tool you do not have? Have you simply lost the gift?"

When the smaller man shook his head, the big man sighed. "Only reason he keeps you alive now is he's contrary. He thinks you'd rather be dead, and I bet he's bloody right."

Even at this the silent man did not speak.

The big man sighed again.

She followed them on silent feet and didn't get too close. She waited. By the time the big man had gone, the moon was spent; now the light was pale and wan, but it was enough to find what she was looking for. The old kiln had been abandoned since the foreign glassmakers had completed the rose window. Their work had been good, but not as good, not nearly as good, as the work that Will Glazier had done, she'd heard. Oh, she'd heard quite a lot, in the dungeon.

She rolled a rock to the window, stood upon it, and saw within the man—unwashed, and hungry, and frightened—who startled at her sudden appearance in the window. The madwoman was slight, and old, but her hands were strong. She felt all over the bars, detecting where the iron was sturdy and where it was weak, all the while talking gently but firmly to the man, the way a midwife might talk to a mother in the pain of birth, and she broke him free from his prison in the old kiln and guided him out into the dawn.

He resisted her, at first. And, oh, how well she

understood what it was like to be some time away, to be imprisoned, to forget you once were someone with a gift. But gently Lucy reminded him who he was, who he had been, and she talked about the people who had loved him. And when the sun rose full and the city gates opened, she would take him to the apothecary—dear Tom, yes, he'd take them in if he yet had breath in his body—and she'd help him climb to the attic, and she'd lay a soft bed with a pillow. She'd feed him weak ale and strong soup, and she would hide him there till she decided what to do. She promised that all would be well—wasn't that what the child had said? She almost believed again that it would.

She had a feeling.

John Book Meets His Match

Outside the walls of the city, a small party approached. It was Bertram and Henry and the borrowed slow, fat pony. Bertram had brought his gift for Margaret, and he intended to present it to her with his good wishes: that she be healed and that she might walk straight and without pain. He knew not if the water was holy away from its source at St. Winifred's Well, but still he had filled the bladder of his bagpipe and stoppered it, and they'd traveled three days from the holy shrine and come to Isobel's Gate. But their arrival was ill timed, and now the gates were shut. They would have to spend the night outside the city walls.

Bertram looked left and right as they moved into the woods, on guard for ghosts and sniffing the air for brimstone, and so he jumped when they came upon two figures. Flesh and blood, thank the saints, the man and woman were arguing, and gesturing at the large, prone body of a man at their feet. Off a short distance, a girl dressed in a grain sack sat comfortably on the ground against a tree trunk and watched the goings-on with some amusement.

Brother Henry frowned. "They bicker as skilled as puppeteers," he said to Bertram.

Bertram smiled and urged Gertrude onward to see about setting a place to sleep, when his attention caught on one word: Mags. His ears perked. He listened more closely.

"If you hadn't spun us all round the compass like a top, north and east and west and east again, well, woman, I swear my eyes have crossed!"

"If you hadn't stolen her crutch to begin with!" said the woman.

"It were a fair trade!"

Bertram strode to the woman, and Henry followed.

"Do you speak of Margaret Church?" Bertram asked.

"No," she said shortly over her shoulder, and kept up her verbal attack on her companion, but Bertram interrupted.

"Margaret the Crutch, then?" he said.

The woman turned fully to him. "Ye-es," she said.

"Are you called Minka?"

"Yes!"

Henry pointed at the figure prostrate on the ground. "Drunk?"

"No."

"Dozing?"

"Dead!"

🍃

A short while later, Minka and Bilious and Urchin and Bertram and Henry, having accomplished the introductions, sat together round a glowing fire ring, the tired horses not caring a whit for the story Minka told.

"Bad luck is ever my lot!" she began.

"Oh, just tell it!" Bilious bellowed.

Minka scowled at him, and then began again.

"We'd just come out the city gates, hiding Mags with us in the cart—"

"What? Why?" Bertram interrupted.

Minka shushed him with a wave of her hand. "It's a long story and we'll get to it in time," she said, "I promise you." She looked up at the moon. "We've got all night," she added, and began a third time to tell her tale.

🍃

The moment the gates had closed them out and Margaret in, Minka had begun to cry and wring her hands.

"Bad luck is my lot!" she'd cried, and Bilious had quieted her with a look.

"She said to meet her at the almonry, and by God we will, but we cannot till the morrow as well she knows! What is she about, and what are we to do?"

Urchin spoke. "She's got our Pip," she said, then sucked on her teeth.

"Fat good that rodent will do her," said Minka.

Margaret was in danger, and alone, and they were locked out of the city for the night.

There were others camped outside the gate. A merry band of players donned their masks and rehearsed their play. Some distance away, a lone harpist plucked a mournful tune.

And so they'd sat in the shelter of a copse of maples in view of the gate and in range of the River Severn's stink, to wait for they knew not what.

It soon arrived: the thief John Book.

John Book and his band took what they wanted from Bilious's cart—hides and brass pots and dull knives—and then, perceiving no threat (the mummers and the harpist had got up and disappeared like vapor), they sat down with Bilious and Minka and took what food they had and ate it right in front of them. Bilious cursed John Book as him who had murdered his dear wife. John Book laughed and put his face in Bilious's and said, "She were a lovely bit of business. We had us a bit of fun, we did. A fair creature, she were, a bonny beauty. She laughed like a fairy, like tinkling bells."

"You plainly don't even recollect her, you brute!" said Bilious, his voice quivering. "She, which you murdered outright, did not ever laugh like tinkling bells, but rather wheezed like a bleating bagpipe! But she were my wife!" and he spat in John Book's face.

The crew of outlaws laughed nervously. "John Book doesn't like that," muttered one of the men. "Not one bit. If there is one thing John Book does not like, it is being spat at." They watched to see what their leader would do. He wiped the spittle from his cheek and glared at Bilious, then drew his knife.

At a sound like a bellowing elk, everyone turned. It was Minka, bearing down on the thief with Bilious's— Margaret's—crutch held high. She brought the thing down with all her might and knocked him sideways, after which he fell over and struck his head upon a rock.

"I'll wager that's another thing John Book doesn't much like," Minka said, and brushed off her hands on her skirts.

The other bandits laughed and capered, expecting Book to rise and smite poor Minka. Only one among them did not laugh and jig about: a woman with a long, dark braid. When Book did not rise but lay dead, the outlaws waited a respectful moment, then searched his pockets. Minka then raised the crutch threateningly, and they ran off without their—Bilious's—loot.

"Just deserts, I say," said Minka. Bilious, slack-jawed, said nothing but stared at the dead body.

"Close your mouth, Bilious; you'll catch flies."

He snapped his mouth shut, gulped, and finally grinned. "Well done, Minka! Well done!" he said, and grabbed her up in a fervent embrace, which caused them to tumble, laughing, to the ground. Overcome, he tilted his face and puckered his lips and moved slowly closer, and closer. . . .

"Stop!" cried Minka, holding up a hand.

For her gaze had hit upon something familiar in the hoard.

❧

Minka leaned forward now, to poke the fire with a stick, and she looked at her listeners, one by one. "It were Margaret's satchel," Minka said. "And in it, magic mirror."

Moonlight winked on the glass. It was enough to see by.

"It shows the beholder's own true love," Minka said, turning it over in her hands. She had looked in the glass earlier, at the feet of the body of the thief John Book. She'd thought to see Sweetheart again, her true love. When the face of Bilious had appeared instead, she'd shaken the mirror up and down with vigor, but could not knock the image free. She saw Bilious in the mirror again now. She glared at him crossly. But when he smiled with his four teeth, she smiled back. "Oh, holy mercy, saints preserve me," she muttered. She passed the mirror to Brother Henry as if it were afire.

"I dare not seek the face of God in a trinket," he said, and turned the mirror over. *"Lux Vera,"* he said, and looked around at his companions. "It's writ across the back." He rubbed his chin. " 'The True Light,' it means."

Bilious grunted. "I've always seen just what I longed to see, when it were mine. Give it here." Sure enough, Bilious saw Minka holding a cup of ale in each fist. "Wondrous vision. And a truer light I never saw, Brother," he said with a chuckle. *"Lux Vera.* Take a turn, lad?"

Bertram accepted the mirror from Bilious. He prayed he wouldn't see a bagpipe. He raised the mirror, and in it saw Maggie. But the vision was dark. The only way he knew it was Maggie was by her limp. As he watched, she stopped and rested her forehead on her crutch— the crutch he'd carved. Then she lifted her head and pressed on.

He looked around at his companions. "The vision is dark" is all he said.

"But there will again be light," said Henry. "There will always be a light."

The Reunion in the Almonry

When the gates creaked opened at dawn, an early mist dampened the air, and a fine fog surrounded Minka and Bilious and Urchin as they marched straight up Church Street to the cathedral, and along St. Mary's Churchyard to the almonry door. With them were Bertram and Henry.

Also in the throng were a madwoman and a glazier, who passed unnoticed.

"Good job the priests pray with such regularity as we can meet here in secret," Bilious said with a wink as Margaret answered their knock.

Margaret surprised herself by bursting into tears at

the sight of Bertram, and she threw her arms about him, nearly knocking him off balance.

"I came to see you wed," he said.

"Then you'll be disappointed," she said, "for there is to be no wedding."

"No?" he said, a grin across his face.

"No," she said, and smiled back. He shifted his bag-pipes, and Margaret noticed that the bag jiggled like a jelly.

Margaret presented Petra and Emma and related the happenings of the night: how Petra was never in the country but in the dungeon all along, and how they'd freed her and left the castle by way of a wheelbarrow and a well-placed blow to the head.

"I didn't marry badly three times without learning how to knock a man senseless," Emma said. "I shot off a prayer to St. Wilgefortis and heaved ho with the night watch's own sword."

"But it was Pip who carried the day by squirreling out the key," said Margaret, placing the sleeping Pip in Bilious's cupped hands. "You should be very proud."

"I am," said Bilious solemnly, with a sidelong look at Minka.

"Now, you'll want this back," Minka said, ignoring Bilious and holding up Margaret's satchel, "it after all being what got us all started on this winding road." Minka thrust the sack at Margaret, who took it and slid out—yes!—the magic mirror.

Even as her blood raced and her heartbeat pulsed in her ears, Margaret's mind calmed, for she trusted the mirror's magic to show her something. She noticed the words etched in fine script across the back: *Lux Vera*.

" 'The True Light,' " Brother Henry read over her shoulder.

Minka elbowed the person nearest, who was Bertram, and rolled her eyes. "She hopes to see a wild-eyed man."

"I know," said Bertram. "She doesn't seem worried about the danger and the death."

"Eh?" said Minka.

"Never mind," said Bertram glumly.

Margaret lifted the mirror and gazed into its surface. There he was: the wild-eyed man. She smiled to see him, as if she had known his company in life and missed it. Strange, she thought; something was changed. But the vision was dim, and she could not have said what was different from what she'd seen before. Was it his eyes? Were they not so wild?

"Let me!" begged Petra, and grabbed the glass from Margaret and held it to her face. After a moment, she laughed wickedly. "The mirror surely shows my heart's desire and, I hope, the future, for I see my dear father locked in his own dungeon. Ha! May he find himself at home there soon," she said.

There was much shy gladness, but little time. The almonry was not the safe haven it had been, for there would be almsgiving following morning prayers, and the annex would soon be hopping with priests and poor alike.

Margaret frowned. "There is that great wooden coffer we might hide in—"

"And suffocate," said Minka.

Bertram snapped his fingers. "It's a simple matter to get hold of a few masks," he said. "There are groups of mummers in the city just now, fitted out for their plays, and so disguised we could move about."

"I can pinch 'em," Urchin offered happily.

"Thank you, Urchin," said Petronilla, "but I am a royal princess with ample resources." She reached for a purse that wasn't at her waist. She'd come, after all, straight from the dungeon.

After a few silent moments of patting around pockets and purses, they realized that none among them had any coin.

"Even Pip would come up empty," Bilious said.

As the bells rang the midmorning hour, one by one they turned and looked at the church collection box.

"Oh, I'll do the deed," said Petra, "but someone please remind me to refund the amount and more, for I'd hate to meet my father in hell come Judgment Day."

Henry set off for the abbey herbalist, to see if he could determine the contents of the liquid that yet remained in the vials of elixir that Margaret had carried out of the dungeon.

And Bertram, with Urchin to help, set out to procure an assortment of mummers' masks.

An uncomfortable hour had passed in waiting when the pair at last returned. "The Devil and Old Vice," Bertram said, handing one ugly mask to Petronilla and an even uglier one to Minka, "and an angel." He delivered a beautiful silver-faced mask to Margaret, and then he flushed. "They're what came soonest to hand." To Margaret he also gave a painted cloak, to hide her fine gown and her crutch. Petra's gown was too bedraggled to be mistaken for the clothing of a princess. He and Bilious donned masks of ladies' faces, and Emma and Urchin wore masks of plain white.

The "mummers" wandered the streets the better part of the afternoon, picking up food and drink (with yet more borrowed coin) and listening for news. The pleasant hours passed in browsing and pretending, and Margaret could almost forget their terrible cares as a cheerful sun traversed the sky. She reveled in an anonymity she had not enjoyed in many weeks, if ever: even with her telltale crutch she felt, for once, invisible.

They met Henry as planned in the alley beside the Crown and Bean.

"The herbalist is still testing the mixture, but already he's detected skullcap and lavender, which herbs induce sleep and visions and numb the senses and the mind," Henry explained. "But there is another ingredient, beyond a doubt, and damning: belladonna—deadly nightshade. In careful dosage it brings on euphoria, followed by sleep. Too much, and it causes death. The monks at the abbey won't even speak of it. But they grow it in their gardens as a cure for boils." Henry smiled, eyes agleam. "Yes, this will do to charge him on some count," he went on. Lord Geoffrey's daughter *and* his ill-treated horse might be avenged after all, God willing. And Armand, rest his soul. "Princess Petronilla's testimony will not be discounted as *in parte insana,* not with the evidence of the elixir."

"It's my word against his," said Petra. "Judgment runs deep as the Severn," she added, "and rumor stinks as strong."

Everyone reluctantly agreed.

"But we have no other proof of Lord Geoffrey's crimes," said Bertram, "excepting the word of a bandit."

"Whom you kilt!" said Bilious to Minka.

At this a head turned, unnoticed: a woman with a long, dark braid.

"For your sake I done it!" Minka exclaimed. "Would that I'd known he'd be of use!"

"Dear, foolish woman," Bilious muttered, and pulled Minka to his side.

The braided woman turned and disappeared into the alehouse.

"Emma, would you be so good as to fetch the sheriff to the castle?" said Henry.

"My pleasure, to be sure," Emma said, eager to add dog-kicking to the list of Lord Geoffrey's crimes.

"Tell him he'll find the body of a thief outside the gate," added Minka. "The law might do well to hire me on," she said, to no one.

Emma went off to locate the law, and Bilious went with her, on account of Minka and the matter of John Book.

Brother Henry shook back his cloak and cracked his knuckles with enthusiasm. "Bertram? Let's go see a man about a horse." Off they went toward the castle, and Lord Geoffrey.

❧

The masked companions went out again and after a while found themselves on Smithen Street, where smiths practiced their trade, and merchants sold items of quality both delicate and brute. Margaret glimpsed through the slits in her mask a wild-looking blacksmith raising his hammer high and bringing it down with a clang. Her thoughts went to the wild-eyed man, and, first noting the location of her friends browsing trinkets at a stall some paces away, she slipped the mirror from her satchel, turned her back on the street, and peered into it. Hello, there he was.

"Watch out" and "step lively" came shouts from nearby, and Margaret glanced up to see the cause of the small commotion: a pony coming up Smithen pushed the foot traffic to the sides of the street. Someone passing jostled Margaret from behind, and into the mirror rippled a vision that replaced the wild-eyed man: a gray-headed woman at play with a sturdy child—a little girl—dressed in a gown of green velvet.

Margaret's breath caught in her throat. Green dress, green velvet—who had caused this vision in the glass?

She pressed the mirror to her chest and, darting round, caught sight of an old woman, stooped but nimble . . . the madwoman? Lucy? Yes, it was she.

Confused, Margaret looked again into the mirror, but the vision had gone. She stuffed the glass into her satchel, adjusted her crutch, and beckoned to her friends. "Quickly! Follow me!"

What Happened at the Apothecary's House

They made a strange parade: a girl with a crutch and a painted cloak, followed by a robust matron with a squashed hat, one girl dressed in a grain sack, and another in soiled silks, all in masks of varying ilk, and all hurrying to catch up to a crone—stooped but cursed fleet.

As she kept Lucy in sight, Margaret told the others what she'd seen in the mirror.

Lucy turned onto Claremont Street and disappeared through a low doorway, beneath a sign picturing a mortar and pestle. Margaret turned the latch. The shop was dim, brighter by the hearth.

"Closed," said a voice. "Apothecary's out."

Then the old woman turned from the fire, rising from a crouch with bellows in hand. Her face lit with astonishment, then went vacant, open-then-shut like the shopkeeper's door, as one by one the party shed their masks.

"I don't know nothing about nothing," the madwoman uttered, as if she could read Margaret's thoughts. Then she turned her back and picked up a poker to rattle the embers, snapping as they shifted and licked now with flame.

"I set you free," Margaret said. "All I ask in return is your story."

"I'm not ready," said the crone, with a shake of her gray head. "I—I'm not ready," she said again, and her voice cracked. "I've work to do."

"Please," said Minka, and Margaret turned to her in surprise, having never before heard the word pass Minka's lips. The madwoman moved her head a fraction and watched Minka out of the corner of her eye.

"This one has traveled far to learn the truth," Minka said, pointing at Margaret. "And that one," she said, pointing at Petronilla, "has endured much in the covering up of it. We've reason to think you know sommat of the truth."

Margaret had seen the old woman in the glass—the crone *would* speak! "Tell us what you know!" she cried, as she yanked the mirror from her satchel and shook it in the air.

The old woman stood still. She gaped at the mirror. Twice she opened her mouth and shut it, squinting hard. She frowned and cocked her head. Then her shoulders drooped as if yielding to a heavy burden, and, setting aside the poker, she turned to face the small party again.

"Listen, then," she said at last.

She was a midwife, she told them. Years ago, before her imprisonment.

"And why *were* you imprisoned, Lucy?" Petronilla interrupted. "You seem hardly mad at all," she added, but the old woman waved a dismissive hand.

"I did deliver the child, the daughter of Queen Isobel and Armand, the first king consort." The woman turned and poked the fire again, disturbing the embers to burn with more heat. "She were a dear baby, full of piss and vinegar, yet sweet as honey, too." She paused, staring into the fire. "A person doesn't guide a baby into this world without she gets some feeling for the child," she murmured.

The madwoman half turned to Margaret, eyes narrowed. Light from dancing flames slashed her face. "They say that child is you," she said, "all grow'd up and come back. The child Beatrice . . ."

Petronilla cleared her throat. "She never knew her given name, and goes by Margaret now."

"Aye." The crone nodded. "They say it's you," she said, "but they're wrong."

Everyone began to sputter and object and crease their brows and talk at once, uttering "what?" and "why?" and "who are you to say?"

All at once the madwoman reached and grabbed Margaret by the hair! Margaret yelped in surprise and confusion, but before the others could react (though Minka's hand shot out for Maggie's crutch), the crone let Margaret loose. "You are not she!" she said. "You are not she!"

The room went silent, but for a soft rustling from above—mice? Too loud, too large a sound for mice— and the hiss of water on the boil.

"As I thought—as I *knew*—you are not she," the old woman said again. Tears ran down her cheeks, and for a moment she squeezed her eyes shut.

"How—how do you know?" Margaret was stunned as much by the woman's tears as by the hair pulling. She rubbed her nape where it smarted.

The crone shuffled to the single chair in the small room and sat heavily. "Beatrice were born with a mark," she said, wiping at her cheeks, "as if the skin were pinched between God's finger and thumb. Shape of a wishbone."

Minka narrowed her eyes.

Margaret stared at a spot in the air two feet in front of her, seeing nothing. A memory was dawning. The feel of the crutch beneath her arm, a crutch that she could use like a lance, to defend against—

The madwoman looked at Margaret and shook her head. "You haven't got the mark."

"And you say her given name were Beatrice?" said Minka, with a glance at Urchin.

Lucy put a shaking hand to her lips and nodded. "Just as I say."

Margaret's face went slack. For she did know a girl with a mark on the back of her neck. She knew Beady, the beggar girl she'd once met along the riverbank. . . . Two little girls, standing together side by side . . . She knew the girl who'd been run out of town, beaten and bloodied, and who visited her in dreams, searching for the truth.

Margaret looked at Minka. Minka returned her gaze.

"Beady Bone," they whispered as one.

Minka pivoted slowly and moved across the room toward Urchin, who, noting Minka's eye upon her, and with an instinct to run when attention turned to her, began to back away.

Petra stomped her foot. "Tell me what is going on! Who is this Beady Bone?"

Margaret's head hung, as if it were suddenly unbearably heavy. "Did Lord Geoffrey know of this mark?"

Because now Margaret recalled him lifting her damp, clean hair from her neck the day they first met, how proudly she'd worn her hair down and long, to dry, scented with licorice and cinnamon. She'd thought he was checking for lice.

The old woman gave a slow nod. "He did," she said, still nodding. "Oh, yes."

"I do *not* understand!" said Petra.

Margaret paled, legs gone weak. She lurched toward the table and leaned on it. So he'd known all along that Margaret was not the rightful heir, but he would have wed her anyway, deceived her and the people of the kingdom, and his own daughter, her sis—

Oh.

They were not sisters, then. Margaret gripped her crutch, her knuckles white. She and Petra were never sisters at all.

The bells of the cathedral began to ring the hour.

But now Margaret wasn't listening. She was remembering a scene from long ago.

Sommat else, then. There: the voice of the little beggar girl. Margaret, so young, so small, had stood up to Thomas the miller's son, poked him in the eye with the end of her crutch, and she'd given the beggar the penny meant for market. And the beggar had tried to give Margaret her dolly, which was really a stinking hank of hair, and Margaret had said no.

Sommat else, then, for stabbin' that boy and givin' me a whole penny.

And the beggar knelt and rootled around her meager

belongings, and there it was, the pale mark of birth—*a wishbone!*—and Margaret made a wish.

I want not to be so alone.

The beggar girl raised her head—*Here's sommat!*—and took Margaret's hand and pressed into it her gift. And there it was, upon her small palm.

A comb.

The carved horn comb she'd convinced herself had come from her mother, the comb that had convinced Petra they were sisters.

Now Margaret took a sharp breath and pushed herself from the oaken table. "Thank you," she managed; then she turned and fled out into the street.

$$\approx$$

It was Petra who found her, huddled against a doorway.

"How terrible sad," Margaret said, her sobs slowing to a hiccup. "Beady was someone with a mother and a sister who loved her," she said, with a longing look at Petronilla, "and now she's likely dead, and she never knew it."

"Then she, this Beady—this Beatrice Bone . . . she was my sister?" said Petra. "And we . . . are not?" she finished.

Margaret shook her head and fought off tears for poor Beady, for herself, for Petra, all of them growing up motherless, sisterless. Petra helped her to her feet and put her arms around her. Maggie slipped into Petra's hand the horn comb that did not, after all, belong to her.

"Holy Mary!" came a cry, and they turned to see Minka moving as fast as ever she had, arms pumping, forehead damp with sweat.

"It's Urchin!" she cried. "*She* is Beatrice Bone!"

What Happened on the Field

Minka had glimpsed the mark of the wishbone when she'd shoved Urchin in the river, back in Sackville Proper.

"But with that blasted squirrel wrapped around the girl's throat for dear life, I haven't seen it since. Plain as day, once I grabbed her up and looked just now," Minka said. "I wonder as she ever knew it was there, the poor wretch."

Margaret's chin quivered, and she fought the tears that threatened again. Her sorrow stung, because she'd come to love Petra, and sisterhood, and all that she'd found in herself, and none of it was true, none of it would hold. But muddled with sorrow was gladness, too, for it was Beatrice Bone, known to herself as Urchin, who had carried the comb of Queen Isobel. Urchin, beloved by a mother. Urchin, a sister. It was Urchin who would be queen now. Margaret smiled. Then she began to cry a little, and then to laugh. If Maggot was an unlikely queen, Urchin was unlikelier still.

"But where is she?" said Margaret, wiping her eyes with the back of her wrist.

"Gone! Gone!" Minka cawed. "She wants nothing to do with it!"

"Why didn't you stop her?" cried Petra.

Minka puffed like a broody hen. "You try holding down a scrawny little eel who won't be held! You'd think I meant to cut her up and put her in a pie!" Minka shook out her arms. "Good luck making her into a lady. She bit me!"

They spent the better part of an hour in a vain search. While they wondered what to do and where she might have gone, Minka began noticing groups of people walking briskly in the same direction, some of them even running, toward the two-towered gatehouse. So she called to a passing town boy, "You, there, what's going on?"

The boy did not stop, but called back as he ran, "A joust at the high meadow!"

"Who is in the lists for jousting?" demanded Minka.

The boy stopped and turned. "Lord Geoffrey did cry

the tournament—a duel, it is, a trial by combat. To the death!" He grinned wickedly and ran on.

The boy's father walked more slowly, and fell in beside them. "The castle is in an uproar," he said. "Lord Geoffrey's been faulted for high crimes, and has called for a duel with his accuser, as is his right." The man pursed his lips. "And no matter his guilt or innocence, he will live, and the rival will die, for His Lordship's armor is fine and oiled, and his opponent . . ." He shrugged. "Well, they say he is a monk!"

"By the Mary!" Minka gasped. There could be no search for Urchin, not now.

Margaret hitched her crutch beneath her arm. "Hurry!"

They joined the crowd climbing the hill to the field in the high meadow where the joust would take place. Emma came across the field at a run, holding up her skirts, with Bilious close behind.

"You'll have heard, then," he wheezed.

"What's taken you so long? You've missed everything!" Minka cried.

"We sought the sheriff hither and thither, only to find him at home and in bed and not to be roused," Bilious said.

"A drunken stupor, no doubt," Emma said. "It's at these great men's pleasure to call a duel, but—madness!"

Bilious wiped his brow. "What have we missed?"

"It will wait," Minka said. "The world's gone upside down, is all, but it will wait."

They went and stood along the south side of the field, where the bank rose up behind them to form a natural amphitheater, and pushed their way through the crowd. The orange ball of the sun hung low in the sky to the west over the red roofs and church spires, and Margaret raised her hand to shield her eyes when it came in and out from behind the clouds, which sped hurriedly over the city as if they wanted no part of what would happen next.

Bertram hurried to them from the other side of the field, carrying Brother Henry's robe. He and Brother Henry had gone at once to the castle, he told them, and presented Lord Geoffrey the evidence of the elixirs meant to keep his own daughter half-dead and easily manipulated. They accused him of imprisoning a ruling princess. Geoffrey was most agitated to discover Petra gone. He scoffed and bluffed and spewed, mocked Henry openly for giving up his knighthood, and challenged his old acquaintance to a joust for his insolence. Henry insisted they wait for the sheriff, but Geoffrey called for a judicial duel.

"And he set a hurried time of one hour hence! The duel is nigh upon us. To the death."

The two horses stood one at each end of the great field. Lord Geoffrey sat high in his saddle astride his enormous destrier, armored in a shining full-length hauberk of chain mail, leggings, and an iron breastplate and backplate. Plates of armor covered too his elbows and arms, his thighs, shins, and feet. The warhorse champed and pawed the ground, flinching as Geoffrey's lance scraped his side. Geoffrey held a helmet beneath the crook of his arm, a cocky smile upon his face.

Brother Henry, sitting astride Gertrude, wore an overlarge coat of mail and breastplate borrowed from the brother of the butcher, killed in the wars. A helmet, ancient and dented, rested at Henry's thigh. His lance, also borrowed, he wielded with the easy manner of old acquaintance. But at present the tip of it rested on the ground, for Gertrude stood but fourteen hands.

"He appears strangely calm," said Bilious, "for a man so doomed."

Bertram set his teeth and gripped the folded cassock in his arms. "He is certain God will not spare the guilty. And though ill-clothed and poor-mounted, my cousin has not forgotten his training. But look!" Bertram pointed at a stout rowan tree on the west side of the field, upon which was hung a colored shield that bore the lord regent's coat of arms. "I've something to set right."

Bertram ran across the field to the shield tree and flung the friar's cassock over a low-hanging branch. The woven brown cloth flapped and then settled wearily, and Bertram raised his fists in the air, as if he'd draped a fine banner.

The two riders took up positions at either end of the field. Lord Geoffrey's horse, to the west, pawed the ground; to the east, Gertrude bent her head and munched the sparse grass at her feet.

To the death—Henry, good, kind Brother Henry, would be killed. A sob of rage and frustration caught in Margaret's throat. Had she never gazed into the magic mirror, had she never set out to find the wild-eyed man, whoever he might be, Brother Henry would never have arrived at this moment on the field, and for that she felt deep regret, and a kind of shame for wanting so dearly and so much.

Margaret clenched her jaw. But it was not she who had ordered the child Beatrice's death, who had made of her the miserable beggar Beady Bone, scurrying from town to town like a rat. It was not she who had stolen Petronilla's and Beady's childhoods. It was that man: it was Geoffrey.

Lord Geoffrey's guard stepped onto the field.

"He's been chosen *chevalier d'honneur,* and will see the rules are upheld," said a bystander.

Bilious spat. "And does he enforce the rule that Henry should have to ride with the blasted sun blinding him?" he muttered.

A stout boy joined the *chevalier d'honneur* on the field and announced Lord Geoffrey. There was a smattering of applause.

Then Bertram ran onto the field. "Brother Henry, of the Brethren of the Holy Cross, of Dale's End Friary, does engage in trial by combat," he called out. "God will aid the innocent but not the guilty!"

Henry urged the pony to raise her head as Bertram

went on. "He does accuse Lord Geoffrey of drugging and imprisoning the Crown Princess Petronilla, His Lordship's own daughter!"

The crowd broke out into a wave of uneasy murmurs. Petronilla squeezed Margaret's hand, and Bilious pulled Minka close.

"On whose say?" came the clear, unhurried voice of Lord Geoffrey, from atop his high mount at the west end of the field. "The word of my daughter, the Princess of Hearts?" Geoffrey laughed. "A madwoman?" His horse stamped a heavy hoof, driving up dust that coiled like the smoke of a waking dragon.

Petronilla stepped from the protection of Bilious and Minka and Margaret and stood two paces inside the pawed ground of the field. Geoffrey's cocky smile slipped. Petra stood regally, the light wind blowing back her gown. "If I have been mad, it's because you made me so with your poisonous elixirs and lies."

Geoffrey's horse stamped again, and his master tugged the reins savagely; the horse cried out.

Minka guided Petra back into the ring of the crowd, and Geoffrey chuckled and slowly shook his head. "Nonsense. I never gave my daughter any poison. Herbal tonics! I drink the stuff myself."

"Excuse me, uh, my lord." Now a monk stepped from the audience. He looked around, wringing his hands. "I was given a vial," he began. He scratched his head, swallowed visibly, and glanced at Brother Henry. "I have tested its contents, believed to have been administered to the Princess of Haaar . . . hmm, rather, the Princess Petronilla. . . ." The monk flushed, and scratched his head again. "Belladonna! It's deadly nightshade in the vial!"

The crowd gasped.

"*Brother* Henry may have given you such a vial, but . . ." Lord Geoffrey shrugged. "The *source* of the vial, who can say? Now *I* say again," he called, smiling as if charmingly befuddled, "who has any evidence on which I may be charged with any crime?"

The people murmured and muttered.

"*I* have evidence!" came a shout from the crowd. "I bear witness to a crime!"

Now the people turned this way and that, searching for the speaker. And then the crowd parted, and out of the gallery, a stone's throw from Margaret, stepped a woman, tall and slender and with a long, dark braid.

Geoffrey went rigid in his saddle; his destrier snorted and danced, and again he yanked the bit hard between the horse's teeth.

Something familiar about her, Margaret thought. That braid. Where had she seen the woman before?

"Step aside!" Geoffrey shouted at the woman.

But the woman did not yield. "I will speak!"

"At your peril," Geoffrey said, his voice gone low and threatening.

"So be it!" the woman cried. Her voice rose and

carried, and she pressed a fist to her chest. "I will speak of another crime! This man . . ." She pointed at Geoffrey and gathered her words. "I am she what took the child Beatrice to John Book's camp twelve years ago. For my offense I may perish," she called, "but I'll not conceal your crime to save myself!"

The people murmured. Guards approached uncertainly from the far side of the field.

Geoffrey's horse pawed the ground. "Silence!" Lord Geoffrey roared.

"No!" The woman's words tumbled out now, as if she knew she had but a moment to say what she would. "I found the little princess! The one who fell into the river and drownt, only she did not drown! I pulled her out, and I brought her to the camp, and once I knew who she was, I should have done different, but—"

"Silence, I command it!" Geoffrey's horse gave a few nervous high steps.

The woman would not be stopped. "But then *he*"— she pointed at Lord Geoffrey—"paid the thief John Book to do away with her! To have the girl kilt!" She looked around at the stunned faces. "I'm sorry for my part, I'm cursed sorry!"

Geoffrey's face flushed with rage. The horse pranced in place, jumpy, and tossed his head.

Henry put out a commanding hand. "See reason, Lord Geoffrey! The truth has set the field against you!" he shouted. "Let us discuss these revelations in private.

There is no need of this foolish duel—throw your helmet down."

All was quiet as the people looked from west to east, waiting to see what the lord regent would do. No one spoke; there was no sound. No tweet of bird or rustle of squirrel or puff of breeze broke the silence.

Henry threw his own helmet to the ground. "Enough, Geoffrey."

Geoffrey looked long at the braided woman. Then he dropped his head to his breastplate and let his helmet fall.

It was over.

The crowd gave a sigh; Henry drew his leg across his pony and slipped to the ground. Margaret smiled at Petra with relief, and they embraced.

Then came the scream of a mighty destrier. Geoffrey dug his heels into his horse and rode hard down the field, teeth bared, his mark the braided woman, who froze in terror, then lowered her chin and closed her eyes as if accepting her due.

Henry leaped up onto Gertrude's back and urged the pony across the field, bearing down, but the field was long. Geoffrey would reach her first.

Margaret saw the braided woman fall to her knees, clasping her hands in prayer. She heard the pounding, felt the furious hoofbeats through the ground in the sole of her good foot and straight up the grain of her crutch, and her heart thundered; the air went still, and over the city to the west the spires of the cathedral pierced the sun.

And into the fast-closing space between charging horse and kneeling woman, Margaret limped—*clump-slide*—onto the field. She raised her crutch high, like a lance, and held it steady.

Margaret the Crutch

"No!" cried Bertram.

"Hear me, God and all the saints!" screamed Minka.

Margaret stood her ground. The charging horse was almost upon her. She squinted against the sudden blaze of orange light that streamed out of the west around the spires of the church. By what faith did she think she could stop the charging steed? By what faith did she believe her crooked leg would hold her steady? Margaret squeezed shut her eyes against the onslaught of the horse. And then, just as suddenly, she threw aside her crutch and yanked the mirror from her belt, and, using every ounce of strength to stay standing, to stay strong, she held the mirror to the sun.

Geoffrey's mount screamed, a sound to curdle the blood, to visit in nightmares, terrible and heartshattering. With the sun reflected into his eyes, the horse reared and twisted, and his hooves came pounding to the ground inches from where Margaret stood, mirror clutched high in both hands. The earth shook, Margaret fell, and the mirror flew from her hands and through the air. It landed at the feet of the mighty horse, who trampled the shining thing as if it were a snake. In the next moment the horse bolted wild and ran Geoffrey underneath the friar's banner on the shield tree. There sounded a terrible crack! The horse galloped on, and Geoffrey fell senseless to the ground.

The shards of the shattered mirror, blinking and broken and beyond repair, reflected the orange sun. Margaret, on her knees, blinked back.

The sheriff appeared now that everything was over, ordered Lord Geoffrey taken into custody, broke up the crowd, and turned to the few who remained. "Er, a few questions," he said, and sighed. Twenty-odd years on the job, and somehow he always managed to snooze through any bit of excitement. Made it blasted difficult to get a story straight.

The braided woman's name was Alice, and she was John Book's wife. They'd not been wed at the door of any church, but married just the same these many years, and no escape. She told of the night she'd pulled the little girl from the River Severn and taken her to their camp. She told of the night Geoffrey was supposed to pay ransom for the girl and collect her, and how instead he'd paid for her death. She told of how she'd comforted the little girl. How John Book had allowed her to keep the child, how he'd used the gift to bind her more tightly to him. But much as Alice had loved the sweet girl, she'd feared for the life she would lead with that lot. She could not subject another to *her* fate.

"One night while the men slept, I took her into town and left her in a henhouse. I figured the hens'd keep her warm, and she did so love to guzzle raw eggs," Alice said fondly. "I told John she run away, and then, quick like, I told him I seen a rich party traveling heavy by the road, and him like a magpie, he forgot about little Bebe and we went after those people and took 'em for all they had."

She sagged. "It pained me. Little Bebe, she were sweet as butter, and I loved to play at being her mum. She used to clutch my hair for comfort; it would soothe her crying. So I cut off my braid what she seemed to like. It's all I could leave her with. I cut it off and give it to her. I hoped she'd remember me not unkindly, poor chick." She was weeping now. "When my hair grew long again, I felt I'd betrayed her. I knew not whether she lived or died. And yet my hair went on ever as before."

The woman wiped her eyes. "I look for her wherever I go, these dozen years." She looked hopefully at the party. "Knows you what became of 'er?"

Until an hour or so ago, Margaret had believed it was she. Putting a hand on Alice's arm, Margaret whispered, "She lived," and the woman smiled through fresh tears.

"I lives" came a voice. Urchin wiggled her way around Minka, behind whom she'd crept up unawares.

Everyone stared. A cricket could be heard fiddling in the grass.

Then: "Holy Mother of the jumped-up!" Bilious gasped.

"The wily thing," Minka muttered. "Surprised?" she said, elbowing Bilious. "Not I. And *you* didn't want to take her in!"

Brother Henry beamed. "God's hand guided you, Minka," he said, to which Bilious gave a snort.

Bertram moved close to Margaret and grinned from ear to ear.

"Who'd have thought," Emma said, gawping.

The sheriff scratched his head.

Urchin stepped slowly to Alice's side, with little Pip wrapped around her neck. Then she reached into the belt that cinched her grain-sack tunic, withdrew a matted hank of hair, and held it out. Alice alone did not grimace or cringe. For a few long moments no one spoke, and then Alice rose and pulled Urchin to her, and Urchin did not refuse her embrace. She stood tolerantly and let herself be smothered, while Alice's long braid fell across her shoulders.

"And how then did you go from the henhouse to the streets?" Bilious wanted to know, but Urchin only shrugged and worked a tooth with her tongue.

The sheriff cleared his throat, and Alice released Urchin and turned to him.

"I did come to the city with John Book once before, lately," she told him, "on what 'e called pressing business."

"And what was the pressing business John Book had in the royal city?" the sheriff asked.

"Blackmail." Alice sniffed loudly, and Henry passed her a cloth to blow her nose. "He wanted more money for taking the child from Lord Geoffrey."

"Did he get the money?"

"He did."

"Will you swear it?"

"I will."

❧

Brother Henry walked with Alice and the sheriff down the hill and into the city.

Petronilla was eager to know her sister "once my sister has known a bath," so Minka and Bilious and Emma took charge of Urchin and promised Petra they would spare no effort to get her clean and to the castle. That left Petra and Margaret and Bertram, who sat together in the grass of the high meadow, picking shards of the ruined mirror from the dirt.

There wasn't anything to say, really. All this time spent wishing for some bit of magic. Finding and then losing the mirror, again and again. She might as well have tried to hold the moonlight, or the wind.

Margaret tossed a tiny piece of useless, sparkling mirror into the dirt. The bridge of her nose began to sting, and she thought she might cry. "I thought I had a sister," she said. "I was so sure." She was only Margaret the Crutch, then as ever.

"Just look-alikes," said Bertram, after a moment. "Like looking in a mirror. Strange."

"None so strange as a two-headed goat, I suppose," said Margaret, and they tried to laugh.

"Not sisters," Petra said, "but friends. Always and ever, our blood oath will stand."

Blrrr-blrrr! There sounded all at once a trumpet.

They turned toward the sharp tones and saw approaching in the distance a band of riders some twenty strong, outfitted in traveling cloaks and many in armor and mail. And then came the loud, matched tones of high minstrelsy—the curved horn, the blaring trumpet and drumming nakers—and such shining in the sun of the instruments of combat and music-making blinded the eye and thrilled the heart. And finally came into view the standard-bearers holding aloft the banner as all approached the grand gatehouse, and on the banner rode the colors of the Duke of Minster.

Blr-blrrrr! sounded the trumpet, and again, *blr-blrrrr!*

"God's wounds!" cried Petra, craning her neck and smoothing the crumpled silk of her skirts. "Did no one send a messenger? It's Frederick de Vere!" When Margaret showed no recognition, Petra flung out her hands in vexation. "It's the Toad!"

What They Found in the Wood

Margaret and Bertie watched Petra stomp down the hill, as it was her duty to greet the travelers.

Margaret wasn't sure what to do. The mirror was no more. The magic was truly gone. What had it all been for?

The city spread out before them like a tapestry. At one end the cathedral, at the other the castle, and all in between the rooftops and spires, the river and the bridge, and beyond the west wall the wood. Margaret bit her lip and studied the scene.

Bertram cleared his throat. "Maggie, this might be poor timing, considering, but . . . my bagpipe, you see . . ." His voice faltered. "Maggie, I've something—"

"The wood." Margaret grabbed Bertie's arm and sent the bagpipe tumbling to the grass, where the bladder lay rippling and round. "Knightsbridge Wood, Bertie, where none but outlaws dare to go." She pointed carefully beyond the cathedral, as if lining up to let fly an arrow into the dark mass of trees.

"And ghosts. Don't forget the ghosts. But, Maggie—"

"It's time we venture in!" Margaret said, interrupting Bertie and grabbing her crutch. "I came on this long journey in search of the man in the mirror. The wild-eyed man could see the rose window from his chamber, Bertie," she said. "The only place from which such a view can be seen has got to be Knightsbridge Wood, and now I won't be stopped from going." She clambered to her feet.

Bertram rose to stand beside her. "But the outlaws, Maggie!"

"And the ghosts, I know, I know," said Margaret, "and the danger and the death, but we must go there, Bertie." And she began the walk, *clump-slide*, down the hill.

Bertram followed, his bagpipes sloshing.

❧

The sun had dropped below the tops of the trees, and the wood, dark and dense, was eerily quiet. They searched the edges of the forest for a way in, and after a while they found a thin trail that, to one desperately looking, might seem to be a path.

"Never follow a path in the woods," Bertram said. "Everyone knows that. They never lead anywhere. It'll only get us lost." He glanced around nervously. "Deer paths," he muttered, "or wolf. Oh, let me," he said, and he stepped in front so that he could hold back the branches for Margaret to pass more easily.

After a while they came to a place where the trees thinned, and the way was easier, and then the wood opened up into a small clearing. And there in the center, plain to see in the dusk-softened light of the clearing, was a sort of hut. It was about the height of two men at its highest point, and the sides sloped to the ground like a haystack, or a beehive. There was an oaken door with a heavy lock, and a high window with iron bars. Margaret put out her hand, and Bertram took it. Eyes wide, she looked back over her shoulder in the direction of the city. Yes. There it was. From here she could see the spires of the cathedral rising above the trees, and between the twin spires the great rose window.

Margaret's heart thumped in her chest, and she was grateful for Bertram's hand in hers. She squeezed it, and he squeezed back. She licked her dry lips and stepped— *clump-slide*—toward the strange little hut.

"Hello?" she said. "Hello? I'm here! I've come!"

No answer.

They crawled up onto the rock beneath the window and, finding the bars loosed in their frame, they climbed into the hut. They saw inside the furnace it housed, the wood table, the tools and the shards of glass, designs drawn on paper, words.

Bertram knelt and picked up a small square of parchment upon which were inked two words.

Lux Vera, Margaret read.

But no one was there. The chamber was empty. The wild-eyed man was gone.

The Wild-Eyed Man

It was full dark and beginning to rain when Margaret and Bertram stumbled out of the wood. They'd followed the edge of the wall to Isobel's Gate, and now they stood just inside. Margaret leaned on her crutch, the rain patting her hair and her cheeks and the backs of her hands, and wondered which way to go. Back to the castle? She didn't belong there. Not now, not anymore. The cathedral?

"Curfew is nigh! All must be in for the night!" the guards called out into the dark.

Margaret felt tears prick at her eyelids. She couldn't bear another minute of this day. Beatrice Bone, the thundering hooves, the shattered mirror, the shattered hopes. Of course, it wasn't curfew that worried her; she knew she'd be taken in tonight. But what of the next day? And the day after that, and all the days and nights to follow?

Out of the dark at that very moment, carrying a torch to light the way, came of all people the madwoman.

Lucy's heart beat fast and strong. Just because she had no use for magic didn't mean she didn't believe in it. "Come now, with me," she said. When Margaret said nothing, Lucy put out her hand. "Please," she said. "You've nothing to fear from me."

Margaret stared.

"Please. I know you are weary. Follow me."

"Curfew!"

Follow follow follow went the rain.

"Quickly, now." Lucy glanced at Bertram and back at Margaret. "Just you," she said.

Bertram stepped close to Margaret. "It's all right, Bertie," Margaret said. She'd decided. "I want to go with her. I'll see you in the morning."

Bertram adjusted his bagpipe on his shoulder and nodded, with a suspicious glance at the old woman.

"All will be well," Lucy told him. "But your instrument sounds ill."

"You should hear me play it," he said balefully.

So Margaret went to the apothecary's house on Claremont Street for the second time that day. She leaned heavily on her crutch. She was hungry, and tired, and sad.

Lucy opened the door and pushed it wide, and ushered Margaret in. "All right, now," she said. "It's all right." And there was a man sitting beside the hearth, and the light from the fire flickered warmly over his tousled fair hair, and he was looking at Margaret, and she saw that his eyes—not wild, not now—were green.

"He's accustomed to be awake in the night," Lucy was saying in a calm voice, knowing her guests were nervous and confused. "It's when he did his work, so none would see the smoke from the kiln. He kept him there, Lord Geoffrey did, all these years, under orders to make another magic mirror. But he never succeeded."

Who—but how—and why— Margaret didn't know where to begin.

He stood. The bench gently teetered, toppled, and fell. Margaret's crutch seemed to take root in the floor, to grow branches, to leaf out, and to flower, all in the space of time it took for the questions to leave their lips:

"Are you my father?" and "Are you my child?"

Tom the apothecary ladled bowls of hot soup, fragrant with herbs and thick with good potato and onion and leek, and then quietly left his houseguests to their supper and Lucy's tale.

It began the night Princess Petronilla was born. The midwife had seen Will Glazier brought into the castle under guard. And she had a feeling.

So she slipped down to the dungeon. Said she needed a hair off a criminal's head to make a poultice for the queen, and the guard believed her. In hurried whispers Will told her about the magic mirror—what he'd seen— and begged her to go and find Catherine behind the kiln. Help her get away. And get word to Queen Isobel of Lord Geoffrey's true nature.

So Lucy had gone to the wood. But—too soon, too soon—Catherine began to labor. Lucy had strength and skill and time enough to save but one life that night: she saved the child. She promised the fading mother she would.

The guards had come looking, kept on looking for the midwife, the baby. So they had to keep moving, place to place. They lived like that near two years. She made herself small, and kept to the shadows, mostly. She doted on the child, bought her a fine dress of green velvet and a pair of tiny shoes, dotted with beads, like a princess would wear. All the while she kept the mirror tucked away.

One day she slipped behind the stair at a tavern

where she'd found work, and took out the mirror and gazed into it. As always, she saw herself with a little girl, a mum with a child of her own. Wasn't that why she'd found her way into midwifery? Didn't it show her she'd done right to keep the child?

Lucy was still smiling and gazing when there came a riot of noise. Out of the tavern she ran. First she saw the little beaded slippers in the street. And there was her little girl, beneath the wheel of a milk cart. She'd toddled into its path while Lucy's attention was far away in the mirror.

She did what she could for the leg, but it wouldn't heal right. And she wrapped the mirror up in linen and sealed the package shut, never to gaze again upon it in her life. She wondered if she should return the child to Will the glazier in the royal city, despite the danger there. She could try. She could see if he was still a prisoner. But she loved the girl, and she never went.

Then one day a knight came. Lucy recognized this red-bearded one—Harold? Henry? A favorite of Isobel's. Though she felt sure he'd not know her, she took to the shadows behind the tavern stair to watch and wait, as was her practice, and that was where she was when the royal messenger came in.

"The Princess Beatrice is missing and thought dead. The queen lies ill and dying of grief. All the queen's men are to return to Knightsbridge."

The heir to the throne missing, or dead? Lucy instantly suspected Lord Geoffrey of foul play. Will Glazier had seen Lord Geoffrey murder Armand, in the mirror. She had to get word to Isobel. She would give this knight the magic mirror to take to the queen.

She must take the risk, and so she did. The knight gave his word of honor that he would deliver the mirror.

But Lucy must also protect her child. And so she ran.

So practiced was she at moving, and so few were their possessions, that within minutes Lucy and her little one had hopped into a wagon with a farmer leaving town. On the road they were overtaken by the red-bearded knight, riding hard. Good, she thought, and smiled at the little girl. It's done.

They came into a town where a crowd was gathered. Hours before, a man had been killed on the road, and now the law was there. She saw the royal messenger. Did he recognize her? She slipped from the wagon and sought a place to hide, ducking into the sanctuary of a church. Later she went to see if the way was clear. *I'll be back in two shakes of a lamb's tail,* she told her darling crooked girl. Back soon.

There was no sound but the embers shifting in the hearth. Lucy looked at Margaret. Looked down.

"The royal messenger caught me," she said. "I have been in prison—in every way—from that moment until last night."

Lucy blew her nose. "And there you were, that day you ventured down with the princess. After all these

299

years," she said, "after all this time. The moment I saw you, I knew. It wasn't the odd likeness to the princess. It wasn't even that bit of green velvet.

"I saw my crooked girl. And I had a feeling."

Margaret's brow creased in thought, and she was silent a while, sitting on the righted bench beside the green-eyed man. Her father, they said. Her father. "You told me you didn't guide a baby into the world without getting a feeling for the child," she said, after a time. "Did you have a feeling," she asked, "when I was born?"

"I had a feeling you were made of love and magic." Lucy nodded. "Mayhap they're one and the same."

"Did my mother . . . what did she call me?" Margaret asked.

Lucy took in a breath. "Vera," she said, with a long look at Will Glazier. "She called you Vera."

A Right Reflection

It happened, after all, that there was a wedding on St. Petronilla's Day.

In the morning, Emma helped Petra dress. Her gown was full and flowing, sky blue and trimmed with gold brocade, and woven into her coiled hair were flowers made of gold. Margaret's gown was of imported cloth from Camulon, purple and red, and fastened low around her hips she wore a jewel-studded belt.

It took the strenuous efforts of Emma plus two kitchen maids to wrestle Urchin into her clothing, and even with that the green ribbons that crisscrossed her chest hung loose and refused to stay tied, so despite all the finery she still looked less royal than ragamuffin. The squirrel on her shoulder didn't help. But when she dutifully curtsied to the young lady in the glass, she gawped and let out a great guffaw, for she recognized the young lady was herself.

By midday the sun was lighting the square before the cathedral so bright that some in the crowd had to shield their eyes from its blazing glory as they nodded to their neighbors, smiling and talking. There was music in the air alongside the smells of game and meat and baking bread. A mother swiped her boy's cap from his head and hit him with it. "Remove your hat, you clod; we're witness to a wedding!"

Frederick de Vere, no longer known as the Toad, hummed and tapped the stylishly long toe of his shoe and watched Castle Street. When he caught sight of Petronilla approaching, his round face broke into a grin, and he waved charmingly, standing high on his toes to see. The throng before the church parted to allow the Princess Petronilla through. Smiling, she came and stood beside Frederick and took his arm. Petra had invited him to stay on, for it would have been very rude to send him away after such a long journey when it was hardly his fault he hadn't got the message the wedding was off. Besides, there was no sign of any drool, and he was kind and funny and a fair dancer, too. Rumors of Frederick's idiocy had been greatly embellished; indeed he was quite as clever and canny as Lord Geoffrey, but with a pleasant result.

It was not Frederick and Petra who stood at the door of the cathedral to wed, however, but Minka and Bilious. Minka, after seeing that Bilious had replaced Sweetheart in the mirror and shaking the thing and deciding after all that it showed the truth of her heart's longing, agreed, or rather demanded, to wed. "You'll have me, Bilious Brighton," she'd said, "or my name's not Minka Pottentott!" And Bilious granted it was, and of course he would.

"It was luck we met," Minka had said.

Margaret's jaw dropped. "Luck? Luck, you say?" she sputtered. "Plain, ordinary luck?"

Minka bristled. "How many times I've said to you, Mags, the coin of life has but two sides, the good luck and the bad! To each of us a turn at each side. I'm sure I've always said it thus!"

Minka had never said it thus in all her days. But she had also never looked so happy.

Now Father Sebastian began to speak the holy words.

"Wait!" Brother Henry pulled the ring from his little finger, the one he'd worn for twelve long years, and put it into Bilious's hand.

"Most unusual," said the priest.

"For luck," said Brother Henry, and Minka turned to Bilious, who tried the ring first on Minka's middle finger, then her third finger, and finally her pinkie. It was a perfect fit. She wondered why the ring looked somehow familiar, and shrugged. She would ask Brother Henry later, if she remembered to.

And with the giving over of the ring, Brother Henry felt strangely lighter. He looked heavenward and whispered a prayer of deep thanks, but for what, exactly, he wasn't sure.

Father Sebastian completed the holy sacrament of marriage, and then, too, the sacrament of baptism, for Margaret had never been baptized; she did not mind the taste of the salt on her tongue, nor the cold dousing of holy water, not one bit. Will Glazier stood by her side, and when the priest asked who did sponsor her into the church, he answered, "I do. Her father." His green eyes sparkled.

"The alchemy never worked again," Will explained to Maggie later, as they watched the dancing in the square. "I was so full of terror and sorrow I couldn't speak. I went a little mad, you see," he said, and scratched the back of his neck. "Chamomile, was it? Monkshood? Common things, but . . ." He shook his head. "I was so full of hope and love and expectations when I made the mirrors—perhaps *that* was the missing stuff. Well, never mind," he said with a wink, and tapping his toe to the music. "I'm only a simple glass-painter."

Released, restored, Will Glazier had gone straight to work in the kiln that had been his prison, sketching designs and cutting the glass for a window to honor the new queen. Urchin scowled at the title Queen Beatrice, but she had already issued her first decree—a wordy scroll having to do with bread and blankets. Petra would help her navigate the rest.

"But is it the right sort of thing?" Margaret had asked, when her father had eagerly shown her the drawings: a boy and a beggar. And a girl the very image of herself. "For a window, I mean?" The only stories she'd seen made of glass were from the Bible, saints and martyrs, and those on the workbench were common folk.

"Oh, yes," said Will Glazier, nodding vigorously, his hair alert in all directions. "God and St. Winifred and you, the squirrel and the peddler, magic mirror, humble crutch—all of it the same mosaic." He pulled on his chin. "The same, er, tapestry. The same soup," he said, and patted his stomach. "I'm hungry."

And then he'd asked if Margaret would like to learn what he could teach her.

"Yes," she'd said. "Yes." They'd smiled, master and apprentice, father and daughter.

Indeed, they could scarcely stop smiling.

❧

The wedding celebrations went on long into the afternoon. Frederick de Vere called for Bertram. "My minstrelsy lacks only the bagpipes! Bertram, will you do me the honor? Accept, and the job at court is yours!" He clapped Bertram sincerely on the back before dancing off.

Petra leaned toward Bertram. "Poor Freddy," she said in his ear before following de Vere to the dance, "he's tone-deaf!"

Margaret, alone now with Bertram, watched them go. "His poor ear works in your favor," she said. "No offense."

Bertram tipped his head. "None taken. I, too, have a quest of sorts, and I am ever learning. You'll see one day! You'll see!"

Her fingers moved along the designs that Bertie had carved into the wood of her crutch, and the letters there. M-A-G-G-I-E. Not Margaret the Crutch or Margaret of the Church or the Quest. Just Maggie.

"Maggie."

She started from her reverie and realized he'd spoken her name more than once. "Yes, Bertie?"

Bertram reddened, and he shifted the bagpipe on his shoulder, where it squirmed like a piglet. "My bag . . . ," he began. "I filled it with holy water from St. Winifred's Well, Maggie." He spoke quickly. "I've wanted to give it to you, but there was Petra, and Urchin, and the joust, and the wild-eyed man, and . . ." He held the bag out to her, and it sounded a gentle sloshing. "For you." He made a courtly little bow and tapped his heels together. "That you would be healed."

Margaret's chest filled up with something large and breathless: *Just because you limp doesn't mean you can't heal. . . .*

"Thank you, Bertie," she managed to say. "Looks as though I'm in for another dousing!"

Bertram took the plug from the bag, and on the spot

he poured the holy water all down her crooked leg. They stared. They waited. The holy water pooled at her feet, a puddle like any other. She stepped and staggered, and as ever relied upon her crutch.

"Mayhap to drink it," he said, his voice bleak as a goat's. "There are yet a few drops."

He held the bag for her to drink, and she swallowed a spoonful. It tasted of must and leather. Music came boisterous from across the square. Again they waited for a change that did not come.

"I'm sorry," Bertram said at last. His voice choked in his throat, and his eyes glistened. "I thought—I believed—I prayed you would be healed."

Margaret was quiet. All her life she'd limped along, marked by God's displeasure. And yet she had journeyed. She looked across the square. In front of the cathedral, the music played on. Petra laughed at something Frederick was saying in her ear, Minka linked arms with Bilious, Brother Henry turned a cartwheel and took up the hands of Alice and Urchin. And there was Lucy the midwife dancing with Tom the apothecary. And Margaret's own father was chatting quietly with the soldier who'd kept watch over the kiln all these years, and petting Walter, scratching behind his ears, straightening his red ribbon. Margaret had come to find a family, after all, and a place. She was not alone. God had not kept these riches from her.

Margaret leaned on her crutch and looked long at

Bertram, and she felt her own heart, big and brimming and bursting over with love.

"But, Bertie," she said, "I *am* healed."

The puddle at Margaret's feet shimmered, and she glanced down and saw her face in the surface of the holy water. She smiled into the puddle, and her reflection smiled back. If she still had the mirror, wouldn't she see, wouldn't everyone see, this very scene upon the magic surface of the glass?

Margaret shoved the crutch beneath her arm and took hold of Bertie's hand. "And I don't need any magic mirror to show me that I long to dance," she said. She nodded at the bagpipe, empty now of holy water but full of possibility, and stepped, *clump-slide, clump-slide,* out into the square.

"Now, play, Bertie," she said, laughing. "Play!"

Acknowledgments

Jeanne Birdsall, Sarah E. Brune, Heather Vogel Frederick, Kelly Garrett, Heather Henson, Alice and Ronald Hill, Don, Mike, and Sara Hill, Kristi Wallace Knight, Kirby Larson, Literary Arts, Barbara O'Connor, Augusta Scattergood, Heather Schroder, Karen Sherman, Nancy Siscoe, Chris Struyk-Bonn, Kim Winternheimer, and others who read, responded, and encouraged: thank you. To Matt, to Molly, to Eliza: love and thanks beyond alphabetical order.